The Superstar Scandal

This is a work of fiction. Names, characters, places, and incidents either are the product of the author's imagination or are used fictitiously. Any resemblance to actual persons, living or dead, events, or locales is entirely coincidental.

Copyright © 2021 by Sara Martin

All rights reserved.

No part of this book may be reproduced in any form or by any electronic or mechanical means, including information storage and retrieval systems, without written permission from the author, except for the use of brief quotations in a book review.

ISBN 978-0-473-59573-9 (paperback)

ISBN 978-0-473-59574-6 (hardback)

saramartinauthor.com

1

In one swift motion, the attacker clamped his hand around my wrist like a vice. The contact caused a shockwave through my body. I tried to move but my feet were frozen to the ground. Towering walls surrounded me in every direction and I was trapped, helpless, as they started to close in on me.

Then, a voice. Soft at first but becoming clearer.

"You can do it, Chloe!"

Shin Jina?

That's right! The walls crumbled as I hurtled back to reality, remembering why I was here and what I had to do. A spike of adrenaline thrust me into action—a set of moves as practised as a dance choreography.

Step one: I lifted the arm the attacker was attached to and held it upright, palm facing my chin.

Step two: My other hand came up and grabbed him under his wrist.

Step three: I abruptly rotated my hips, breaking his grip.

Step four: I swung my foot towards his groin.

I came dangerously close to actually making contact with

his crotch, but he dodged and stumbled backwards, falling on his butt with a smooshing sound on the thick foam mat beneath us.

I did it. I really did it. Maybe I wouldn't have been able to without Jina's encouragement, but still…

Applause and cheers erupted from the group of women around the mat. A surge of pride lit me up. I beamed, chest puffed out, shoulders back.

Damn. That actually felt pretty good.

The attacker got to his feet and faced me.

"Well done," he said with a smile. "You'll get the hang of this in no time. Keep up the good work."

"Thank you, *Seonsaeng-nim*." I tilted my head in polite acknowledgement before stepping down from the mat.

Jina welcomed me back to my spot beside her, grinning. "Yay! You did so well. I'm proud of you."

Despite the active nature of the self-defence class, she was wearing full makeup and was doused in a flowery perfume. At least she had the good sense to wear appropriate clothing—a loose sweater over high-rise leggings. Her hair had grown out of its pixie-cut style, and she wore it pulled back in a tiny ponytail, though many short strands escaped confinement. Despite the messiness of it, she still managed to look super chic.

"Thanks for suggesting this," I said. "It's not easy, but I can already tell that it's going to help me a lot."

Even if I never had to confront a physical attack from one of Jinseung's *sasaeng* fans again, knowing how to defend myself would give me much peace of mind.

We were inside a large Taekwondo studio with white walls and a red-and-blue-squared floor. Various pieces of fitness equipment lined the perimeter, along with wooden cubby holes and a picture of the Korean flag. Squishy foam mats in various colours lay strewn across the floor. The teacher stood in the middle of the largest mat, his arms folded across his chest. He was a small, slim man, but the muscles rippled in his arms, betraying his strength. He had hair down past his ears, and a short, wispy beard. His face was youthful except for his eyes which looked ancient and wise. I had no idea how old he was.

"Who's up next?" he asked, scanning the room.

None of the women made a noise or even moved. Many of them actually shrank backwards, as if to minimise themselves so they wouldn't get noticed.

"No volunteers? Then I'll have to pick someone at random. Hmmm…"

He pointed his finger and moved it in the direction of his gaze around the room, eliciting nervous jolts from everyone it passed.

I placed a hand on Jina's back and gave her a slight nudge forward.

"Hey!" she snapped.

"Come on, *Unnie*," I whispered. "You should have a turn. It will make you feel good. Promise."

She grimaced at her freshly manicured hand. "What if I break a nail?"

"Trust you to get your nails done right before a self-defence class."

She pouted. "I had a standing appointment and left it too late to reschedule. Do you know how difficult it is to get an appointment at Haejung's salon?"

"Jina-ssi, are you volunteering?" the teacher asked, drawn by the noise of our whispered conversation.

She cringed and covered her face with her hands. "No, no."

"He's going to make everyone come up and do it eventually," I said. "Might as well get it out of the way."

"That's right," the teacher said. "Come on up. I don't bite. I *will* grab you, though."

"That's not very reassuring," Jina grumbled. She reluctantly made her way forward.

They stood at opposite ends of the mat, then without warning, the teacher lunged at her. Jina flailed her arms, but he still managed to grab onto her wrist. She let out a high-pitched "Eep!"

"Do you remember what to do?" he asked.

"Uh, I think so." After taking a breath, she proceeded through the practised movements, up to raising her foot to strike.

The teacher had already relinquished his grip. He backed away from her.

"Good. Well done."

Everyone clapped as she hopped down from the mat. She turned to me.

"I was pretty good, wasn't I?"

"Now who's all confident?" I chided.

The same process continued until every student had had a turn. Some struggled more than others, but everyone eventually managed to break free. Many of the women in the class had dealt with physical assault in the past, so I knew better than anyone how difficult this was for them. That's why I yelled my support from the sidelines at the top of my lungs.

"That's it for today's lesson," the teacher said, stepping off the mat. "I'll see you all next week. Keep practising in the meantime."

The students bowed and thanked him then began to filter out of the studio.

Jina dabbed her hairline with a pink hand towel from her gym bag. "Whew. That was a tough sesh. I think we deserve a treat. D'you want to grab a tea?"

"Sounds good."

I'd never turn down an opportunity to hang out with Jina for a little longer.

We threw our winter coats and scarves on over our exercise gear and headed to a nearby bubble tea outlet. The interior had a pastel colour scheme and walls decorated with pictures of its cartoon giraffe mascot. We sat on high stools at a wooden bar by the window, looking out through the rain-speckled glass onto the dreary street.

"How's work going?" Jina asked, sipping her honey milk tea. "You've barely told me anything about what it's like to work at KAM Entertainment."

I shrugged. "What's there to tell? I don't work there much. It's pretty much a ruse arranged between me, Jinseung, and Mr. Kim, to get me a visa. I wouldn't have been able to come back here without it."

"Yeah, but you still get to teach English to Jung Jen and Go Yoojin, right? That must be so cool." She had a dreamy look in her eyes.

"I guess it's pretty cool. Though the dazzle did wear off after a while. Now they're just like regular people to me."

"What's Jung Jen like? I haven't seen much of her on TV since...*you know*."

Jung Jen had been one of the top actors under management at KAM Entertainment...until she got involved in a big scandal. She got caught dating San Seung, the most popular male idol in South Korea. Then it came to light that she was also dating Lee Changho, his number-one rival, at the same time.

There was a huge furore, with fans from both sides turning against her. Her own fans didn't like it either.

Jung Jen's argument was that she was seeing them casually, and that she hadn't agreed to dating either of them exclusively. San Seung and Lee Changho remained tight-lipped on the subject. Neither of them were seen with her again.

While the male idols' entertainment careers continued to flourish, Jung Jen's took a major nosedive, going from lead roles to bit parts at most.

"It's a shame she got so much backlash," I mused, resting my head in my hands. "She's actually a lovely person. I think I believe her side of the story."

Jina swirled her straw in her drink. "Fans can be so brutal."

"Tell me about it." I sighed. "Anyway, what about you? Been getting many modelling jobs lately?"

"I have. Surprisingly."

"Why surprisingly?"

"Well, you know how old I am."

"You're hardly old."

"Old in the modelling world."

"I suppose."

"Just a little while ago I thought my contract wouldn't get renewed, but now I'm busier than ever. I've had to cut back my shifts at the cinema."

"That's good, isn't it?"

"Yeah, I just wonder how long this will last."

"A long time, I'm sure. You're still drop-dead gorgeous, and I don't see that changing anytime soon."

"Really?"

"Absolutely."

My phone dinged, interrupting my little pep talk. I swiped at the screen.

Jinseung: How was the class? When are you getting home?

"Who's that?" Jina asked. "*Dongsaeng*?"

"Mmhmm."

"Meeting's over then?"

His meeting. I had been so preoccupied with the self-defence class that I had completely forgotten. I cringed. "Oh. The meeting."

Jinseung had been on hiatus for the past few months to support me through my recovery, but he still had weekly meetings with Mr. Kim. They always made me anxious for one reason in particular.

"Don't look so worried," Jina said. "I'm sure it's just general admin stuff, as per usual."

"I hope so."

"Finish your tea and go home. I'm telling you it will be fine, but you should talk to him and see."

"Yes. You're right."

I picked up my phone and replied to Jinseung.

Chloe: I'll be home soon. Talk then?

Jinseung: OK. See you soon.

I finished the last gulp of my peach green tea and hopped down from the stool.

"See you at the next lesson." Jina slung her gym bag over her shoulder.

We shared a brief hug before parting.

As I drove the short distance home in Jinseung's car, I couldn't help fixating on the meeting. I had a terrible feeling about it. The meetings were usually on Thursdays, so why was this one on a Tuesday? Something must have been different about it, that was why, and if my suspicions were correct then my life was about to be thrown into turmoil.

Changsoo's work van was outside the house when I arrived. This escalated my fears since he didn't usually stick around after dropping Jinseung home. I parked in the garage and opened the door into the house, a vortex of trepidation whirling in my stomach.

When I entered the living room, I saw Jinseung and Changsoo sitting with tensed-up shoulders and serious looks on their faces. That was all the confirmation I needed.

2

Jinseung immediately lit up at my presence, though I could tell his cheerful smile was forced. Changsoo didn't make a similar effort, sitting there with a heavy scowl on his face.

"Hey," I said meekly, approaching.

Jinseung patted the space next to him on the couch. "Hey. How was the self-defence class?"

I swallowed the lump in my throat and sat down. "Good. Difficult, but good. I'm glad *Unnie* talked me into it."

"I'm happy to hear that."

A moment of awkward silence hung in the air. Both Jinseung and Changsoo didn't seem to want the job of bringing it up first, but if I had to wait a minute longer, I'd explode with pent-up tension.

"So, how did the meeting go?" I asked, keeping the tone casual though my anxiety must have been written all over me.

Jinseung's smile abruptly faded. "About that…"

"We need to talk to you about something," Changsoo said,

crossing his arms. "Though I'm sure you've already worked it out."

I nodded solemnly, hands clasped together in my lap.

"Mr. Kim wants me to resume a full schedule of work," Jinseung explained, "starting tomorrow."

Just as I feared. Even so, tomorrow was much sooner than I expected.

"We all knew this day was coming," Changsoo said. "It'll be difficult to put it off any longer. It's already been three—almost four months. The fact that we've gotten away with it for this long astounds me."

"Mr. Kim pretty much gave me an ultimatum," Jinseung explained. "Get back to work or else my contract won't get renewed. I haven't said yes yet, but he wants an answer by tonight."

"Surely he should give us more time," I stammered. "There's a lot to consider…"

"I agree, but you know what Mr. Kim is like."

"I…I don't know what to say." My brain was mush. I couldn't process my thoughts.

"How do you feel about me going back to work?"

"Well, not good, obviously."

Jinseung frowned. "I know it will be hard for you. You're still recovering. You still have nightmares, panic attacks…"

I sighed, staring down at my lap. "I suppose you don't really have a choice."

"He'll be forced out of the agency if he doesn't agree." Changsoo glared at me with a look which told me not to screw things up.

I groaned, face in my hands. What could I do? If Jinseung went back to work I'd be left alone for long periods while he went on shoots. I wasn't ready for that, but I couldn't ask him to say no, could I? I'd be asking him to sabotage his career, and I had already done far enough damage as it was.

"*Hyung*, could you please leave us to discuss this in private?" Jinseung asked.

Changsoo's mouth narrowed to a thin line. "Certainly." He stood up, pulled his messenger bag over his shoulder, and closed his coat buttons. "Call me once you've made a decision." He caught my eyes on the way out, sending me a silent warning.

My posture slouched when he left. At least I didn't have to contend with him anymore.

Jinseung moved closer and laid his hand on my shoulder. "So, anything you want to say now that Changsoo's gone?"

"I...don't know." Head bowed, I anxiously twiddled my fingers in my lap. *Mr. Kim wants an answer by tonight.* My mouth was dry. My heart thudded in my chest.

Jinseung silently reached for my hand and stroked it soothingly. The gesture did little to comfort me.

Perhaps I should just be honest. *I don't want you to go back to work yet.* I wouldn't make him say no, I wouldn't give him an ultimatum like Mr. Kim had, but he would be free to make the decision knowing exactly how I felt.

I spoke up. "Jinseung-ah."

"Hmm? What's on your mind?"

"I..." *No. I can't do it. I've already asked so much of him.* "Never mind."

"It's okay, tell me."

I looked him in his deep, dark eyes, trying to work out what he was thinking. "You're going to say yes to Mr. Kim, right?"

He wore an inscrutable expression on his face. Several seconds passed before he nodded slowly.

3

A pair of malicious black eyes glared at me, penetrating my soul, filling me with a deep sense of dread. I couldn't move. She had me pinned to the ground, her hands pressed hard on my wrists, sharp fingernails digging in, my back flush with the floor. I thrashed beneath her, completely powerless.

"You can't escape," she said, voice cold and laced with malice.

I opened my mouth to scream but no sound came out.

Her thin lips curled into a smirk. "You will die now."

Pressure built on my neck. Her eyes were blown wide, the pupils dilating as my throat began to constrict. I couldn't breathe. Everything became a blur except the beady pair of eyes, ablaze with determination to end my life.

Wake up. I know this is a dream. Please, wake up.

I tried to wrench my heavy eyelids apart, but they were sealed shut.

Wake up!

With a burst of focused effort, I cracked my vision open a

sliver. A battle between the real world and the dream world ensued, flashes of my bedroom interior interlaced with the scene of my ongoing nightmare. The mental tug-of-war continued until I finally awoke with a sharp gasp, snapping into a sitting position, hands grasping fistfuls of the duvet, heart pounding.

The bedsprings creaked and the sheets swished as Jinseung rolled towards me. His warm hand came down on my arm which was clammy with cold sweat.

"You okay?" he asked. "You're shaking."

I couldn't reply until I regained my breath.

"A nightmare," I said at last.

The nightmares were far less frequent these days but just as vivid. Going to bed was a game of roulette—would I have pleasant dreams or nightmares?

Jinseung heaved himself onto his butt and wrapped me in his arms.

"Everything is okay," he murmured, rocking me gently. "Oh Sejung is locked up. She can't harm you. No one can harm you, not as long as I'm here with you."

His words rang hollow despite the sympathy in his tone.

"But you won't be here with me, will you?" I spluttered. "You're going to go back to work, and you'll be so busy that we'll hardly see each other."

Jinseung clenched his jaw and didn't say anything. Spurred by his lack of reassurance, I burst into uncontrollable, heaving sobs.

He tightened his embrace and stroked my hair. "Shhhh."

The truth I had kept pent up inside came gushing out. "I don't want you to go back to work. I want you to stay here with me. It's selfish, I know, but I can't help it. I'm sorry. I'm so sorry."

He wiped my tears. "It's okay. Shhhh. It's okay. I'm glad you told me. You don't always have to put on a stoic front for my sake. I completely understand what you're saying."

"But what will you do?" I choked between sobs. "Are you really going to go back to work?"

"I'll try to negotiate something with Mr. Kim. Maybe we can come to some kind of compromise."

"But you already called and told him yes, didn't you?"

He shook his head. "I had a feeling this might happen, so I said I needed an extension."

I looked at him doubtfully. "That worked?"

"He hasn't given me long, twenty-four hours. I'll meet him again tomorrow evening—tonight, I mean. He wants my final answer then."

"What will you say?"

"If he won't let me continue my hiatus, I'll tell him I don't want to come back to work full-time...a lighter workload... modelling, commercials, nothing more strenuous than that."

I perked up a bit but still had my doubts. "Do you think he'll agree?"

"I don't see why not. He's strict, but I know he doesn't want to lose me. That's why he let me go on hiatus in the first place and why he helped get you a visa. He wouldn't do all that if he considered me expendable."

"Good point."

"Then it's settled. I'll ask to extend my hiatus, and if he says no, I'll try to get him to compromise with part-time work. I know it's not ideal, but—"

I threw my arms around him and kissed him on the cheek. His solution was so much better than I had hoped for.

"No, that's perfect. I couldn't ask for more. Thank you."

"You should've spoken up sooner."

"I didn't feel like I could."

"Please don't feel that way. We should be able to tell each other anything—*everything*. I love you, Chloe."

"I love you too."

He continued to hold me for several minutes, riding out the last soft wave of my sadness. When my eyes and cheeks had dried and my shoulders stopped shaking, he gently let me go.

"I know it's hard, but try to get some more sleep. It's still early. You have teaching in the morning."

I glanced at the digital alarm clock on the bedside table. 3:04 a.m. I lowered myself with a sigh, my head sinking into the feather and down pillow. Jinseung draped an arm over my waist and snuggled against me, his chest to my back. Sleep tugged at my eyelids, but I kept them open, just in case I drifted back into the same nightmare and it continued where it had left off.

At some point, Jinseung rolled away from me and dozed off, one arm curled above his head, the other resting on his stomach. His hair was mussed and his crumpled white t-shirt was askew, half exposing his abs. I watched his broad chest rise and fall in the even rhythm of his breath.

What did I do to deserve a boyfriend as kind and understanding as you?

I resolved never to hold back my true feelings from him again.

My body began to ache. I groaned and turned onto my tummy, planting my right cheek firmly on the pillow. I continued to hold my eyes open, resisting sleep until pale morning light seeped into the room, illuminating the dust particles in the air. Birds chirped in the camellia tree outside the window.

Jinseung awoke with a grunt and stretched his arms above his head. He turned to check the time, rubbing his eyes.

"Good morning," I said.

"Mornin'," he replied groggily. "Did you—" he yawned "—manage to get more sleep?"

I shook my head. "I didn't want to."

"Because of the nightmare?"

"Mmhmm."

He gave me a sympathetic look. "You're gonna be tired today."

"Maybe I'll have a nap when I get back from work."

"Okay. Well, I'm gonna get up now. What about you?"

"I'll get up."

"I can make breakfast while you shower, if you want."

"Yes, please." I pulled back the covers and hopped out of bed, bare feet finding the soft, springy carpet.

Despite my lack of sleep, I felt much better. Talking with Jinseung had settled my fears. He wouldn't abandon me. Everything was going to be okay.

By the time I emerged from the bathroom and got dressed, Jinseung had already set the table and served breakfast—a vegetable omelette with side dishes of rice, seasoned tofu, and radish kimchi. The savoury scent of soy sauce, fried egg, and chilli pepper tingled my nostrils. My stomach growled.

"Wow. What's all this?" I asked.

"Since I might have to work a little bit from now on, and we might not get to eat together as often, I thought I'd make a proper breakfast today. Hope you're hungry."

"You know me. Always hungry in the morning." I grabbed my chopsticks, cut off a small piece of omelette, and tucked it into my mouth. "Delicious!"

Jinseung smirked. "You're easy to please."

"You're a good cook."

"Only you think that."

Buster whined at my heels as I ate, begging for food.

"*Ya*! You've had your breakfast already," Jinseung scolded.

Seemingly chastised, Buster gave up and trotted to the corner where he circled twice then lay down.

When I finished breakfast, I got ready for work.

"Take my car," Jinseung said. "Changsoo will drop me off later."

Since revealing our relationship, I no longer took public transit for fear of getting recognised, so Jinseung let me use his car whenever I needed, and at some point I would probably get my own. I still wasn't used to driving in Seoul, and the icy winter roads were difficult to navigate, but I needed the privacy more than anything.

I took my coat down from the hook by the door and put it on, closing the tie tight around my waist.

"Don't forget this," Jinseung said, coming towards me with my wool scarf.

"Thanks." I reached for it, but he snatched it away.

"Allow me." He stood close as he coiled the thick, warm scarf around my neck. "There. Feeling better today? Any more concerns you wanna share before you go?"

I shook my head. "I think I'm okay. Knowing that you're not just going to give in to whatever Mr. Kim says is reassuring."

"I can't promise anything, but I'll do my best."

I believed him with all my heart.

———

The first time I met Jung Jen, I was completely starstruck. She looked every bit as beautiful as I had seen her in countless K-dramas, magazines, and advertisements. She was tall and slender with long, straight black hair and creamy, blemish-free skin. Bright blue contact lenses and soft pink lipstick completed her trademark look. I had hearts in my eyes when I looked at her.

Despite her recent fall from grace, I had still blushed and stammered my way through my first lesson as her English tutor. Since then, I had become used to her presence, and I learned to treat her just like anyone else. Both of us were more comfortable that way.

She entered the lesson room late—as usual, casually dressed in faded black jeans and a baggy sweater, hair thrown back in a messy low ponytail.

"Good morning, Jen," I said in English.

"Good morning, Chloe," she replied with a weak smile, lowering herself into the seat opposite me.

I noticed the dark rings under her eyes, the hollows in her cheeks, and the grey cast of her skin. I didn't ask if she was feeling okay, because I knew she wasn't. A combination of overwork, extreme dieting, and lack of sleep would make anyone sick. Jinseung used to get similar bouts of exhaustion. Even so, Jen looked quite a bit worse than usual. I decided not to push her too hard this lesson.

We started by reviewing the English lines in her latest script. She was playing the small part of a doctor in an ensemble drama, and she had a few scenes with a patient who spoke English. I worked through the lines with her, making sure she understood the meaning of each sentence, then checking her pronunciation.

Going through the script took much longer than I anticipated. Jen kept yawning, she was scatterbrained, and I often had to repeat myself.

"Sorry," Jen murmured as she massaged her temples. "I just can't think today."

"Stressed out?"

"Yeah."

I didn't think there was much I could do to help but offered to lend an ear anyway. "Anything you want to talk about?"

She hesitated. "No."

"Okay. Well, take as much time as you need."

After going over the script several more times, we reached a point where I didn't think I'd be able to squeeze much more improvement from her, so we put it aside.

"How about a listening exercise?" I asked.

"Sure." She didn't sound very enthused.

I couldn't blame her. Regardless, I handed her the sheet of paper with a list of pre-prepared questions. "I'm going to read a short story aloud. I want you to write the answers to the questions, in English. Got it? I'll read the story three times and pause so you have plenty of time to write. On the first read, you can just listen."

"Okay."

Jen chewed the tip of her pen as I read the story. She had a blank expression on her face, and I wondered how much she was taking in. Not much, it turned out. By the end of the third read-through, I glanced at her paper and saw that she had only answered two questions out of ten.

"Could you read it one more time?" she asked.

"Of course."

I cleared my throat and began again. Jen concentrated on the question sheet, her forehead wrinkled from the strain. This time she managed to answer a couple more questions.

I had started going through the answers with her when someone knocked sharply on the door. Her manager, Jeong Daeshim, walked in—a short, stylishly dressed man in his mid-forties. He was neatly groomed and smelled like grapefruit-and-ginger-scented cologne. I didn't like him. Not sure why. Something about him just rubbed me the wrong way. He didn't acknowledge me when he came in, speaking directly to his charge instead.

"Dermatology appointment in fifteen minutes," he said brusquely. "We better get going."

Jen gave me an apologetic look. "Sorry, *Seonsaeng-nim*. I'll see you next time."

"No problem. Hope you manage to get some rest."

This kind of thing happened more often than not. English lessons weren't considered a top priority on the actors' schedules so they usually ended up missed, rescheduled, or cut short.

Jen got up and followed Manager Jeong out of the room, closing the door behind them. I sagged in my chair.

Jen was taking English lessons to improve her chances in getting roles overseas. Her reputation was damaged in South Korea, but in America she could start fresh. Unfortunately, she'd never make any progress in English at this rate. *Oh well.* At least I got to go home early. I packed up my teaching materials and went on my way.

As I walked across the concrete floor of the basement carpark, I didn't realise that someone was following me. I unlocked the car, hopped into the driver's seat, and was in the process of pulling on my seatbelt when there was a sharp rap on the window, making me jump. I let go of the seatbelt in shock and it retracted with a whoosh. *What the heck?* I looked out the window and saw Changsoo standing there. His face was red and shiny with sweat. He was puffing. He must have chased me. What did he want that was so important? I'd never known Changsoo to *run* before. I wound down the window.

"Manager Bong, everything okay?"

"Thank goodness I caught you," he huffed. "Jinseung is on his way for an emergency meeting with Mr. Kim."

I screwed up my face in confusion. "Emergency meeting? Is this about Jinseung going back to work?"

I thought he had twenty-four hours…

Changsoo shook his head.

"Then what?"

"He just received his draft notice."

4

I always knew this day would come, but I never expected that it would happen so soon and so out of the blue.

Just like every young man in South Korea, Jinseung would have to serve in the military. And the worst part? There was absolutely no way he could get out of it. End of story. Even famous people had to enlist. The whole dilemma of him going back to work or not was moot. This was worse. Much worse.

I opted to wait at KAM HQ until the emergency meeting concluded. Changsoo had gone in with Jinseung and left me sitting at his desk in an office which smelled of weak coffee and warm printer paper. The framed photograph of him and Jinseung making a heart-sign pose still took pride of place on his neat and tidy desk, now joined by two other similar shots. All of the other desks in the room were unoccupied except for two where a very young man and woman worked. I hadn't seen them before. *Interns?* The pair kept stealing covert glances at me. They definitely knew I was Jinseung's girlfriend.

I caught the young woman's eye and she averted her gaze, blushing.

"Do you happen to know what's going on in the meeting?" I asked her. "I don't know anything except that Jinseung got his draft notice."

She grimaced. "Wish we could help, but we honestly don't know more than that either."

"You're Chloe Gibson, right?" the man asked.

"Yes."

"*Aigoo.* You're so pretty."

"Um, thanks."

I wasn't in the mood for flattery. My head whirred with the consequences of the latest turn of events. Jinseung would be away for around twenty months, leaving me to fend for myself. There would be no one to comfort me when I woke from a nightmare. No one to share the house with so I wouldn't be all alone, feeling paranoid about stalker fans breaking in. No one to notify the police if I got kidnapped again and didn't come home. I knew my fears were irrational, but that's what trauma does to your head. Although I had come a long way in the last few months, I still hadn't fully recovered and wouldn't for a long time yet. I sighed into my hands.

This is terrible. What am I going to do?

I wasn't keeping track of the time, but the painful hunger pangs in my stomach told me it had been hours since Jinseung and Changsoo entered the meeting room with their colleagues and Mr. Kim. What were they discussing that could possibly take so long?

My ears pricked at the sound of movement in the corridor. The office door swung open. I got to my feet as Jinseung, Changsoo, and their cohort entered the room, all of them straight-faced and speaking quietly or not at all.

At first glance, Jinseung looked calm and untroubled, but

then I noticed one telltale sign of distress—his tightly clenched jaw, which clenched even further when his gaze met mine. I didn't want to make a scene in front of his colleagues, so I restrained myself from running over to ask all the questions racing through my mind.

Everyone returned to their seats, apart from Jinseung and Changsoo who remained standing. The sounds of typing and mouse-clicking seemed amplified in the otherwise quiet office. A phone rang, but no one answered it.

Changsoo was first to break the uneasy silence. "Why don't I take you two home? I'm sure you have a lot to discuss—in private."

"Chloe has the car," Jinseung said. "I'll drive us home, you take care of things here."

"Right. Call me if you need anything."

Jinseung turned to me. "Let's go."

He didn't say anything else until we sat down in the car. He crumpled in the driver's seat, deflating like a balloon.

"I'm sorry," he murmured. "I thought I had more time. Next year...several months, at least... That's why I never said anything."

"You think I didn't know this might happen? Of course I did. I just didn't want to think about it. I pushed it to the back of my mind."

Jinseung sighed, smiling wearily. "Talk about bad timing."

"Do you have to serve in the army? Can't you do public service work instead?"

I had heard of some men being able to work as public servants if they weren't capable of participating in the army.

Jinseung raised an arm and flexed his bicep. "Look at me. Do you think they'd let me go to waste as a public servant? I'm far too fit and healthy."

"Can't you just, I don't know, get an injury or something?"

Jinseung laughed.

"Hey! I'm serious."

"No. I can't just get an injury or something. How bad would that look?" He abruptly started the engine.

The heater came on, thawing me out. I pulled on my seatbelt. "What did you talk about in there, anyway?"

"Well, my contract is going to expire while I'm away, for one thing."

"Ah. So what's going to happen with that?"

"I'll make a decision when I get discharged. So will Mr. Kim. For now, he wants me to work up until I leave."

I snapped my head around to face him. "What? He won't let you stay on hiatus?"

"No. He was firm about that."

Damn. How could Mr. Kim be so harsh? Expecting him to work, with such limited time to spend with family and friends before joining the military.

"But it won't be too much," he stressed. "I obviously can't take on any big projects at this stage."

Well, that was true, but still…

One question remained. The biggest question of them all. *Do I dare ask?*

I swallowed the lump in my throat and forced it out. "How long until you leave?"

"Four weeks."

I gasped. "Four weeks!"

There's much less time than I thought.

"I'm lucky to get that much notice, to be honest."

I absorbed the news in silence while Jinseung drove out of the carpark. *Four weeks. Just four weeks.* Then we'd be separated for nearly two years. *How am I going to cope?*

Jinseung's gaze flicked back and forth between me and the frostbitten road, a wrinkle of concern deepening between his eyebrows.

"*Jagi*, don't be sad. I know it will be hard, but we'll get through this. Together. Look at it this way: once it's over and done with, we'll never have to worry about it again."

His calm reason fell on deaf ears.

"Why, oh why did this have to happen now?" I wailed.

"Would it be any easier in a few months or a year's time?"

I opened my mouth to respond but didn't know what to say. He had me there.

"No. It wouldn't," I admitted.

"You see."

It would take a lot more than a few months or even years before I recovered from my trauma—if I ever did. Deep down I knew Jinseung was right. Better to get it over with now instead of living with an undercurrent of low-key anxiety, knowing that he could get sent away at any moment. The twenty months apart would be a short, sharp, shock to the system in the long-term scheme of things. Like a vaccine jab—once taken, I'd be protected.

"I've got an idea," Jinseung said, steering carefully on the icy road. "Why don't you consider going back to the UK while I'm gone? It might be easier—"

My answer came before I even gave the notion a brief thought.

"No. No way. Uh-uh. I'm not going back."

"Okay. It was just a suggestion."

I didn't know why I was so averse to the idea. Perhaps I equated it to a giant step backwards when I wanted so badly to keep moving forwards.

"I'll stay and wait for you here," I said with resolve.

Jinseung smiled, obviously relieved. "Then I'll visit you as often as I can."

"And you'll keep in touch?"

"Of course. One good thing is they're not so strict on phone usage in the army anymore."

"Really? Whew. That's comforting."

We continued our homeward journey, discussing the ins and outs of his pending military service. The more we talked, the more reassured I began to feel. It wouldn't be so bad. We'd chat on the phone every day, and he would visit me whenever he had a break. Twenty months would fly by before I knew it. In the meantime, I had my friends—Shin Jina and Yang Bora. I knew I could rely on them to keep me company and make sure I was okay.

I heard Buster before we even drove into the garage. How could such a tiny dog yap so loudly? He came running to us as soon as we walked in the door. I wasn't in the mood for petting him.

"Shush," I said, lightly batting him away as he pawed at my leg, whining.

I barely made it to the couch before collapsing in a heap.

What an overwhelming day.

Jinseung sat by my side and placed a steady hand on my knee. He said nothing. The lines etched on his face told me he was deep in thought.

It suddenly struck me how self-centred I was being. All I had done was worry and complain about my end of the bargain. What of Jinseung's plight? He'd have to leave his comfortable lifestyle behind for the drudgery of the army. I had heard stories of the hazing that goes on—the harsh treatment of new recruits. I wondered if he would be okay.

"Are you scared?" I asked.

He snapped out of his solemn trance and smiled his usual heart-warming smile, the corners of his eyes crinkling, dimples in his full cheeks.

"No. I'll be fine. If I can survive the entertainment industry, I can survive the army. Don't worry about me. Focus on taking care of yourself."

I had heard that idols and actors usually did okay in the army since they were already highly self-disciplined and used to rigorous training, but I still felt wary. Would he really be okay?

"Hey," he said, shuffling closer to me. "Cheer up. I don't like to see you sad."

"But I'm going to miss you."

"Me too." He lifted my chin and stroked my cheek. "But don't you think I'll look good in army fatigues?"

So this was his tactic for changing the subject and taking my mind off the bad things. The mental image invaded my thoughts before I could stop it. I pictured him in a camouflage uniform, looking tough, strong, and undeniably sexy.

"Now that you mention it, that does sound kinda hot," I said with a smirk.

He grinned. "Oh yeah?"

"I can't wait to see it."

"There, now you're smiling."

My smile turned to a pout just to tease him.

He wasn't having any of it. He grasped my face in his hands, pulled me to his lips, and kissed me roughly. I closed my eyes and let all the unhappy thoughts dissolve as I reciprocated, wrapping my arms around his waist and drawing him closer. He deepened the kiss, tasting my tongue, turning me weak and unable to think straight.

Chapter 4

A ringtone suddenly assaulted my ears. I pulled away but Jinseung brought me back to his lips, insistent.

The ringing seemed to last forever, and when it finally stopped, only a few brief seconds passed before it started up again. It was far too distracting to simply ignore.

Jinseung reluctantly broke away, growling in annoyance. He grabbed the offending phone off the coffee table and checked who was calling. "Damn. I better take this."

I presumed it was Bong Changsoo or Mr. Kim calling—but the shrill female voice I heard definitely wasn't either of them.

"*Eomma*, is everything okay?" Jinseung asked.

So, the caller was his mother…

He tensed up in reaction to what she was saying.

"What?…You're in Seoul?…You're coming here?…Now?"

My wide eyes met Jinseung's.

5

Half an hour later, Mrs. Woo and Mr. Shin arrived on our doorstep with luggage in tow.

Oh my gosh. Do they plan on staying the night? I tried not to let my horror show. Judging by his grimace, Jinseung was equally concerned.

"My dear son!" Mrs. Woo said, smiling fondly. The tall and elegant woman enveloped him in a hug, bracelets jangling on her wrists.

When she finally let go, Jinseung turned his attention to his father—a kind-looking man of average build, who wore round spectacles which looked far too small for his large face. They nodded wordlessly at one another.

I hid behind Jinseung, but Mrs. Woo's keen eyes found me.

"Chloe, my dear," she cooed. "How lovely to see you again. We haven't seen each other since you visited Tongyeong all that time ago."

"Uh, hello."

Jinseung hadn't told his parents the he was dating me until we had already moved in together, though Mrs. Woo had been suspicious about the nature of our relationship since I met her in Tongyeong. The fact that we were an unmarried couple living together had initially upset her, but she quickly got over it and had since accepted me as her precious son's girlfriend.

Something that Mrs. Woo and Mr. Shin weren't aware of was the kidnapping and attempted murder I had gone through. They knew I had suffered an altercation with a *sasaeng* fan, but that was the extent of their knowledge. I hadn't wanted them to make a fuss over me. We would have to tell them at some point, though, or they would learn the full story from the media once it inevitably got out. *That can wait*, I told myself.

"No need to be shy, dear. Come and give me a hug." Mrs. Woo held out her arms and I awkwardly stepped into her embrace. She smelled strongly of floral perfume. I held my breath to stop myself coughing from the sickly scent.

"*Eomma, Appa*, what brings you to Seoul with so little notice?" Jinseung asked. The tinge of annoyance in his voice went unnoticed by his parents.

"You could say it was a spur-of-the-moment decision," Mrs. Woo said. "We thought it would be a nice surprise."

"Does *Noona* know you're here?"

"Yes, we called her too. She'll come to dinner with us tonight."

Jinseung eyed the luggage warily. "Are you going to stay here?"

"*Aigoo*. What's with all the questions? You have plenty of room, don't you? Your sister doesn't have a spare room and lives with a flatmate, so naturally we should stay with our dear son."

"Naturally," he repeated with a forced smile. "So, how long do you intend to stay?"

"Just a few nights."

A few nights! I thought one was bad enough.

"Won't you invite us inside? It's cold out here." She wrapped her arms around herself and shivered exaggeratedly.

"Of course. Come in and make yourselves comfortable." He stood aside so they could get past.

Mrs. Woo shed her fur coat and I hung it up on the rack of hooks by the door. She studied her surroundings with her nose wrinkled in a mild look of distaste.

"How long have you lived here now? Looks like you could use the help of an interior decorator."

"There's no need. We like it how it is," Jinseung said, brushing her comment off.

Playful barking filled the hallway as Buster bounded towards Jinseung's parents. His tail wagged with furious excitement. He used to live with the couple so no wonder he was so thrilled to see them.

"Buster, my sweet puppykins!" Mrs. Woo bent down and scooped the little ball of white fluff into her arms. She kissed him all over, and he licked her with his tiny pink tongue.

"Let me take your luggage to the spare room," Jinseung said. He relieved his mother of her many bags, most of which were emblazoned with luxury designer logos—Louis Vuitton, Prada, and Gucci.

Not wanting to be left alone with the couple, I took Mr. Shin's single plain black suitcase and followed Jinseung away.

As soon as we were alone in the guest room and out of earshot, Jinseung threw me a look of sympathy.

"I'm so sorry about this."

I drew a weary breath. "Don't worry. It's okay."

It wasn't really okay with me, but what could I do? It would be totally inappropriate to kick them out. Such concepts as filial duty and respecting your elders were a big deal in Korea, and I didn't want to make a bad impression.

Jinseung squeezed my shoulder. "Thanks. I know this isn't ideal. I'll make it up to you. I promise."

"You better," I teased. "Well, at least you get to break the news of your conscription in person now."

"Yeah. I better tell them."

Once we were all sitting down together in the living room, Jinseung brought it up as soon as there was a lull in his mother's constant stream of chatter.

"*Eomma*, *Appa*, I have something to tell you." He spoke in a neutral tone which gave little away.

Mrs. Woo's face brightened. "Oh, let me guess! You two are going to get married!"

My mouth gaped in shock and I felt my face turn red. *Where did she get that idea from? Wishful thinking?*

"No. That's not it," Jinseung said, unruffled by her outrageous assumption.

"Then…you're going to have a baby? You should get married first."

A baby! It just gets worse.

This time her remark provoked a stronger reaction from him. "*Eomma*! It's nothing like that."

Mr. Shin spoke up, a serious look on his face. "You're going to the army."

At least one of his parents has sense.

Jinseung nodded.

Mrs. Woo's mouth snapped shut, all the brightness fading from her features. "Of course that's it. I should have known."

"I just found out," Jinseung said. "Got my draft notice this morning."

"Well, every man must do his duty. It's about time you

went to the army. It will be good for you. Besides, just think how handsome and manly you'll look in your army fatigues!" she gushed, hands clasped together under her chin and a dreamy look in her eyes.

"I hope I live to see the day conscription gets scrapped," Mr. Shin grumbled.

"What are you talking about?" Mrs. Woo said. "The army is an excellent opportunity for young boys to become men. Of course they should enlist."

"You wouldn't say that if women were drafted too."

Mrs. Woo waved her hand and tutted. "Nonsense."

He dropped the subject, unwilling to argue with her. "Have you told your sister yet?" he asked Jinseung.

"No. Not yet."

"You can tell her at dinner tonight," Mrs. Woo said.

"Dinner? Are we going somewhere?"

"I booked us a table at a lovely Japanese place. Since we now have good cause to celebrate, you should eat and drink as much as you want. Our treat, of course." She turned to me. "You've met our Jina, haven't you?"

"Yes. We're good friends, actually."

"Wonderful!"

With a couple of hours left before we would leave for dinner, the four of us filled the afternoon discussing army life. Mr. Shin recounted grim memories of harsh toil and bullying which sometimes bordered on torture. The knot in my stomach tightened with each word.

"Stop it. You're frightening them," Mrs. Woo scolded.

Mr. Shin attempted to ease up on the negativity. "Fortunately, things have improved since then. I'm sure you won't have the same experience as I did. You're a strapping young lad too, so that's in your favour."

Chapter 5

On the other side of the coin, Mrs. Woo's memories were rose-tinted and nostalgic. Her days as fiancée to the active-duty solider were full of romantic correspondence and wedding planning, longing for the day that he would return so they could finally marry.

"It was well worth the wait," she said, taking her husband's hand and giving it a gentle squeeze.

The gesture caused Mr. Shin to break into a shy smile. "Knowing you were waiting for me helped me get through it."

At seven o'clock, we piled into Jinseung's car and headed to dinner. Jina planned to meet us at the restaurant.

Haru was not your typical Japanese ramen or sushi joint, but a classy and modern establishment with minimalist decor in subdued tones, soft lighting, and floor-to-ceiling windows providing expansive views of metropolitan Seoul. All around, smartly dressed couples and small groups dined on fancy sushi platters while sipping drinks and making quiet conversation.

A waiter led us to our table—the most privately positioned in the restaurant.

"Nice place," I commented, taking a seat next to Jinseung and opposite Mrs. Woo.

"I dined here a few years ago and have wanted to come back ever since," Mrs. Woo said. "I hope it's still as good as I remember."

Jina arrived and joined us shortly. She looked stunning with her short hair tucked behind her ears, false eyelashes on, and her signature fuchsia lipstick which would look over-the-top on most people yet suited her to a T. Somehow her simple ensemble of slim black trousers and a cream sweater looked ultra stylish. I supposed with her model figure anything would look good on her. She greeted her parents then took a chair at the end of the table.

"It's been a while since we all got together as a family like this," she commented.

"We should do it more often, as I'm always saying" Mrs. Woo said.

"Well, now that we're all here, shouldn't we order soon?" Mr. Shin asked.

Mrs. Woo touched his sleeve. "Aren't you forgetting something?" She directed a meaningful glance towards Jinseung.

He coughed. "Right. Jinseung-ah, why don't you tell your sister the news."

"Oh?" Jina turned to him, brow raised. "*Dongsaeng*?"

"I received my draft notice today," he said.

Her mouth dropped open slightly, eyes widening. "Ooooh."

"I'll enlist next month."

"Funny how something so expected can still take you off-guard." She reached out and squeezed his hand. "You'll do great."

He smiled. "Thanks."

"But what about Chloe? And I wonder what will happen with the trial and everything. Will they let you take leave to be a witness, or even just to watch?"

My stomach tightened. The confusion radiating off the siblings' parents was palpable.

"Trial?" Mrs. Woo asked, brows knitted.

An awkward silence descended before Jina gasped and brought a hand in front of her mouth.

Damn. The cat's out of the bag. Now I'll have to tell them...

"Oops," Jina said. The wide-eyed frowny look she gave me said, "My bad."

"Could someone please explain?" Mrs. Woo demanded,

Chapter 5

eyes flicking between me and her son. "What's this about a trial? And witness? Did something happen?"

Jinseung spoke up before I did. "This is between me and Chloe—"

"It's okay," I cut in. "We should have told them after it happened. I just...don't like explaining it over again."

Recounting my ordeal and having to answer a million questions about it was the bane of my existence. I had already done it enough in my lifetime to be completely over it.

"What is it, dear?" Mrs. Woo asked, face softening into a sympathetic expression.

"I'm not sure this is something we should discuss over dinner," Jinseung said. "Let's at least wait until we get home."

"That sounds fair to me," Mr. Shin said.

Mrs. Woo sulked and pouted but didn't say anything.

"Enough chitchat. I'm going to order." Mr. Shin pressed a button which alerted a waiter that we were ready.

A man in a crisp white shirt and black trousers arrived at our table momentarily. Mr. Shin placed an order for the priciest sushi platter on the menu, along with a vast array of side dishes and some premium-label sake.

Jina leaned in towards her brother, head resting in her hands, elbows on the table. "So, *Dongsaeng*, when will you be having a goodbye party?"

"Hmmm. Haven't thought about that yet," Jinseung said. "Not even sure I will have one."

"Of course you will! You must!"

"That so?"

"You haven't even had a housewarming party yet, have you? You should invite everyone over."

Jinseung rubbed his chin in thought.

"I think it's a good idea," I chimed in. "I haven't even met most of your friends yet. You should introduce me."

We rarely had guests over to the house or visited other people. I think Jinseung was trying to be considerate and not stretch me too much while I was still recovering, which was sweet but a bit unnecessary. I actually wanted to meet his friends.

"See? Chloe thinks so too," Jina said.

A grin spread across Jinseung's mouth. "Well, in that case…"

"You'll do it?"

He nodded.

"Yes! Can't wait. I *will* be invited, won't I?"

"Absolutely."

"And what about your parents? Will we get an invite?" Mrs. Woo asked.

Mr. Shin shot her a warning look. "Don't be ridiculous. He won't want his parents there spoiling the fun."

"No offence, but I think I'll just have my friends over," Jinseung said. "But you're welcome to come and see me off on the day I leave for training camp."

"We wouldn't miss it for the world," Mr. Shin said.

Dishes began arriving at the table, fragrant with the mingling smells of sesame oil, soy sauce, and wasabi.

"Let's eat," Mr. Shin said, grabbing a pair of chopsticks.

I looked over the spread of options, trying to decide what to eat first. Too bad my appetite wasn't all there. My stomach twisted into knots with anxiety. First, the news of Jinseung's conscription and now this. The thought of having to dredge up the details of my horrible experience yet again made me feel sick to my stomach. The feeling only intensified throughout dinner. At one point I had to excuse myself and go to the bathroom, thinking I might throw up. Fortunately, as I leaned over the toilet bowl, nothing came out of my mouth except my heaving breath.

When I emerged from the bathroom cubicle, Jina was standing with her back to the row of basins and mirrors, frowning with concern.

"Are you okay?" she asked.

"It's just…It's been a long day."

That was truth enough.

"Hey, I'm sorry about…you know."

"Don't worry about it. We should never have kept it a secret this long, and it's better they heard it from you than the media."

I leaned over a basin to splash my face with water. Jina held my hair back. The cold water refreshed me.

"Feeling better?" Jina asked.

I dabbed my face with a paper towel. "Yep. Good to go."

I stepped towards the door, but Jina grabbed my arm.

"Before we go back in, I want to give you something," she said.

"Oh?"

She fumbled in her Kate Spade handbag and emerged with something small, wrapped in fuchsia paper that matched her lipstick.

"I was going to give it to you after dinner, but since we're here, might as well give it to you in private."

I took the gift-wrapped object, wondering why she'd buy me something when it wasn't my birthday or any other special occasion.

"What is it?" I asked.

"Go ahead. Unwrap it and see."

Curious, I tore open the bundle.

6

I don't know what I expected but it sure as hell wasn't this.

"Cool, isn't it?" Jina asked, beaming.

I stared at the object in my open hand. A keychain with two items attached—a mini flashlight and a small spray canister. I had a general idea what it was supposed to be but didn't know the specifics.

"So, er, what is it exactly?" I asked.

"A self-defence kit. The flashlight doubles as a stun gun. The other thing is pepper spray."

"Oh, I see. I thought it might be something like that. Did the self-defence workshop give you this idea?"

"Uh-huh. I asked *Seonsaeng-nim* which one to buy."

A strange gift, but it made a lot of sense. I didn't know why I hadn't thought of it myself.

"Thank you. I'll carry it with me whenever I go out on my own."

"I got one for me and one for Yang Bora too. I'll give it to her the next time I see her."

"She'll love it."

"I know, right? Though I can't help thinking she might be overzealous with it."

I cracked a smile. "I know what you mean. She'd use it without hesitation. Some poor guy might get hurt for no good reason."

"I better tell her to be careful. Come on, let's go back out. They'll start to think you really are sick."

With the kit safely stowed away, I followed her out.

The rest of the dinner carried on without incident. I barely touched the food but hoped everyone was too focused on their own meals to notice.

After Mr. Shin paid the bill, we said goodbye to Jina and left the restaurant.

Mrs. Woo's cheeks were puffed out as if she were holding her breath. She barely lasted one minute in the car before she burst.

"It's the *sasaeng* fan, isn't it? I didn't know you pressed charges. You should have told me, I could have recommended a good lawyer."

"We have a good lawyer, thank you," Jinseung said. "Let's talk about this when we get home." He turned to me and mouthed, "Don't worry."

But I did worry. Very soon I'd have to open up my wound again so they could leer at it. That was what it felt like, anyway.

At home, Jinseung managed to sneak a quiet word with me while his parents were in another room.

"Let me take care of this," he said. "I'll tell them everything while you go and have a relaxing bath then go to bed."

I stared at him in disbelief. He made it sound so easy. Was it really so?

"Go on," he urged. "They'll understand why you don't

want to talk about it."

I stood on my tiptoes and planted a kiss on his cheek. "Thank you."

"And I'll tell them not to make a fuss the rest of the time they're here."

"You're wonderful, you know that?"

"Go. Enjoy your bath." He playfully shooed me away.

I didn't feel guilty hiding out in the ensuite bathroom. I felt relieved. *What a crazy day*. I sank into the hot bathwater loaded with epsom salts and tried not to think about the conversation going on in the living room or Jinseung's imminent enlistment. The meditation techniques my last therapist taught me came in handy. Focusing on nothing but my breath, I watched my belly expand and contract with each intake of air. Slowly, I began to relax, my muscles loosening, body slipping further under the water.

I didn't want to come out while Jinseung's talk with his parents was still in progress. I stayed submerged until my skin was wrinkled up like a prune.

Finally satisfied that the talk would be over, I stood up, water dripping off my naked body, and pulled the plug. I dried off in the steamy room and slathered myself in body cream. Before doing my skincare routine, I had to wipe the misted mirror with a cloth so I could see my reflection.

Hair pulled back with a pink bunny-ear headband, I got to work. My regimen had become a lot more extensive than it used to be, thanks to recently implementing the ten-step method.

A plume of steam rushed into the air when I emerged from the bathroom wrapped in a fluffy robe. The bedroom was empty—Jinseung hadn't come to bed yet.

Would it be rude to go straight to bed without saying goodnight to his parents? I contemplated this a moment before deciding that yes, it would be—at least his mother might think so. Just a quick "Goodnight," then I'd disappear to safety again.

I opened the bedroom door and tentatively stuck my head out into the hallway. All was quiet and still. I made my way to the living room, but the lights were off and the curtains drawn. Did they retire to their room? Where was Jinseung?

I walked up the hallway and saw light coming through the open door of the spare room they were staying in.

I'll just walk by and say goodnight.

As I approached, I heard voices—Jinseung and his mother.

"Please, take it," Mrs. Woo urged.

"I don't know," Jinseung said. "Won't *Noona* want it?"

"Don't worry about her. She'll be taken care of as well."

"…Are you sure?"

"It's my mother's ring and I want *you* to have it."

I stopped in my tracks before I reached the door. I didn't mean to eavesdrop, but before I could turn and walk away, I caught a few more words of their private conversation.

"All right," Jinseung relented. "I'll take it."

"Wonderful!"

I quickly tiptoed back to my room.

What did I just hear? My head fell on the pillow. *This is more than I can process right now.*

An awkward silence reigned at breakfast the next morning. Jinseung, his parents, and I sat around the table avoiding eye contact as we ate the pastries Mrs. Woo had bought from a nearby bakery. The sounds of chewing food, sipping drinks, and crumpling page turns of the newspaper Mr. Shin was reading filled the void. I noticed Mrs. Woo taking furtive little glances at me. She practically trembled with the effort of self-restraint. I knew it would only be a few seconds before she erupted.

Five…four…three…two…one…

"I can't take this anymore," she snapped.

Here we go.

"Why are we being so quiet?" she asked. "Someone needs to say something."

"*Eomma*," Jinseung warned.

She ignored him. "Chloe, you poor dear…If I had known… Oh, it just breaks my heart. All that you've been through…We could have done something. If you ever need anything, we are here for you. If you ever want to talk about it—"

"I went through this with you last night," Jinseung said firmly. "She doesn't like to talk about it."

"But I just can't ignore it. I can't."

I knew this would happen if we told them. Mrs. Woo wasn't the kind of person who could just leave things alone, she had to get herself involved. That didn't make her a bad person, but being smothered in pity was the last thing I wanted.

"Thank you for your concern, Mrs. Woo," I said, "but I have all the support I need and I'm recovering well."

"Is that so? What about when Jinseung leaves? However will you cope?"

"I have my friends."

"Friends who will always be available to look after you when you need them?"

"Yes." I wasn't going to let her make me second-guess the quality of my friendships.

"Well, you have us too. Right, *yeobo*?" She tugged her

husband's arm.

He glanced up from his newspaper. "Yes," he grunted.

"Thank you," I said. "I appreciate that. I'll let you know if I need anything."

Mrs. Woo shook her head and clucked her tongue. "You poor, poor thing…"

Oh, great. Was the rest of their stay going to be like this? If so, my patience was going to wear through very quickly.

When we had finished eating, I took the dishes to the kitchen just to get away from everyone. Jinseung followed me inside and massaged my shoulders from behind as I rinsed the plates.

"I'm so sorry about my mother," he said. "She can't help it."

"I know she's just trying to be nice, but…Just how long are they planning to stay?"

"I'll tell them I'm going to be too busy to spend any time with them, so there's no point staying very long."

"Do you think that will dissuade them?"

"I'll put my foot down if I have to."

I bent over and put the dirty dishes in the dishwasher.

"Changsoo *Hyung* will be here in a minute," Jinseung said.

I straightened and faced him. "Are you going to work?"

"Yes. Like I said, Mr. Kim wants me to work up until I leave, and I should at least go in today and find out what he's planning for me. Not too much can get arranged at this late notice. It's not like I'll have to be out on shoots all day or something."

"I suppose that's okay."

As much as I hated it, perhaps seeing less of Jinseung in the lead-up to his departure would help ease me into daily life without him. Or that was how I justified it to myself, at least.

"I know it's not ideal," Jinseung said, caressing my cheek. "I'd like to spend as much time with you as possible before I leave, but I don't want to argue with Mr. Kim and find out that I no longer have an agency when I return."

"I do understand. Just…please don't take on too much."

"I'll do the minimum required. Enough to keep Mr. Kim happy, and that's it."

The rumble of a car engine outside pulled my eyes to the window. Changsoo's work van rolled up the driveway.

"He's here," I said.

"Then I better get going."

We emerged from the kitchen. Mr. Shin was still absorbed in his newspaper. Mrs. Woo looked at us expectantly.

"Are you off somewhere?" she asked.

"I need to go into KAM," Jinseung replied.

"And leave us alone here? The whole point of coming over was to spend time with you. I thought you were on hiatus?"

"Not anymore. If you had given me notice of your visit then maybe I could have arranged something."

Mrs. Woo hung her head and let out an over-the-top sigh. "What will we do? Our trip is spoilt."

Mr. Shin folded his newspaper in half. "Don't be so dramatic. I'm sure we can find something to do. We're in Seoul, after all."

Mrs. Woo suddenly lifted her head, face brightened by a spark of inspiration. "Oh, I know! Chloe, let's go shopping together."

I shot Jinseung a panicked look. No way could I survive a day being dragged around expensive shops with his high-maintenance mother.

"Uhh…" Jinseung flicked a nervous glance back and forth between us.

Chapter 6

Changsoo honked the horn outside, making my chest jump. I had forgotten he was already here.

"Why don't you come to KAM with me?" Jinseung asked her. "I'm sure someone can give you a tour. You've always wanted a tour of my workplace, haven't you? Potentially spot some of the other talent…"

This idea seemed to pique her interest. Her thin eyebrows shot up, mouth forming an O shape. "Well, I wouldn't say no…"

"Sounds good to me," Mr. Shin said, abandoning the newspaper and rising to his feet.

Whew. Nice save.

Changsoo knocked on the front door now. Jinseung normally didn't make him wait this long.

I answered the door while Jinseung and his parents got ready to leave. Changsoo stood on the doorstep, poking his head in, forehead furrowed in curiosity.

"Is something going on?" he asked. "There's another car here."

"His parents are here," I explained.

"Ohh…"

"They'll be with you in a minute."

He cocked a brow. "They?"

"Yeah…He kinda told his parents they could have a tour of KAM HQ."

"He *what?*" Changsoo threw his head back in disbelief, hands clenched into fists at his sides. "I s'pose I'll have to be the one to arrange this tour," he grumbled.

"Sorry, Changsoo-ssi, but someone needs to keep them entertained. Better you than me."

"*Aigoo…*"

7

Two days later, Shin Jina and I said goodbye to Mrs. Woo and Mr. Shin. Jinseung was at work, so Jina had come over in his stead. She had also spent the previous day with her parents, kindly taking them off my hands.

The sky was overcast and misty rain wet us as we helped load her parents' luggage into the back of their car.

Mr. Shin closed the car boot with a thunk when we were done.

"Take care," he said, bowing his head to each of us in turn. "We'll meet you in Hwacheon County next month to see Jinseung off to the training centre." He removed his glasses, wiping a speck of rain off the lens with his coat sleeve.

"Goodbye, my darlings!" Mrs. Woo said, eyes shining with dramatic tears. She hugged each of us, lingering on me in particular.

"You poor dear," she repeated for the millionth time. I wondered if she'd always call me that from now on.

"Let's go," Mr. Shin said, opening the car door.

Mrs. Woo slowly backed away from us with a melancholy

smile. Jina and I stood on the doorstep waving them goodbye. I held my breath until the iron gate clanged closed across the driveway exit and their car disappeared down the street. My shoulders drooped with the release of pent-up tension as I exhaled.

Jina chuckled. "You look relieved."

"I admit I am."

We went back inside, closing the door on the gradually worsening weather.

"I'm not used to surprise visits," I said.

"Sorry they imposed on you like that. If I had known, I swear I would have warned you."

"Don't worry. It wasn't too bad. Thanks for looking after them yesterday. You really saved me."

"No problem. They're my parents, after all. Now, since I'm here, let's talk party arrangements." She rubbed her hands together with glee.

"Party arrangements?"

"You know, the housewarming-slash-goodbye party. There's so much to organise—the guest list, food, music, security…"

"I haven't even thought about it yet."

"*Dongsaeng* isn't going to have time to plan it himself, is he?"

"Of course, you're right. I'll have to plan it."

"And I'll help you!"

"Thanks. Event planning isn't really my forté."

"Well, I looove planning parties. Let's start brainstorming some ideas, shall we?"

"Okay."

We moved to the living room. Jina took a sparkly pink

notebook and pen from her bag which she had tossed on the couch.

"Before we get started, want something to eat?" I asked.

"I *am* feeling a little peckish. Anything's fine."

On my way to the kitchen, I checked my phone to see if Jinseung had answered the text I sent him a while ago. Still no reply. I sighed and slipped my phone back into my pocket. After months of Jinseung's hiatus, I had almost forgotten what it was like to be unable to contact him. Oh well, at least he *would* come home. All of his upcoming activities were based in Seoul, so I wouldn't have to spend any nights alone.

I scoured the pantry shelves for snacks and emerged with a packet of honey butter chips then grabbed two cans of Diet Coke from the fridge.

When I returned to the living room, Jina's head was bent down as she furiously scribbled in her notebook. I placed a small wooden bowl on the coffee table. The packet rustled as I poured the chips in.

"What are you writing?" I asked.

"Names of some people I could contact about music and catering."

"Good thing you know so many people."

As I sat down next to her, my phone pinged. *Jinseung?* I checked it again.

> **Bora:** Hey, Chloe. Thought you'd want to know that the press release is out.

Intrigued, I clicked the link she sent. A web page loaded.

"Here it is," I said, registering the subject of the press release.

"Here what is?" Jina glanced over my shoulder.

Chapter 7

"KAM has sent out the press release about Jinseung's conscription."

I read it aloud. "'Hello from KAM Entertainment. Today we confirm that Shin Jinseung has recently received his draft notice and will be enlisting as an active-duty soldier to fulfil his obligation as a male citizen of South Korea. There will be no public send-off as per Jinseung's request for privacy when he enters the training facility on the twenty-third of March. We ask for your patience during Jinseung's absence from all promotional activity until he returns from military duties. Please wish for Jinseung's safety and personal growth during his time with the military. Thank you.'"

"So, we can talk about it freely now," Jina said, reaching a manicured hand into the chip bowl.

"Yeah. As long as we keep the time and location of his entry to the training centre under wraps."

"That goes without saying. Now, back to party planning. Let's make a checklist of all the things we need to organise."

"Sounds good."

We got to work. Thank goodness I had Jina's help, because this would be a much bigger party than I had ever organised before.

After a couple of hours, the sun began to set underneath thick grey clouds.

"I better get going," Jina said, checking the time. "I'm meant to be going out with Scarlett for dinner tonight."

"Your flatmate?"

"That's the one."

"I see. Well, thanks for all your help today."

"You're welcome. I'll be in touch with more party ideas as they come up." She wound a pink cashmere scarf around her neck and grabbed her bag. "See ya, Chloe."

"Wait, have you got an umbrella? Looks like there's gonna be a storm. Maybe I should give you a ride?"

"Don't worry about me. I've got an umbrella and I'll catch a taxi. Oh—is that a car coming up the drive?"

We turned our heads to the window. Sure enough, Changsoo's van had entered the gate. The automatic light turned on outside the house, illuminating the driveway.

"Nice timing," Jina said. "I'll ask Manager Bong if he can drop me off."

She bounded to the front door. I followed. A blast of frigid air swept inside.

Jinseung was halfway out of the van when he paused, seeing his sister emerge from the house.

"*Noona*, you're here."

He was wearing makeup. Must have come straight from a photo shoot.

"Yep," Jina said. "Keeping your girlfriend company."

"Are you leaving? Why don't you stay for dinner?"

"Can't sorry, I'm meeting Scarlett."

"Oh. Maybe next time." He closed the van door.

Jina tapped on the driver window. Changsoo wound it down a smidge.

"Are you heading back to town?" Jina asked.

"Yes," Changsoo replied impassively.

"Can I have a ride, Changsoo *Oppa*? Pretty please." She fluttered her false eyelashes at him.

A snicker escaped my mouth. If she thought flirting with Changsoo would work, she was sorely mistaken. That man was totally immune to womanly charms.

"Go on, *Hyung*," Jinseung said. "It's going to pour down any minute."

Chapter 7

Changsoo relented. "All right. Get in." He brusquely gestured to the passenger seat.

"Yuss!" Jina hopped inside the van.

Lightning flashed in the sky. We didn't linger outside. As soon as I shut the door, heavy rain started to pelt down and thunder rippled through the atmosphere, making the walls vibrate.

Jinseung headed straight to the living room couch where he slumped with a groan of exhaustion, his coat and scarf still on. I came to his side and gently helped him remove the excess clothing, which I folded and placed on the adjacent armchair. He wore a silky, black shirt and tight, black jeans underneath. His fingers were decked out with rings of various thicknesses and colours, and chains hung around his neck. The flashy outfit wasn't his normal style, so it must have been what he wore for the shoot.

I didn't bother asking if he was tired—that much was clear. Even under the heavy makeup I could see the shadows below his eyes.

"Three months off work and I seem to have lost all my stamina," he growled into his hands. "All I did today was photo shoots for the fan meeting merch and I'm exhausted."

"What else is on your schedule?" I asked.

"Apart from the fan meeting, let's see...I'm going to have a variety show appearance, a magazine interview, and I'm going to be a guest DJ on NCD Music...and probably some other things I'm not aware of yet."

"You work so hard," I murmured.

I wasn't crazy about him spending so much time working in the lead-up to his departure, but I understood he had little choice in the matter.

Another thunderbolt pierced the sky, lighting up the living

room like an X-ray. A fresh downpour pounded on the roof and windows.

"Romantic, isn't it?" Jinseung said.

"The storm? Only when I'm safe and warm inside with you."

"Come here." He beckoned me to his open arms.

I enthusiastically obliged.

"Thanks for putting up with my parents," he said, hugging me and stroking my back, "and for being so good about everything else."

"I've even surprised myself how well I'm holding up," I admitted.

"You need to give yourself more credit." His hand travelled from my back, up my side, and to my cheek, which he gently caressed. "I'm so lucky to have you."

I basked in the warmth of his affection. Once upon a time I doubted his love for me, and now I couldn't fathom why I ever felt that way.

He took my hand, guided it to his lips, and kissed it. Just this small action had me release a little sigh of pleasure. Spurred on, he pressed his lips to the inside of my wrist, then, pushing my sleeve up, to the underside of my arm, and in the crease of my elbow, which was surprisingly sensitive.

"Oh," I mumbled.

"Do you like that?"

"Y-yes."

He pressed another kiss into my elbow, this time sucking and biting a little. I squirmed in my seat. This was driving me crazy.

"Chloe," he rasped. "Let's go to bed."

8

Jinseung's best friend, Young Jae, had a wicked grin on his face as he held an electric razor above Jinseung's head.

A mixture of laughter, gasps, groans, and cheers filled the room, blending with the music pumping from the sound system. One of the groans came from Yang Bora, who stood next to me, watching on with trepidation.

"I can't look," she said, lifting her hands to shield her eyes.

"I'm sure it won't be that bad," I consoled.

Jinseung had worn very short hair for his role in Hidden History, but this would be even shorter. The shortest it had ever been. I wasn't worried, though. He would always look good to me—short hair, long hair, no hair.

It was the night of the farewell party for Jinseung, and shaving his hair off was the main event. He sat on a chair in the middle of the living room, a sheet draped around his shoulders to keep the hair off his clothes. The carpet would inevitably get messy, but a vacuum cleaner stood nearby at the ready.

The audience's anticipation intensified as Young Jae flicked the razor on, emitting a loud buzzing sound. He brought it closer to Jinseung's head. Bora took a sneak peek then quickly re-covered her eyes. "Just tell me when it's over," she said.

The first tuft of black hair fell to the floor.

Then another.

And another.

Soon enough, hair was flying everywhere.

Young Jae chuckled away with a look of pure delight. Meanwhile, Jinseung grimaced, eyes clenched shut, hands gripping the sides of the chair. Perhaps he didn't trust his friend not to cut him or do something else stupid, like shaving a pattern into the back of his head. Seemed like the kind of thing Young Jae would do based off my first impressions of him.

After a while, there was more hair on the floor than on Jinseung's head. A few more strokes with the razor and the haircut was over. Young Jae turned the razor off. Military buzz cut complete.

Jinseung's boyish good looks had disappeared along with the hair. He looked much older now. Older, but no less handsome. I didn't mind the new style at all. The less hair he had, the more his impressive facial features stood out. He looked sexy.

"Is it over?" Bora asked, lifting a finger so she could peek through her hands.

"Yep."

She slowly lowered her hands and fully opened her eyes. She frowned at the sight of him. "Poor Jinseungie!"

"Come on. It's not that bad!"

"You know how I feel about his hair!"

"Yeah. You're weirdly obsessed with it."

Chapter 8

"I just like his usual image. That so bad?"

Another one of Jinseung's friends held up a mirror. Jinseung examined his reflection. He eased up, apparently satisfied with his new look. He fist-bumped Young Jae.

"Thanks, man. Looks good."

Bora could barely look at him. "Ugh. I need a drink."

"I'll have one too," I said.

We walked to the kitchen. There were two staff waiters circulating the party, but food and drinks were mostly self-service, laid out on the kitchen island and stored in the fridge.

"What would you like?" I asked.

"Anything. A beer, maybe."

I grabbed two cans from the fridge and two clean glasses which were set out atop the bench.

While I poured our drinks, Shin Jina walked into the room. She approached the island, reaching for an open bottle of sparkling wine to refill her empty glass.

"Hey, guys," she said. "What you think of the buzz cut? Looks smart, doesn't it?"

"All his cuteness is gone," Bora complained.

Jina scoffed. "You would say that. What about you, Chloe? Your opinion matters most out of all of us."

"Well, I think it looks quite good, actually," I said. "He has the head and face structure to pull it off."

"I agree. He suits his hair in any style. Did you know that as a kid, he went through a phase of really long hair? He looked like a girl."

"Really? I would've liked to have seen that."

"I'm sure my parents have photos. Next time you visit them, ask to see an album."

"Ha! I might just do that."

"*Dongsaeng* will be so embarrassed. Tee hee."

"Won't there be embarrassing photos of you in there as well?"

"Oh yeah. Didn't think of that! I don't mind if you see them, though."

As we chatted in the kitchen, a male guest whom I hadn't been introduced to sidled up to us.

"Hey, girls, what you drinking?"

He seemed a little out of it, whether from alcohol or something else. I didn't like his vibe.

"The drinks are in the fridge," I said simply. "Help yourself to whatever you want."

He ignored me and focused his attention on Jina. "So, *Noona*, Dowoon tells me you're a model."

"Uh, yeah."

"I've always wanted to hook up with a model."

She screwed up her face in distaste. I was equally grossed out by him. *Who even says something like that?*

"Wanna go somewhere?" he asked, seemingly oblivious to Jina's discomfort.

"Can't you see she's in the middle of talking with her friends?" I shot back.

"Whatever," he grumbled.

"Hey, *Unnie*, let's go." I pulled her and Bora away with me towards the hallway. I took them to my bedroom, closed the door, drew the curtains, and turned on the lamps by each side of the bed. Now we could drink and chat in peace.

"Thanks, Chloe," Jina said.

"Who invited *him*?" Bora asked. "What a loser."

I shrugged. "Don't know. Jinseung wrote the guest list, but surely that's not one of his friends. He has better taste than that."

"He mentioned Dowoon," Jina said. "Maybe Dowoon brought him here."

"Should've stipulated no plus-ones." I sighed.

Too late now. If he kept behaving badly, I could ask the security guard to kick him out of the party.

The three of us sat on the bed together, sipping our drinks.

"It's funny," I mused. "Part of the reason we planned this party was so I could meet Jinseung's friends, yet I've spent most of it hanging out with you two."

I wasn't complaining. Jinseung had taken his time introducing me to everyone, but it had been overwhelming, surrounded by all these celebrities and cool and fashionable people, so I gravitated back to Jina and Bora.

"You can go back out there, if you like," Jina said. "Don't worry about me."

"Nah. I'm enjoying myself. You guys are the only company I need."

"What about *Dongsaeng*?"

"I'm sure he just wants to catch up with his friends. It's been a while since he's seen them."

I didn't think he would miss me. We had been lavishing each other with attention every spare moment over the last few weeks. Now he had time to focus on his friends for once.

Jina held her head in her hands, elbows propped up on the plump pillow in her lap. "Just over a week to go…"

"I know. Don't remind me. I'm kind of dreading it."

"Still feel scared to be on your own after what happened?"

I nodded.

"You know, you can always rely on me and *Unnie*," Bora said. "If you ever have flashbacks, start to panic, or anything at all, let us know and we'll do whatever we can to help you. Just 'cause Jinseung's not around, doesn't mean you have to go through this alone."

"Awww. Thanks, guys. It's not just that, though. I'm also worried about Jinseung. I'm scared about the abuse that goes on in the army, scared that he'll actually have to fight…"

"I know what you mean. I'm scared about that too," Jina said with a frown. "But we shouldn't underestimate him. He's smart, fit, and strong. If anyone can survive the army, it's *Dongsaeng*."

"*Unnie's* right," Bora said. "He's tough, physically and mentally. Besides, he wouldn't want you to worry about him. He'd want you to focus on taking care of yourself."

I cracked a faint smile. "That's exactly what he said."

"See? Don't worry so much. Let's all take care of each other while he's gone."

"Agreed," Jina said.

Their little pep talk really did make me feel better. I was so glad to have them on my side.

"Thanks, guys. You two are the best."

They beamed at me, blushing slightly from both the compliment and, I suspected, the alcohol.

"Shall we head back out to the party?" I asked, grabbing my drink off the bedside table.

"Wait—" Jina said. "There's one thing I wanna ask while we're here in private."

I paused. "Okay. What is it?"

"Has *Dongsaeng* been acting strange or anything lately? Like he's got some kinda secret?"

"No. Why?" Now I was intrigued.

"Well…" She suddenly became reluctant to spit out whatever she was going to say.

"Well?" I repeated.

"Oh, never mind. It's probably nothing. I shouldn't have said anything."

"Come on. You have to tell me now."

"You've got me curious too," Bora said. "Tell us."

With a little cajoling, Jina relented. "Okay. This is kinda silly, but I've been thinking about how my father proposed to my mother just before he entered the army. It made me wonder if *Dongsaeng* might be planning something similar."

My eyes widened. "You mean...do I think he's gonna propose?"

The thought had occurred to me. Mrs. Woo had given him a ring, after all. I just hadn't wanted to jump to conclusions, nor did I even think I was ready for such a big step in the first place. I doubted Jinseung was either.

"I know, it's silly," Jina said. "That's why I didn't want to say anything."

I rubbed my chin in thought. "We haven't been together that long. I can't imagine him making a big move like that."

"Yeah," Bora agreed. "And why would Chloe know anything if he was planning to do that? Maybe you should ask him yourself if you suspect something."

"Nah," Jina said, shaking her head. "We're not that close. He wouldn't tell me. None of my business, anyway."

I didn't tell them about the conversation I overheard in the spare bedroom. I wasn't even supposed to know about it.

"Let's go back out," Jina said. "He's probably wondering where we all disappeared to."

"So will Dowoon's friend," Bora commented. She stuck out her tongue and made a face like she was going to puke.

"It'll be okay," I said. "If he tries that again I'll get him kicked out."

Back in the living room, the party was still in full force—

music blasting, lively chatter, the sound of drinks being poured and snacks being munched on.

"I've been looking for you," came a voice behind me. Not Jinseung—his friend, Young Jae. *Why would he be looking for me?*

"Oh. I was just with my friends in another room," I said casually.

"Wanna go outside for a minute and talk?"

"Um…"

"I feel like we should get to know each other a bit better. You're my best friend's girlfriend, after all."

"Sure, why not?"

Separating from Bora and Jina, I grabbed a jacket from the coat rack by the front door then met Young Jae out on the deck. The pretty garden was bathed in moonlight. It felt secluded, tucked away from the street behind tall zelkova and maple trees.

"Mind if I smoke?" he asked, pulling a pack of cigarettes from his jeans.

"Go ahead."

He lit up. The end of his cigarette glowed orange-red in the night air.

Young Jae was an attractive guy. Same age as Jinseung. He had a bulkier physique and an edgier appearance overall, wearing a baggy white t-shirt over his low-riding jeans, his hair dyed brown and spiked up a little, a tattoo on his arm, and a pair of gold earrings in his ears.

"So how'd you and Jinseung meet?" he asked. "I've heard his perspective, now I wanna hear yours."

I told him my story—how I came to Seoul to teach English but ended up acting in Hidden History instead, how Jinseung took me under his wing, and how we became friends, then more than friends. One thing I left out was the whole saga involving Oh Sejung. As always, it was something that I didn't want to dredge up again.

"Jinseung said pretty much the same thing," Young Jae said, taking another puff on his cigarette.

"And what about you? How do you know Jinseung?"

"We did idol training together. For a while I thought we were gonna debut in the same group, but Jinseung ended up getting dropped at the last minute."

"Wait—are you an idol?"

"Nah. Well, I was one, briefly. A rapper. The group wasn't successful. We disbanded after one album."

"Oh. That's a shame. What was the group called?"

"X-Tream. You wouldn't have heard of it. Like I said, we weren't successful. Jinseung was lucky he didn't end up in the group. Took an acting opportunity instead and look how well that turned out."

"So, what do you do now?"

"I'm still a musician, but I'm in production now. Sound mixing and all that."

"Sounds cool."

"It's a pretty sweet gig. I get to work with a lot of top groups."

"You must get to meet idols all the time then. I'm jealous."

"I'm sure you've met a few famous people too. Some are even at this party."

"Yeah, that's true."

Young Jae leaned back against the wall, exhaling a cloud of smoke.

"Have you done your military service yet?" I asked.

"Uh-huh. Ages ago. I enlisted after X-Tream split up."

"How was it?"

"After the stress of trying to make it as an idol, it didn't feel that bad in comparison. Not everyone has such an easy time of it, but Jinseung should be fine."

"Ah. That's good to know."

"Worried about him?"

"Of course. How could I not be?"

Young Jae grinned. "Must be nice to have a girlfriend to worry about you."

"Are you single?"

"Yep."

"I'm surprised. I would've thought a guy like you would be popular with girls."

Young Jae smirked. "You could say that. Unfortunately the kind of girls that like me aren't the ones I want to date anymore."

"Why not?"

"Well, this might sound kinda lame, but—" He shuffled awkwardly on his feet. "I'm looking for something authentic. You know what I mean. The kind of connection you and Jinseung have. Seriously, I've never seen him so in love."

I blushed so hard I felt sure he could see my red cheeks even in the dark.

"Jinseung is a lucky guy," he said.

"I'm just an ordinary girl. What's so special about me?"

"The fact that you would even say something like that, for one thing."

"There are plenty of girls out there like me. You just need to expand your horizons."

"Is that so?" He said it more like a statement than a question.

A chill wind suddenly picked up. Young Jae noticed me

shiver in my jacket. "You're getting cold. Go back inside if you want."

"I think I will. It's been nice chatting with you."

"Hey, can I give you my number? So you can call me if you need anything while Jinseung's away."

"Sure. That's so nice of you. What's your number?"

The more allies I had during Jinseung's absence, the better. I typed his number into my phone as he said it aloud.

"Thanks," I said. "Well, see you around."

"See ya. I'll tell Jinseung I approve."

"Approve?"

"Heh. Never mind." He lit up another cigarette.

The front door swung open. I could hear a commotion from the hallway. Young Jae and I exchanged confused looks. Someone got shoved out of the door. Dowoon's friend—the guy who had made that inappropriate comment to Jina.

"It was an accident!" he wailed, squirming and clutching at his nether regions, practically in tears.

Jinseung cut an imposing figure, arms folded across his chest, dark eyes glaring with fury.

"You groped my sister's butt by accident?" he spat. "I don't think so."

"Is everything okay here?" The security guard stationed outside, tall and broad, wearing all black, approached the scene.

"This guy's just leaving," Jinseung said. "Right?"

The man briefly considered his options before turning his back on Jinseung.

"Fine!" He marched away in a huff. "Your sister's not so hot, anyway."

Jinseung swore after him.

Young Jae and I approached the open door where Jinseung continued to stand, seething with rage.

"Is *Unnie* okay?" I asked.

"Yeah. She had the good sense to kick him right in the nuts as soon as he copped a feel."

Young Jae winced. "Ouch."

"He deserved it."

"Wow. I can't imagine her doing that," I commented. "Those self-defence classes have really come in handy."

9

If the weather could match my mood, it would be gloomy, dark, pouring with rain. The weather gods had other plans, however.

Glorious sunshine descended from the heavens. Birds twittered in the trees and puffy white clouds like candy-floss drifted across the azure sky. The grass was lush and bright green, glistening with dew. Plump-budded plants threatened to burst into flower at any second.

Too bad I couldn't appreciate the beauty of my surroundings. All my effort went towards stopping myself from breaking down in tears.

The congregation in front of the training centre entrance in Hwacheon County, Gangwon Province, consisted of a small number of Jinseung's colleagues, friends, and family. No media present—the time and exact location of the gathering had been a closely guarded secret.

Jinseung, dressed casually in sweatpants, hoodie, and a puffer jacket, mingled and took photographs with his group of close companions. I wanted to be glued to his side but had to give him space so he could properly say his goodbyes one-on-one with each member of the congregation. Jina stayed with me instead.

"This doesn't feel real," I lamented. "I can't believe he's leaving today."

"Me too," Jina said. "It happened so fast. He seems cheerful, at least."

"I'm sure he's nervous on the inside."

"I'm sure you're right." She sighed wistfully. "It's a shame Yang Bora couldn't come."

"I know. Too busy with work. She did call him and said goodbye on the phone, though."

"Sweet of her."

I watched Jinseung talk with his parents, exchanging plenty of hugs and kisses. When he brushed a hand over his eyes, I knew that he was crying. My heart lurched.

"Want a tissue?" Jina asked, holding out a small packet.

"Yes, please." I grabbed one and wiped my eyes.

"You can have the whole pack. Plenty more where that came from."

"Thanks. Should've brought my own supply. Wasn't thinking."

Changsoo offered to take a photo of Jinseung with his parents. The trio arranged themselves in front of him—Mr. Shin on the left, Mrs. Woo on the right, and Jinseung in the middle. He aimed his phone and snapped a few shots. Checking the results, he appeared satisfied.

It looked like they were done, but Mrs. Woo stopped her son and husband from dispersing, tugging on their arms. She waved to me and her daughter. "Jina-ya, Chloe! Come here."

I reluctantly approached, feeling like I might look out of

place in a family photo. I wasn't exactly a bonafide Shin family member. Mrs. Woo must have sensed my hesitance. She gently pulled me into position by Jinseung's side, making it very clear that she wanted me in the photograph. Jinseung wrapped his arm tight around my waist and tilted his head close to mine. I glowed with pride at how willingly he claimed me as his partner in front of all his closest companions.

Changsoo stepped back until we were all within frame.

"Say kimchi," he said.

"Kimchiiii!" We all grinned stupidly.

After numerous shots, we broke apart. Changsoo showed Mrs. Woo the photos. She looked delighted and asked him to send them to her straight away.

"I'll get one framed and put it up on the wall," she announced, beaming with glee.

Jinseung had already moved on to chat with others. As I watched him interact with his friends, I became aware of someone else on the periphery—a man wearing a cap and sunglasses, partially hidden behind a leafy tree. He wasn't a member of our party as far as I could tell, but he watched with immense interest.

"What are you looking at?" Jina asked.

"Do you see that man?"

"No—ah! I see him. Just what is he up to?"

The answer was clear when out came a camera lens behind the tree.

Jina's eyebrows shot up. "A paparazzi all the way out here?"

"I don't think so. Probably just an opportunist."

"This was meant to be a private gathering. We better go warn someone."

"Agreed, but let's leave Jinseung out of this. Don't want to ruin his day. I'll tell Changsoo."

I didn't delay. I walked straight up to Jinseung's manager.

"Everything okay?" he asked.

I directed his attention to the man behind the tree, but by then someone else had already noticed. Mr. Kim strode out to confront the man, his laid-back appearance quickly turning intimidating. I didn't know what he said to the man, but whatever it was, the man looked stricken and fled the scene at once.

"*Omo*. Mr. Kim can be scary when he wants to be," I observed.

"He didn't climb all the way to his position by being a nice guy," Changsoo said. "At least it's taken care of."

Mr. Kim returned looking completely carefree and composed. Jinseung hadn't noticed a thing. He was still busy saying goodbyes, giving out hugs, and taking selfies with his friends.

Once Jinseung had worked his way around the entire party, the only person left he hadn't said goodbye to was me. I was beginning to think that he didn't even plan to say goodbye to me. Perhaps he thought that it went without saying. My bottom lip began to tremble and tears gathered in the corners of my eyes. I couldn't help it—I was so emotional about him leaving.

Is this it? Is this how we're going to part?

I was disappointed to say the least.

Jinseung stood near the gate, saying something to Changsoo. I was too far away to hear. He picked up his duffel bag.

I knew it. He's about to leave, and without even saying goodbye.

But he didn't leave. He grabbed something from his bag, pocketed it, then marched straight over to me and took my hand, intertwining his fingers with mine.

"For a moment there I thought you'd forgotten about me," I said, wiping my eyes.

He ruffled my hair. "You fool. Come with me."

"What? Where?"

"Anywhere. Away from here. Come on." He gently yanked my hand, guiding me towards a wooded area away from the road.

A faint dirt trail led into the shade of trees. We walked until we couldn't hear anything but the birds singing in the branches and the gentle rushing sound of a nearby stream. We were completely alone.

"Why couldn't you just say goodbye to me in front of everyone else?" I asked.

"Because then I wouldn't be able to do this." He swept me into his arms and sank his lips down onto mine.

I melted with a soft moan, yielding completely to his lips and tongue, allowing him to explore my mouth with all the urgency and passion of the moment. He held me tight while he kissed me, briefly breaking away to take my bottom lip between his teeth, biting me softly, then returning fully to my mouth, devouring me with such incredible heat and force, rendering me weak at my knees.

I felt his absence as soon as he parted from my lips, even as he still clung to me.

"Wow," I whispered.

Jinseung ran a hand over his head, looking sheepish. "On second thought, I better not get too excited."

I glanced downwards. "Too late. Those sweatpants don't leave much to the imagination."

"*Aish!*" He let go of me at once and stepped back to put some distance between us. "I'll need to give myself a few minutes to recover."

I giggled. "So, you wanted to kiss me? Is that the reason you took me out here?"

"Nah. That was spur of the moment. I actually brought you here because I wanted to give you something."

"Oh?"

He started to rummage in his jacket pocket.

My heart thumped against my ribs as I recalled what Jina said. Was she right? Did Jinseung intend to propose? *I can't believe this.*

He took something out of his pocket, covered by his hands. He approached me, and I half expected him to get down on one knee, but he did not. Instead, he took my hand, then pressed the object into my palm. Contrasting sharply with my expectation of a round and smooth metal item, it felt thin, plasticky, and rectangular. *What the heck?*

As soon as I looked down it was apparent what it was. A credit card.

"What's this for?" I asked, turning it over in my hands.

"My accountant will be taking care of all the usual expenses when I'm gone, but it occurred to me that you don't make much money, and I won't be around to gift you anything."

"You already pay for a lot, and my personal spending isn't much…"

"I know, but should anything come up…if there's anything you really want…I want you to have it."

I stared at the card in my hands.

"I trust you, Chloe, and I don't ever want you to struggle. That's why I'm giving you this. "

It wasn't a ring, but it still signified his feelings for me. I didn't need a proposal, anyway. It was too soon.

I leaned in and kissed him on the cheek. "Thank you. I appreciate this."

"Good. Make sure you use it too. Not like I'm going to be spending much while I'm in the army, so you might as well treat yourself to what you want."

"Okay, but I promise I won't go overboard."

"I know you won't."

I slipped the credit card into a zipped pocket in my coat. "I suppose we should go back. They'll think we disappeared into the woods for a quickie."

He smirked. "Let them think what they want."

"Then, one more kiss?"

"Yes, please."

I held him, revelling in the feel of his broad shoulders, strong arms, and hard chest. We found each other's lips and kissed each other, sweet and soft. He then burrowed his face into the crook of my neck, sighing with contentment.

"I love you," he murmured, breath prickling my skin.

"I love you too," I replied, cheek pressed to his chest.

I wished I could hold onto him forever, but after a while, I let my grip slacken. We simply stared at each other for a moment, taking everything in, savouring the mental image of one another.

He took my hand. "We better not leave them waiting much longer."

I knew he was right, but I still felt a pang of sorrow in my chest. Our last moment alone together was coming to an end.

We slowly walked back to the entry gate of the training centre, my heart sinking further with each step. When we arrived, Jinseung hugged me again, kissed me, wished me goodbye, and told me he loved me. Then he was by the gate, handed his backpack and duffel bag by Changsoo.

"Farewell, everyone," he said, waving goodbye, a charming smile upon his face masking the sadness.

Warm wishes of good luck shouted out from the crowd accompanied his walk, alone, through the gate. He turned back several times, waving and blowing kisses, but eventually he disappeared from view. I clutched at my chest, feeling like my heart was going to explode.

10

I lay my head down, and when I opened my eyes, I realised with a jolt of panic that I was back in the dank basement apartment, surrounded by darkness except for the tiny barred window shining in the distance. Oh Sejung appeared before me, wraith-like, pale-faced, her limp black hair matted. She circled me, watching me with menacing eyes like a beast focused on its prey. Pure terror coursed through my veins.

"He doesn't love you," she taunted. "He left you all alone."

She entwined her skinny fingers around my neck, cold and clammy.

"He's not coming back," she whispered in my ear. "You'll never have him."

I shook my head. "That's not true."

"Oh, but it is. Don't believe me?" Her hands tightened.

I desperately tried to pry them away, but her vice-like grip held strong.

"Say goodbye, Chloe."

"No!"

"Insolent little bitch." She squeezed my neck so hard I thought it might snap.

Twisted visions of violent war scenes played in my head before everything went black, then I awoke coughing and spluttering, Oh Sejung's touch burnt on my neck.

"Jinseung-ah!" I gasped, reaching for him, but his side of the bed was empty, the place where his head lay still imprinted on the pillow from the night before.

I was confused for a moment, then everything flooded back. He had left for the army, and I was alone. Sejung's words echoed in my head.

"He left you all alone."

I groaned and clutched at my chest, an empty ache in my heart as I stared longingly at the vacant space next to me.

Jinseung...

I buried my face in his pillow, trying to comfort myself with the remnants of his scent.

Damn. I miss you so much already.

I stayed glued to his pillow until my muscles relaxed and my pounding heartbeat began to subside. When I had fully calmed down, I groped for my phone on the bedside table. 6:07 a.m. The countdown on my home screen read five hundred and ninety-nine days. I groaned. Perhaps setting that countdown was a mistake. A reminder that it would be so very long until Jinseung's return. I deleted the widget off the screen, vowing to put it back as soon as the number became easier to stomach.

I had two options—go back to sleep and risk having another nightmare, or get up and embrace the morning. It didn't take long for me to come to a decision.

Yawning loudly, I dragged myself to the kitchen and made a strong cup of coffee. When I started tinkering around looking for something to eat for breakfast, Buster stirred on his plush dog bed. He opened his little round black eyes and stood up, stretched, then came padding over to me.

"Do you want breakfast too?"

He yapped in reply, tail wagging.

"All right."

I plonked some dog food into his red paw-print-patterned bowl. He scoffed it quickly then licked the bowl for quite some time after.

I ate fruit—an apple and some grapes that looked like they might not have stayed fresh much longer, plus a handful of nuts.

"I'm up nice and early for once," I mused, staring out the window. The sun had yet to rise, but I could make out the silhouetted trees against the moonlit sky. "What should I do with all this time? Do you want to go for a walk, Buster?"

He leapt up in excitement.

"All right. Let's go."

I threw on a casual outfit, a coat, and a scarf, then grabbed Buster's lead. We headed out the door. Despite the lack of sunlight, the footpath was well-lit from the bright streetlamps. The air was brisk. I couldn't see anyone out and about—just the way I liked it.

Since revealing my relationship with Jinseung, I had been very cautious about being seen in public. So far, I had yet to run into any overzealous fans, and I planned to keep it that way.

I pulled up my scarf to cover the lower half of my face, just enough to obscure my identity. The neighbourhood was usually so quiet that I didn't have to worry too much about someone recognising me, not to mention the fact that most people who lived around here would be much more well-known than I was. It was that kind of post code.

For such a small dog, Buster was surprisingly powerful. He ran ahead of me until the lead was pulled tight. I had to jog a little to keep up.

The houses we passed were large, detached, and hidden behind tall fences. Whenever I walked around the neighbourhood, I liked to peer through the gaps in the fences or gates, take in the grandiose properties, and wonder about the people who lived there. I rarely saw my neighbours. Residents came and went in fancy cars with tinted windows. They kept to themselves.

The first person I came across on the walk was a woman out jogging, headphones on, clad head-to-toe in designer activewear. She passed me by without a hint of acknowledgement.

The next person I saw stopped me dead in my tracks. A dark figure emerging from a shadowed alleyway. That pale face, limp hair, callous eyes…

My breath caught. My blood ran cold.

No. It can't be!

I could hear my racing heart pound in my eardrums, beads of sweat running down my forehead. I felt dizzy, lightheaded. My vision blurred. An intense pain emanated from my head and I pressed my hands to my temples. My knees buckled. I crumpled down onto the hard pavement, groaning. I thought I might die, whether from Oh Sejung or the pain in my head.

No one came to my aid.

When the attack finally began to subside, I managed to properly open my eyes and look around. I was alone. No sign of the woman I thought was Oh Sejung.

Was she a vision?

Chapter 10

My breath began to return. My heartbeat began to stabilise.

It was a hallucination. She wasn't real.

I got to my feet, body weak and trembling, a dull pain persistent in my head. That was when I realised Buster was gone. I must have dropped the lead. He probably got scared and ran away.

"Buster!" I cried out. "Buuuuster!"

He didn't come.

I couldn't muster enough energy to keep shouting his name or properly search for him, so I trudged back to my house, head hung in defeat.

One day without Jinseung and I have a panic attack and lose his precious dog. I can't believe this.

With a heavy heart, I opened the door and went inside. I had a little cry on my bed before recovering enough to call Yang Bora. She didn't pick up, but I left a message.

"Hey. It's me, Chloe. You know how you said that I can always rely on you with Jinseung gone? Well, I need your help. I just had a pretty bad panic attack. Call me back when you get this."

I left a similar message with Shin Jina.

After lying down for a while, I remembered the bottle of pills in the bathroom cabinet. My doctor gave them to me after my last panic attack—a similar episode which occurred when I had passed a random house which reminded me of the one where Oh Sejung had held me captive.

I took one pill with a tall glass of water and a piece of buttered toast. The effects were almost immediate. My body relaxed. My thoughts became blurry and indistinct. I went back to bed because I couldn't operate.

The next thing I knew, my phone was ringing—a sound

loud and annoying enough to penetrate the thick fog in my brain. I groggily reached for it on the bedside table.

"Are you all right?" It was Yang Bora. She sounded concerned.

"I'm just…resting." I couldn't explain anything to her in my current state.

"Do you need me to come over?"

"You have to go to work, though."

"Yes, but Actor-nim has some appointments this afternoon that I don't need to be present for. I'm sure I'll be able to get away."

"If it's no trouble…"

"I'll come over as soon as I can. Call me again if you feel worse, okay?"

"Okay. Thank you."

Jina called me a little later.

"I'm so sorry, Chloe. I'm on a modelling shoot today. There's no way I can get out of it, and it will probably take some time. Not sure how long."

"It's okay. Bora is going to come over."

"Whew. Then at least I know you'll be in good hands. I'll call you again later."

Thank goodness for those two. Now all I had to do was stay calm and rest until Bora arrived. No work to do, so that was one good thing at least. In my mind, I started making a plan to go out and look for Buster, but I ended up falling asleep instead. Deep, dreamless sleep.

When I finally awoke, I felt much better—except when I passed Buster's empty dog bed, reminding me of his absence. *I have to find him.*

I was at the door, putting my shoes on, when I found

myself paralysed. Too scared to go back out in case I had another panic attack. *I better wait until Bora gets here.*

Fortunately, she arrived earlier than I anticipated. A ray of sunshine on my doorstep. She was in her work clothes—slim trousers, a cashmere turtleneck sweater with a blazer over the top. Her red-dyed hair in its usual style—half up in a high bun. Her eyes scanned me from behind her round, gold, wire-framed glasses, searching for answers.

"You came," I said lamely.

"Of course I did. Actor-nim was worried about you too. She insisted that I leave straight away to go check on you. What happened?"

"I was walking Buster this morning when I thought I saw…*her*. I had a panic attack and Buster ran away. I have no idea where he is."

She frowned sympathetically. "Oh dear. We better go look for him. Or if you don't feel up to it, I'll go on my own."

"I'll be okay if you're with me, but do you have time? Won't you have to get back to work?"

She shook her head. "It's okay. Actor-nim is with her assistant and they know I'll be a while. Come on, let's go."

So, Bora and I began our hunt for Buster. Our first stop, the place where I must have dropped his lead.

"It was in front of this alleyway that you had the panic attack?" Bora asked, looking down the narrow path.

"Yes." I averted my gaze from the exact spot I had seen the vision, even though daylight had chased away all the shadows.

"I can see how it would look scary in the dark. There's no streetlight here either. Do you know which way Buster ran?"

"I have no idea. I didn't even see him run away."

"Then let's just have a look around."

Both of us searched the immediate area, but there was no sign of him.

"He could be miles away by now," I grumbled. "I should have gone to look for him earlier."

"You couldn't have," Bora said. "And don't blame yourself. Jinseung *Oppa* wouldn't."

"Wouldn't he? He loves Buster."

"He loves *you* more."

"What about his parents? He was their dog too. His mother will have a fit."

"It's far too soon to abandon hope. We'll find him."

We widened our search area, checking every street and piece of land, and peering into yards he could have scrambled into.

"If we don't manage to find him, I'll make some posters," I resolved.

"And I'll check all the local social media groups," Bora said. "People who find pets usually post about it."

"Good idea."

"Oh!"

"What?"

"Over there, by those trees."

I glanced in the direction she pointed but couldn't see anything except the trees and patch of grass by a fence.

"I thought I saw movement," Bora said. "Maybe it was just the wind."

We continued our search, leaving no corner unexplored. When we ran into another woman walking her dog, Bora approached her.

"Excuse me, have you seen a little white dog walking alone around the neighbourhood?"

"No. Sorry."

Chapter 10

"Ah. Thank you."

The woman strode away.

I was beginning to run out of hope. "Maybe we should head back? We've searched the area pretty thoroughly."

"Yeah," Bora agreed. "Looks like we'll have to move on to Plan B. Posters and social media."

I stared down at my feet. "I really hoped we'd find him."

"Someone's bound to have seen him. He's probably safe at someone's house right now, and once they see a missing poster, they'll contact you."

"Yes. That's got to be the case."

I thought about which photo of Buster to use on the poster. I'd have to crop Jinseung out if I used one with him in it.

"Do you get panic attacks often?" Bora asked as we walked back to my house.

"No. This was my second one. I think I was still half asleep when I left the house this morning. I had a nightmare last night. Maybe that's what set it off."

"You're still getting nightmares?"

"Yeah."

"I wish there was something I could do. You're all alone in that big house now."

"Maybe I should get a flatmate," I joked.

The words had barely escaped my mouth before it dawned on me. I didn't know why I hadn't thought of it sooner. Both of us looked at each other, and I knew she understood what I was thinking.

"Would *you* like to move in with me?" I asked.

"Seriously?"

"Of course. You could have your own room, you wouldn't need to pay any rent, and I'm sure Jinseung would agree to it. Just until he gets back from the military."

"Then, hell yes! I would absolutely like to move in with you."

"You're living with your parents now, right?"

She nodded. "I looked into apartments in town, but they were too expensive and I didn't want to have roommates. If it were you, though, that would be different."

"So you'd be able to move in straight away?"

"Yup. Pretty much. Maybe this weekend."

"Perfect!"

"*Omo*, this is going to be so great! I'm excited already."

I would have been excited too if it weren't for the fact that Buster was still missing. I wouldn't be able to celebrate properly until he returned.

"Well, here we are," I said when we reached the gate to my house. "We didn't find him."

"I'm sorry. Guess I'll head back to work if you think you'll be okay without me."

"I'm feeling better now, so I think I'll manage."

"*Omo*!" Bora clutched her chest.

"What is it?"

"Isn't that…?"

I followed Bora's gaze to the porch. Buster was sitting outside the front door, his little pink tongue poking out.

11

"Does the agency know you're using their van as a moving truck?" I asked Bora when she pulled up in the driveway of my house three days later.

"Maybe," she said dismissively. She slid open the van door revealing a ton of boxes stuffed inside.

"I'll help you unpack," I offered.

"Living together is gonna be so much fun!" Bora said, heaving a large box to the door.

"I know! I'm so excited."

I grabbed two small boxes. Buster, curious as to what was going on, trailed at my feet as I carried them inside. Thank goodness he had turned up the other day. *Such a smart doggy.* He must have let himself in through a gap between the bars in the gate. *What a relief.* I promised myself that I'd never let him out of my sight again. Bora would be able to help look after him too, now that she'd be living here.

We marched back and forth between the van and Bora's new room—the largest guest room, complete with its own ensuite. I released a heavy box onto the floor with a loud thud.

"*Aigoo!* How much stuff do you have?"

"We're not even half done."

"At least there's plenty of space. There's the third bedroom too, if you wanna store some stuff in there as well. I don't use it for anything."

"I think this room will be big enough. I made it work with my old bedroom which was half the size, and I certainly didn't have my own bathroom."

It took several trips to empty the boxes from the van.

"Whew," I said, wiping a hand across my forehead when we were done. My body ached, and even in the cold I was sweating.

"Well, that's the easy part over and done with," Bora said. "Time to put everything away."

I gritted my teeth looking at all the boxes surrounding us, stacked almost to the ceiling. "Just give me a second to recover first. That was quite the workout."

"Yeah. Think I pulled my back muscle." She stretched her arms over her head, straightening her back with a series of tremendous clicks.

I cringed at the sound—worse than nails on a blackboard.

"Ah! Much better," she said, returning to her usual straight posture.

After a glass of water to refresh ourselves, we went back to the room to continue the job. I put myself in charge of storing Bora's clothing while she worked on everything else.

It turned out Bora had a lot of clothes, and my job was slow work because I kept stopping to examine each piece and gush over it.

"You have so many beautiful clothes!" I said, holding up a pretty plum-coloured wrap dress.

Bora grimaced. "Yeah, I know. Think I might have a shopping addiction. Ever since I got my promotion I've been spending up large. The first time in my life I've actually had disposable income and I've gone a bit crazy."

"That's to be expected. You'll get it under control once the novelty wears off."

"It's been over a year already! But you're right, hopefully the urge to shop will die down soon. In the meantime, if you ever want to borrow something to wear, feel free to raid my closet."

"Really? Thanks!" My excitement quickly faded, reminding myself that Bora was at least two sizes smaller than me. "Not that I could fit most of this stuff…"

"I'm sure some of it will work."

I picked up a pair of her shoes and lined them up against my feet. "Looks like we have the same shoe size."

"Then definitely borrow my shoes if you want. Some of them I've hardly even worn. There's my bags and accessories too."

As I went through the rest of her clothes and accessories, I checked each piece and made a mental note of items I'd like to borrow, which made the whole process much more fun.

When everything had finally been put away, we flattened all the boxes and stacked them in a pile to be recycled.

We stood back and admired our handiwork on the room. The sparse and uninspiring space had been transformed, injected full of Bora's personality by her sprawling collection of possessions. The bed was covered in her cushions and throws and her sheepskin rug tossed over the chair. Books, journals, photographs, and souvenirs filled shelves. Perfume bottles, candles, and jewellery boxes stood neatly arranged in vignettes on the dressing table.

"Wow," Bora said when she opened the wardrobe and the drawers in turn.

I had folded and arranged her clothing vertically so everything could be seen at a glance, and the wardrobe was organised by colour and length.

"It looks amazing!" Bora said. "Unfortunately I don't know how long I'll be able to keep it that way. I tend to keep my clothes on the bed or the floor most of the time."

"Haha. Don't worry. I'm not anal about tidiness. But maybe limit the mess to your bedroom, and not the living areas."

"Can do."

"All this hard work deserves a cold drink, don't ya think?"

"You read my mind."

We crashed on the couch with a couple of cans.

"Ahhh!" Bora leaned back and put her feet up on the ottoman.

"You're making yourself right at home," I noted.

"Yup! Gotta feel comfy, don't I?"

"Absolutely. Go for it."

"Hope you won't get sick of me now that we'll be seeing each other a whole lot more."

"It's not like you'll be here all the time, anyway. You work so much."

"True. You know I work strange hours. Sometimes I might not even come home at night if a shoot runs super late."

I nodded. "Jinseung used to have the same kind of schedule, if not worse. Promise me you'll text me, though, so I'm not worried about where you are."

"Yep. Same goes for you." She took a swig of beer then patted her stomach. "I'm starving. Got anything to eat?"

"I thought we could do a big grocery shop tomorrow. For now, let's get takeaway."

"I want pizza."

Just what I had been considering. "Great minds think alike."

I ordered from the delivery app on my phone. One large spicy Italian pizza to share. My tummy rumbled in anticipation.

While we waited for the pizza to arrive, Bora grabbed her tablet. I saw her check her work emails and Go Yoojin's schedule for the next day. She screwed her face up at something.

"What's wrong?" I asked.

"Actor-nim has to do another screen test tomorrow."

"Isn't that a good thing?"

"She's basically been given the role already. Didn't think she would need to do more. I wonder what the point is? Oh well. At least she's actually getting auditions, which is more than can be said for Jung Jen."

"Go Yoojin is more popular than Jung Jen now. That's so crazy when I think about it. Jen is practically a veteran actor compared to Yoojin."

"I know, right? Jen only gets minor roles these days. I've heard Mr. Kim is being super hard on her. She's always in his office for some reason or other. He's probably not happy with the situation. She's a liability."

"I feel so sorry for her. She seems pretty tired and stressed when I tutor her."

"She knew what she was risking when she two-timed San Seung. I don't blame her, though. Two gorgeous guys fawning over her…How could she choose? I'd probably do the same thing."

"Haha."

The intercom sounded, and the thought of hot, cheesy pizza overrode everything else in my head.

"That must be the pizza," I said.

"I'll go get it." Bora got to her feet.

I grabbed plates while she went outside to collect the pizza.

I could smell it even before she returned—mozzarella, olives, pepperoni. She waltzed in the doorway, bearing a square cardboard box stained with grease. What came next happened in slow motion. Buster scurried by her feet. She didn't see him, and as she stepped forward, she tripped over the little white furball. The pizza box left her grip and tipped over in the air, the lid falling partially open. The pizza went hurtling towards the floor.

"Noooo!" I cried, rushing over to try and save it.

Buster got to it before either me or Bora could salvage any pieces which didn't touch the floor.

"Oops," Bora said, rubbing her head sheepishly.

I folded my arms, both amused and peeved by the incident.

"What a waste."

Buster scoffed the pizza with loud chewing and licking noises. It made a terrible mess on the carpet.

"At least Buster is happy," Bora noted with a wry smile.

"I think he did that on purpose."

"Finds his own way home and works out how to get pizza. Smart dog."

12

Where is she? I looked up at the clock on the wall of the lesson room. 1:18 p.m. Go Yoojin was meant to arrive at one, and Bora had assured me that she'd be there as scheduled. I tapped my foot on the floor below the table, restless with impatience.

Another fifteen minutes passed before my phone started to ring, Yang Bora's name on the screen. I quickly picked up.

"Yes?"

"I am *so* sorry." Bora sounded flustered. "I know I told you this morning that Actor-nim would definitely make it today, but something has come up. She's not gonna be able to attend. Can we reschedule?"

"Sure, no problem."

At least I had confirmation. Now I could leave and get on with my day.

"I'll book another time in with you tonight," she said.

"Okay. Everything all right?"

"Yup. We ran into a famous producer and he invited us to

lunch to talk about an upcoming project. Can't let a chance like this slip by."

"Ah. Well, see you tonight."

"Yep, see ya, *Unnie!*"

So much for coming into the office today. I packed up my things and left the lesson room.

At the elevator, I pressed the down button. The metal doors stuttered open momentarily. I caught the eyes of the single occupant—Mr. Kim. I froze for a second, startled to see him. He was sharply dressed in a navy suit and yellow silk tie. He smelled faintly of cigarettes and spicy cologne.

"Are you getting in?" he asked, holding the button down so the doors didn't close.

"Um, yes."

I entered the elevator and reached for the ground-floor button, but it wouldn't activate. I had been so flustered upon seeing Mr. Kim that I hadn't noticed the elevator's direction.

"Oh, it's going up. Whoops."

The doors had already closed.

"I've actually been meaning to speak with you," Mr. Kim said.

His comment took me by surprise.

"With me?" I asked incredulously.

Why would he want to speak with me? My status at KAM was so low, surely I wasn't more than a blip on his radar. Didn't he have other, much more important matters to attend to?

"Yes," he said, straightening his tie.

The elevator doors opened, and he stood between them, preventing them from closing.

"Will you come to my office?" he asked, face expressionless.

Chapter 12

"Uh...okay."

I couldn't have said no even if I wanted to. Mr. Kim exuded that kind of power.

I followed him to his office, wondering the entire way what he was possibly going to speak with me about. Was it my working arrangement? My visa? Maybe it was something about Jinseung. Yes, that seemed like a strong possibility. Hopefully nothing bad had happened.

We entered his office, a spacious room full of shiny glass and black leather. A large bookcase occupied one wall, glossy volumes artfully arranged on its shelves. He closed the door behind us, and I thought I heard the click of a lock, or perhaps that was just my imagination.

"Take a seat," Mr Kim said, gesturing to the leather couch.

I sat down while Mr. Kim continued to stand, leaning against his desk. His bare ankles stuck out of his loafers.

I played with the hem of my shirt, waiting for him to speak.

"I've heard positive feedback about you from Go Yoojin and Jung Jen," he began. "It seems like you're doing a really good job with them, despite how little time they get to spend with you."

I lifted my head to meet his eyes, pleasantly surprised by the praise.

"Thank you, sir."

"English is becoming more and more important since we'd love our actors to work on international projects. We recently signed an agreement with an American agency. Through them, our portfolio of actors will be considered for any suitable roles which come their way and vice versa."

"I didn't know about that. Sounds like a good opportunity."

"Yes, it certainly is."

Maybe Jinseung would get to work on an American drama or film one day. Then again, his English was pretty poor so it seemed unlikely.

"In light of this, I was wondering if you would like some more hours," Mr. Kim said. "We have a couple of new recruits joining our ranks and I'd like you to tutor them in English."

I didn't need to think it over. I had little else to do with my time, anyway.

"Yes. Absolutely."

"Great. I'll put their managers in touch with you and you can sort something out with them." He stopped leaning against his desk.

Was that all he wanted to say? If so, what was the point of asking me to his office? I wasn't talent, and I didn't think he usually got involved with other staff matters. Did my relationship with Jinseung make me different? Perhaps that was why.

I gripped the handle of my bag, prepared to be dismissed from the room, but instead of going to the door, Mr. Kim dropped down beside me on the couch. I instinctively moved over so there was more space between us.

He turned to face me. From afar, he was quite a handsome man, but up close, I could see the pock marks on his upper cheeks and his nicotine-stained teeth.

"I also wanted to ask about how you're getting on without Shin Jinseung," he said. "I know it must be difficult to be on your own after the traumatic experience you went through."

"Yes, I mean, I'm going to miss him a lot, but I'll survive."

"Of course you will. You're a strong woman. I could tell that much from the first time I saw you."

"Oh, um, thanks."

"You'll survive, but I do wonder about Jinseung."

Chapter 12

"What do you mean?"

"Announcing a relationship, taking a four-month hiatus, then joining the military. It's a lot to put himself through. Will his career ever recover?"

There it is. His usual disdain for me was peeking out.

"I don't see why it wouldn't," I returned. "None of those things should affect his ability to act."

He sniggered, and I could tell he thought I was naive for saying that.

"If only that was all that mattered," he said. "No, joining the military was to be expected, but usually people in the entertainment industry don't commit themselves to a relationship at such a young age. He has really sacrificed a lot to be with you."

My face burned.

"I know he has," I spluttered. "And I really, really appreciate everything he's done for me."

"And it's not just Jinseung who has taken a hit," he continued. "So has the agency as a whole. Jinseung was one of our top earners before, now he's one of our lowest."

I didn't know what to say to this, so I stayed silent, looking down at my feet and fiddling with my hands in my lap.

"And we even invented a role for you at the company just so you could come back to South Korea. We've really done a lot for the sake of you and Jinseung."

"I know you have. I'm so grateful…"

"If you recall, I was against your relationship from the beginning, but Jinseung convinced me to make a concession. To be honest, I'm still not entirely convinced I made the right move in allowing it."

I hadn't noticed him edge towards me until his leg brushed mine. There was no room for me to move away, I was already flush up against the arm of the couch. Uneasiness bloomed in the pit of my stomach, making me quiver.

"I'm not saying all this to make you feel bad," Mr. Kim said. "I just want to make sure you know the circumstances that we're facing. I'm on Jinseung's side. I'm fighting for him as best as I can, but how long can this continue? I don't know." He sighed and I could feel his hot, slightly rancid breath on my cheek. "Just think about what I've said, okay?" He patted me on the top of my leg.

I internally recoiled at his touch, yet on the outside I was frozen, too startled to do anything. What was he playing at?

His hand lingered against me. I stared at it like it was a cockroach.

"You're doing great work, but you could be doing more," he continued. "It's a simple matter of give and take. The agency has made sacrifices for your sake, so what can you offer us? Just think about it. That's all I'm asking."

He started to rub his hand up and down a little, stroking me.

For a moment I just sat there, paralysed, but I quickly came to my senses. I had to extract myself from this situation before it progressed.

"I-I've got to go now." I snapped to my feet, his hand limply falling away. "I have an appointment I need to get to."

"Of course. Go ahead." His voice was totally calm and steady, like there was nothing wrong with this situation at all.

I walked straight to the door, but when I pulled the handle, it was as I feared. The door was locked. A coldness washed over me, heart thrumming in my ears. I struggled with the door handle, causing a rattling sound as I tried to work out how to unlock it. My panic must have been palpable.

I didn't hear Mr. Kim come up behind me, but I felt his

presence. I shuddered as he reached over my shoulder, his arm skimming the fabric of my shirt. In a quick, fluid motion, he unlatched the lock, then opened the door for me.

"Goodbye, Chloe," he said. "Enjoy the rest of your day."

I didn't turn around or say anything, I just marched straight out. I even took the stairs down instead of the elevator, not wanting to stand around a moment longer. As I made my way to the ground floor, I remembered Changsoo's words from the day that Jinseung entered the training centre.

He didn't climb all the way to his position by being a nice guy.

Now more than ever, those words resonated, and I wondered what exactly Mr. Kim was capable of.

13

I replayed the encounter with Mr. Kim in my head over and over again as I drove home, so much that I began to question my interpretation of what had happened. His words—did they mean what I thought they meant? His touch—that wasn't supposed to be a comforting gesture, was it? He had locked the door, but then again, he had let me leave without a struggle.

I desperately wanted to give Mr. Kim the benefit of the doubt. Things would be much less complicated if he hadn't meant anything sordid by his actions. I wouldn't have to say anything to anyone. I wouldn't have to cause a stir...

I gripped the steering wheel, my knuckles white. *No.* I couldn't fool myself. My original instinct was definitely correct: Mr. Kim had propositioned me, asking me to do him a favour in payment for everything he'd done for me and Jinseung, and that favour was undeniably sexual in nature.

Sleazy bastard...

Jinseung would be furious if he found out, but what could he possibly do while he was so far away and with limited means to communicate? Was that why Mr. Kim had waited until he left for the military to make his move?

Yes, that must be it. Bastard!

I thumped my fist on the horn, the loud, sharp toot shocking me despite being my intention.

My mood hadn't calmed by the time I got home. I felt as weak as a feather, all jittery and fluttery. I couldn't think about anything else all afternoon. What could I do? Who should I tell? The only thing I knew for sure was that I'd spill everything to Bora. She'd listen to me. She would understand. I didn't want to call her, I wanted to speak with her face to face. I'd wait until she came home, no matter how late that was.

―――

The smells of pork and vegetables, chilli peppers and soy sauce mingled in the air as the pot gently bubbled on the stove.

I heard Bora's voice before I saw her enter the room.

"Oooh. What's cooking? Smells soooo good!" Her cheery smile faded as soon as she set eyes on me. "*Unnie*, is something wrong?"

"Yes," I said.

"Oh no. Another panic attack?"

"No. Worse."

Her face fell even more. "Let's sit down. Tell me what happened."

"I'll tell you over dinner. It's ready now."

"Then you sit down, I'll serve it up."

I did as she said, pulling out a chair. Bora joined me after placing bowls of rice, dipping sauce, and meat and vegetables on the table. She served me a large portion, using her chopsticks to fill my plate before serving herself.

"I'm listening," Bora said from the chair opposite me. "Tell me everything."

I drew a deep breath before explaining what had happened, from the moment I saw Mr. Kim in the elevator, to the instant I left his office.

Bora didn't say anything, but her face grew paler and paler until she looked like she might faint. Her mouth was set in a deep frown. She was shaking so much she couldn't control her chopsticks. I knew she'd be shocked, but her reaction was worse than I anticipated.

I finished my story, and still she said nothing. Did she need more time to fully digest what I told her?

"Well?" I prompted. "Say something. I need to hear your thoughts."

Bora bowed her head and mumbled something indistinct, averting her gaze from mine.

"Sorry, I couldn't hear you," I said.

"It can't be true," she repeated.

My heart dropped to the pit of my stomach.

"What?"

Surely she didn't mean what I thought she meant or else I must have misheard her.

"Are you certain you read the situation correctly?" she asked, still avoiding my eyes.

"Yes," I said, though a tiny bit of doubt crept in. "At least, I'm ninety percent certain."

"Ninety percent isn't enough. No one will believe you."

Her words stung like needles through my chest.

"Do *you* believe me?" I asked.

"...No."

Chapter 13

It was a punch to my gut so hard I felt winded.

"I don't understand," I spluttered. "I thought you'd back me up on this."

"Well, you were wrong."

I felt angry now, my face burning, my hands fisted.

"Are you serious?" I spat. "You're the first person I've told because I thought I could trust you and I thought you'd be able to help me. Why are you being like this?"

"I can only help you when I believe what you're saying." Her voice was cold and harsh, yet weak at the same time.

"I'm telling you the truth!"

"But there's no way Mr. Kim would do such a thing. You've interpreted his actions wrong, that's the only valid explanation."

"But...but..."

Bora got to her feet, her eyes fixed firmly on the floor. "I need to go away and digest this."

"Where are you going?"

"Out." She turned and stormed out of the room and down the hall with heavy footsteps.

"When should I expect you back?" I called after her.

No answer. The front door slammed.

Left alone at the table with two plates of barely eaten food, I burst into tears.

I thought I could trust her. I thought she was my best friend. Why couldn't she believe me? Why would she take Mr. Kim's side instead? She wasn't behaving like her usual self. I didn't understand at all.

But maybe she was right.

Maybe I really did take my interpretation of events too far. It wasn't like he'd actually said or done anything that could outright constitute sexual harassment, had he?

"Arrrggggh," I groaned, clutching at the sides of my head feeling a massive headache coming on.

My phone began to ring and I reluctantly checked who was calling.

Jinseung.

I picked up at once, unwilling to miss the opportunity to hear his voice, despite my inner turmoil.

"Hello," I answered.

"Hi," Jinseung said. "Are you okay? Are you upset about something?"

Trust him to extrapolate my feelings from just one word.

I swallowed my distress until it settled deep in my stomach.

"No, I'm fine. I just miss you, that's all."

His voice softened. "I miss you too."

I couldn't tell him the truth. I needed more time to properly assess the situation first. The moment I told him, he would definitely to do something rash, and I didn't want that.

"I can't believe it's already been three weeks since you left. How are you getting along?" I asked. "You must nearly be done with training now."

"Uh huh. I've been made the leader of my squadron too."

"What? Wow. That's amazing. Well done."

"Thanks."

"So, you're doing well?"

"Very well. Too well."

"Too well?"

"I see others struggling. Guys much younger than me. Guys who aren't used to self-discipline. Guys who are unfit and can't keep up with the drills. For me, it's like a walk in the park. I feel kinda guilty about that. It's easy for me."

"I'm just glad you're not one of the people who are struggling."

"Heh. I don't blame you for thinking that way."

"You never told me what the dorms are like. Are you comfortable?"

"Not really. They're big, sterile rooms full of rows of bunk beds. There's no privacy, even in the bathrooms."

"*Aigoo*. That must be hard for you."

"It was tough, especially in the beginning. Now the other guys are used to me being around. They've stopped staring at me and hounding me for autographs and photos."

"That's good."

"And you? Are you doing okay without me?"

"Well…" My voice broke. "It's hard."

"Are you lonely? I thought Bora moving in would have helped."

Her name stabbed me in the chest. I didn't comment.

"Why don't you give *Noona* a call? I'm sure she'd love to hang out with you."

"Maybe."

"Do it. And remember I gave you that credit card. Treat yourself."

"Are you encouraging me to go and waste your money on frivolous items?"

"Precisely."

"Be careful what you wish for."

Jinseung chuckled. "I better go. My parents are expecting me to call soon."

"All right. Talk again soon?"

"Of course. Love you."

"Love you too."

He hung up.

How long would I be able to keep my secret from him?

The food in front of me had long gone cold, but I shovelled in a few mouthfuls and swallowed them down, merely for sustenance.

Bora didn't come home that night, and I gave up waiting for her. I went to my room, and as I lifted the covers to crawl into bed, I felt sure that I was going to have another nightmare —only this time it wouldn't be about Oh Sejung.

14

Bora didn't come back the next day, or the next day, or the day after that.

About to head off to work, I reached for my shoes on the small wooden shelf by the door but stopped short. A pair of Bora's shoes sat next to mine—pretty red slingback heels. I brushed a finger against the smooth leather, adoring the cute shoes and the woman who owned them.

We have the same shoe size…

A pang of regret squeezed my heart. Having Bora move in with me was the only good thing to come out of Jinseung's enlistment so far, and now look what had happened.

I slid on my ballet flats, remembering they were the pair Bora bought me for my birthday the previous year, which made my heart squeeze even tighter.

I desperately wanted to call her and beg for forgiveness, even though I knew it should be the other way around. She had wronged me. We had fought before but not like this. I couldn't bear it.

After lingering by the door lost in my thoughts for far

longer than I should, I set out. My first trip to KAM HQ since *the incident*.

I hadn't seen or heard from Mr. Kim in the past few days, and I prayed it would stay that way.

When I arrived in the underground carpark, I had to take a few deep breaths to calm myself. I talked to my wary face in the rear-view mirror. *It's going to be okay. You won't see Mr. Kim and he won't see you. The run-in on the elevator was a one-off. It won't happen again.*

Despite my pep talk, I froze in front of the elevator door, my index finger mid-way to the call button. I decided to take the stairs instead. If anything, it would give me a good work-out.

I stopped at reception first to sign in, then continued up yet more stairs. Puffing slightly from the ascent, I settled down in the lesson room surrounded by walls covered in bright posters with English words on them.

Go Yoojin arrived shortly after me. The shock of her sudden entry caused me to spring from my seat.

"Actor-nim, you're here," I said, slightly flustered.

Go Yoojin undid her hair tie, letting her long black tresses fall to her waist. She wore amber-coloured contact lenses which made her eyes look even more intense and cat-like than usual.

"You seem surprised," she said, one perfect brow quirked.

"I wasn't sure whether to expect you or not," I explained.

"Didn't Manager-nim say I would come?"

"No, she didn't."

Bora had rescheduled the lesson in my online calendar without any other form of contact, and there had been no word from her since then. I just had to assume it was still going ahead.

Chapter 14

"Oh. Well, I'm here," she said. "Surprise."

I chuckled sheepishly. "I'm glad. Take a seat."

The lesson plan for the day was to practice describing appearance and personality. We started by describing the pictures of people supplied in the workbook, then moved on to people in real life.

"Can you describe Yang Bora to me?" I asked in English, tensing slightly as the name rolled off my tongue.

Yoojin brought a finger decorated with intricate nail art to her lips in thought. "Umm...She is short and cute. She has long red hair."

"What else?"

"She have glasses."

"She *wears* glasses."

"She wears glasses. She wears nice clothes. She is pretty. Ummm."

"And her personality?"

"She is smart. She is strong. She is kind. She is...de-determin..."

"Determined?"

"Yes. Determined. And she is stubborn."

I nodded along. All those things were true, and hearing them said aloud made my chest ache with longing for my dearest friend. I still couldn't get over the fact that she didn't believe me, and the perfect angel was not as angelic as I had once thought.

I asked Yoojin to describe a few other people. She was doing well and I was about to move on to a different exercise when an idea struck me. There was another person we both knew, and I'd be interested to hear her take on him.

"Can you describe Mr. Kim?" I asked.

Yoojin's eyes widened.

I wondered if she was about to say she didn't want to talk about him, but then she opened her mouth and rattled off several familiar descriptors.

"He is average height and weight," she said. "He has short black hair and black eyes. He wears nice suits. He wears colourful shirts and ties."

"What is his personality like?"

"He is smart. He is funny. He is…" She used her hand to mime a talking mouth.

"Talkative, charismatic, extroverted," I offered.

"Charismatic," she repeated slowly, feeling out the sound in her mouth.

"Anything else?"

"Hmmm…He is scary. A little bit."

I snapped up straight in my seat. "Scary? Why is he scary?"

Yoojin shrugged. "I don't know. Manager Yang thinks so too."

"Yang Bora thinks he's scary?"

Yoojin nodded but struggled to form an explanation in English.

"Why does Yang Bora think he's scary?" I asked, reverting to Korean. I tried to keep my tone light-hearted while panic simmered in my stomach.

"I don't know. She just does. She doesn't let me meet with him alone."

The simmer turned up to a boil.

What does this mean? Does Bora fear Mr. Kim after all? Then why would she say she didn't believe me?

"Why is that?" I asked.

"I don't know. He's just a bit intimidating, don't you think? Even I don't dare talk back to him."

I suppressed my bubbling anxiety.

"Yes. I see," I said calmly.

If I continued this line of questioning, Yoojin would surely get suspicious. I had already pushed further than was reasonable, and I couldn't disguise this as part of the English lesson since we were speaking Korean now.

"Let's do another exercise," I suggested, going back to English.

Yoojin nodded, seeming eager to drop the previous subject.

The rest of the lesson went smoothly, and Yoojin even managed to stay until the end of our allotted time without the usual interruptions.

When I was ready to leave afterwards, I took the stairs again. I didn't expect to meet anyone in the grey, concrete stairwell, so the sound of approaching footsteps made me clench up inside. My initial instinct was to flee, but when I listened closely, they weren't the footsteps of a man. They were light and click-clacky, like a woman's heels. I continued my descent. The click-clack came to an abrupt stop. I looked down and saw Yang Bora. She averted her gaze and continued walking as if she hadn't seen me.

"Hello," I said when we met each other on the same flight of steps.

"Hi," she said in a voice several decibels weaker than her usual bright and lively tone.

We slowly passed each other by. I gave her one final glance over my shoulder and saw that she was still looking at me. She looked sad. Regretful. Then she cast her eyes away and hastily walked away before I could say anything.

15

I woke in the middle of the night to a loud thud. I clutched at my chest, heart racing beneath my flannel pyjama top. *What the heck was that?*

Whatever it was had woken Buster too. I heard his paws thump as he scurried around barking his head off. Not a good sign. My ears pricked at another sound—the creak of floorboards. I gasped.

There is someone in the house.

I shook my head trying to wake myself up from what must have been a nightmare, but as my senses sharpened, all the noises became even clearer.

There is definitely someone in the house.

My pulse quickened. Beads of sweat prickled my forehead. *What do I do?*

I was trapped between the idea of confronting whoever was in my house and cowering underneath my blankets.

A Sasaeng *fan?* How did they get through the gate and into the house without waking me sooner? Surely they would have set off the alarm.

Buster soon quietened, and the creaking trailed away to nothingness. Perhaps it really had been in my head, but I wouldn't be able to sleep until I knew for sure.

My self-defence kit keychain lay on the bedside table. I had got into a habit of leaving it there overnight—just in case. I grasped it in a white-knuckled hand and crept to my bedroom door. Racked with nerves, I slowly, carefully, opened the door, trying not to make a noise. I craned my neck out and looked both ways down the hallway.

All quiet, all still.

I tiptoed towards the kitchen. I was about to enter the doorway when I collided with someone.

I screamed and shone the mini flashlight in their eyes. The other person screamed as well—or more like a yelp of shock.

"Chloe! It's only me." Yang Bora squinted through the powerful beam of light, her open hands raised in the air.

I was so panic-stricken that it took a long moment to realise I wasn't in danger. Eventually, my breath returned and my heartbeat slowed down. I lowered the flashlight.

"I thought you were an intruder," I confessed.

"I tried not to wake you," Bora said.

"Well, you did, and you gave me the fright of my life. You know what I've been through. You should know better."

She cringed. "I'm sorry. I didn't think."

"What was that loud noise before?"

"I tripped over the step by the door."

I didn't bother to ask if she was okay. "Planning to sneak in, take your things, and leave again, were you?"

"No, I was going to stay here the night, and continue to stay here, if you'll let me."

Her answer surprised me. After the way she acted when

we saw each other in the stairwell, I believed I'd lost her forever.

"So…you're back?" I needed further convincing.

"Yes." She was resolute.

I didn't let my relief show. I couldn't let her off the hook that easy after what she did to me.

"I can't live with someone who isn't on my side," I said.

"I *am* on your side." Her eyes were wide and pleading.

"Have you had a change of heart?"

"I've always been on your side. I was just too afraid to admit it."

She sounded so earnest. I couldn't stay angry at her. I was sure she had her reasons.

"Sounds like we better have a talk," I said.

Bora agreed with a sharp nod. "There's a lot to discuss."

We made hot drinks in the kitchen—the sweet contents of two coffee sachets mixed with freshly boiled water—then we sat opposite each other at the dining table, the room lit by a single floor lamp in the corner. Half of Bora's heart-shaped face glowed warmly in the dim light, the other half in shadow. She cradled her mug in her hands and sipped.

"So, you *do* believe me?" I asked again.

"Yes, I do. I believed you the moment you said what you did," she explained.

"Then…why?"

"Because I'm terrified, Chloe. Terrified of what it means. I've worked so hard to get to this point in my career. *So* hard. Has it all been based on a lie?"

"Why would it be?"

"Because I can't work for Mr. Kim if he does things like that. I can't work in the entertainment industry if this goes on and it's considered normal. I've heard stories, rumours, but I shut them out, preferring to believe that nothing like that could ever happen, but now…"

"Wait—have you heard other rumours about Mr. Kim?"

"Not about Mr. Kim—other staff, other companies. I was distanced enough not to let it affect me."

"But not anymore," I said softly, understanding dawning.

"Hearing what you said was overwhelming. I didn't want to accept it, even though I knew deep down you must be speaking the truth. I'm sorry." She looked down at the table with a strained expression on her face.

This must have been eating her up inside for the past few days.

"I think I understand you a bit better now, but I wish you told me this straight away."

"I know. I wouldn't blame you if you hated me right now."

She kept her head hung low, but I could still make out the anguish swirling in the depths of her eyes.

"I don't hate you. I could never hate you."

After all she had done for me over the course of our friendship, the least I could do was forgive her.

She lifted her head a little. "Really?"

"Of course."

I offered her a wry smile, coaxing one from her as well.

"I swear I'll never do something like that to you again. Can we still be best friends?"

"Absolutely."

Her bubbliness returned, filling the hollowness of her cheeks and making her eyes sparkle.

She was back, hopefully for good.

"The question is, what can we do about Mr. Kim?" she asked, suddenly serious again.

"The reason I told you in the first place was because I thought you might know what to do," I explained.

"I'm afraid you've overestimated me. I really have no idea. What he did was bad, but not bad enough that the police would do anything about it."

"What about HR? I could make an anonymous complaint."

"Mr. Kim is part owner of the agency. Filing a complaint against him wouldn't achieve anything."

"Then...the media? They're always looking for entertainment industry scandals to report on."

"A good idea in theory, but I wouldn't advise it. Mr. Kim would counter-attack. He'd get an article written about you which would be far worse. He'd drag your name through the mud to make you sound like a liar."

I sighed through gritted teeth. "You're right."

Bora adjusted her glasses. "We simply can't take on Mr. Kim by ourselves. He'll chew us up and spit us out. And then there's Shin Jinseung and Go Yoojin to consider."

I flinched at his name. "I haven't told Jinseung."

"I don't blame you. Who knows how he'd react? It's probably for the best—at least for now. We wouldn't want him to do anything rash. This is a complex issue. We need to think about it very carefully before taking action."

"And if Mr. Kim approaches me again in the meantime? Takes things a step further?"

"Then we'll have more ammunition to use against him."

My stomach lurched. "I don't know. That makes me feel uneasy."

"There *is* an alternative."

"What's that?"

"Quit working at KAM."

Chapter 15

I shook my head. "I'd lose my visa. I'd have to leave the country."

"Exactly. You could leave all of this behind. Come back when Jinseung is discharged."

"I...don't know."

"Think about it."

Are those really my only two options? Both were untenable. Both made me feel ill.

"Well?" Bora asked, looking unsettled by my descent into deep and thoughtful silence.

"Let's play it by ear," I suggested.

16

Face Mr. Kim or go back home. The choice plagued me for weeks until it began to feel irrelevant.

I hadn't seen Mr. Kim again since the initial incident. Time and space made me believe that perhaps I'd overreacted, perhaps he wasn't as dangerous as I'd built him up to be in my head. So I began to let my guard down.

The clock on the lesson room wall struck 7:30 p.m. I was halfway through a teaching session with Jung Jen, the first time I'd seen her in a long time because she had been busy shooting the medical drama, among other priorities.

Pink lipstick stood out against her ghostly white skin. Had she lost even more weight, or was she this skinny last time as well? I couldn't remember.

As I watched her silently work through an exercise, something Bora had said suddenly came back to me.

I've heard Mr. Kim is being particularly hard on her...She's always in his office for some reason or other...He's not happy with the situation...She's a liability...

Chapter 16

I wondered what Jen thought of Mr. Kim. I had already asked Go Yoojin, perhaps now was my chance to question Jen.

She looked up at me. She must have sensed my enquiring stare.

"What is it?" she asked.

I was about to say, "Nothing," but changed my mind as soon as I opened my mouth.

I have to know.

"Actor-nim, Mr. Kim is your agent…"

Was that a slight flinch at his name?

She narrowed her eyes.

"What do you think of him?" I asked.

No games this time. No disguising it as a part of the lesson. Straight to the point.

She definitely flinched that time. She jolted back in her seat, eyes wide. "Why are you asking that?"

"Just…no reason."

I could hardly tell her the truth.

Her eyes flicked around the room. It looked like she was trying to find something. I followed her gaze but couldn't work out what she was looking at.

"I have no comments to make about him," she said, returning her focus to me.

A strange response, almost like she'd been instructed never to talk about him and it was the automatic reply she gave whenever someone asked. That was my impression, anyway.

"Huh. I see. Forget I said anything."

After that moment of weirdness, the rest of the lesson continued without a hitch.

"That's it for today," I said.

"Thank you, *Seonsaeng-nim*. I'll be going now." Jen tilted her head at me before leaving the room.

I stayed behind for a few minutes, jotting down notes on Jen's progress and ideas for what I could teach her in our next lesson.

Afterwards, I checked the time again, wondering if Bora would be finishing up soon too. It was getting pretty late, after all. Maybe she'd like a ride home. I sent her a text message, but she replied saying she was still held up with work.

I was half out of my chair when the lesson room door suddenly swung open. I was so startled that I gasped and dropped back down into my seat, clutching my heaving chest.

The woman who entered looked at me funny. She wore a plasticky apron and rubber gloves, tugging a cart of cleaning products behind her.

"Sorry," she said. "Should I come back later?"

"No. I'm leaving now." I gathered myself and left the room.

In my flustered state I forgot all about taking the stairs and automatically approached the elevator. As soon as I punched the button, I realised my mistake, but I decided that the chance of seeing Mr. Kim was slim. I'd take the risk.

I watched the floor number on the display panel descend, praying that I wouldn't see him inside. I tensed in anticipation when the metal door lurched open.

"Oh! Hey, Chloe."

I relaxed at the familiar voice. Seo Minjung stood inside the elevator, immaculately dressed as usual, a long trench coat over a sleek turtleneck and high-waisted trousers, her straight black hair secured with a chic tortoiseshell clip.

"Minjung-ssi!" I said, grateful to see her friendly face. "Finished for the day?"

"Yup."

"Me too."

"How are you? We don't bump into each other often."

"I know. I'm not here very often, so it's not surprising."

"Have you met the new recruits yet? I hear you'll be teaching them."

"New recruits?"

"You didn't know? Nam Sungjin and Do Junghwan just joined. Everyone in the office is talking about them."

Of course. Mr. Kim *did* say there would be new recruits. I had been so focused on other things that I hadn't absorbed it as fact.

"Oh! I remember now. Yes, I'm meant to be teaching them but I haven't heard anything from their managers yet."

"You'll probably hear soon. Hope the new actors won't be too much of a handful."

"I'm sure they'll be delightful."

We continued to chat as I walked to the touchscreen by the reception desk to sign out.

"Are you catching the subway?" Minjung asked.

"No. I'm parked downstairs. I don't take public transit anymore."

"Ah, that's right. I forget that you could get recognised these days. To me, you're—"

Her words faded into silence as soon as I saw Mr. Kim. He crossed the glossy floor carrying a black briefcase. He seemed to be moving in slow motion as I focused on him, everything else drowned out by his presence. I tried to avert my eyes but they were stuck to him.

Please, don't notice me…

As soon as I thought these words, his head turned and his eyes locked onto mine. Two cold, black eyes, soulless, just like Oh Sejung's. A bitter wave of dread seeped into my veins and crept through my body.

"Chloe…"

The voice was distant, as if I were underwater and someone were calling to me from the shore.

Mr. Kim no longer looked my way. Time sped back up as he strode purposefully towards the door.

"Chloe?"

Minjung waved a hand in front of me and I snapped out of my trance.

"Are you okay?"

"Yeah. Sorry, spaced out for a second there." *On the verge of another panic attack, more like.* "What were you saying?"

"Nothing, really. Just that I don't think of you as a celebrity, or the girlfriend of a celebrity, but knowing how hardcore some of the fans can be, you're right to avoid public outings when you can."

Little did she know that I had already had a dangerous encounter with one such "hardcore" fan.

"Anyway," she said. "I'm going to go home now. See you around."

"Okay. See you."

Mr. Kim had left the building through the main doors, which meant it would be safe to go down to the carpark.

I drove home thinking maybe Bora had been right. Maybe I should quit working at KAM. Avoidance tactics would only go so far, and I couldn't work in fear of seeing him again. I gnashed my teeth and grumbled. *What should I do?* Having to quit jobs and move was starting to become depressingly frequent, and the thought of going back to the UK was too bleak to bear. I wanted to stay in Korea so I could at least visit Jinseung whenever he had a break from the army. Ending up back at my parents' house in defeat like the other times was the last thing I wanted. My life was here, no matter what.

Chapter 16

Buster was all over me as soon as I walked in the door, yapping and whining.

"Poor boy," I said, petting his fluffy head. "You've been waiting patiently for your dinner."

He followed me to the kitchen, where I filled his bowl with dog food and replenished his water.

After taking care of Buster's dinner, I turned my attention to preparing my own meal. I made enough for Bora as well, in case she didn't have time to eat at work, as was often the case.

I was about to serve the hot Japanese-style curry when I heard the front door open, followed by footsteps directly towards me.

Bora entered the room, a strange expression of determination mixed with concern on her face.

"Bora-ya! I thought you were going to be much later," I said. "There's plenty of food, if you want some."

"You've got to see this," she said. Her mind clearly wasn't on food.

"See what?"

She marched straight into the living room and turned the TV on.

"What is it?" I asked, watching the screen.

"You'll see."

A news programme played. A story about something to do with China's economy. I watched with a furrowed brow.

"Not this," Bora said. "I'm sure it will come on again soon."

After an ad break, the news anchor reappeared on camera.

"And back to tonight's top story," she read, "sexual abuse allegations have been made against a prominent executive in the entertainment industry."

17

A lot of unusual things happened during my next lesson with Jung Jen. The first thing that shocked me was that Jen arrived early. No one ever arrived early. Tight schedules meant the actors were more likely to arrive late, or never, than on time, and especially not early.

The second thing that shocked me was that it looked like she'd been crying. Her eyes had a red tinge and were slightly swollen. Her makeup was blotchy, as if it had been ruined then haphazardly reapplied over the top.

"Hello," she said quietly, taking her seat opposite me.

I was so used to seeing the actors look sick and exhausted that I usually didn't ask "Are you okay?" even when I wanted to, but this time was different.

"Is everything okay?" I asked.

"Yes," she said.

I didn't believe her.

"I know I'm just your English tutor, but if there's something wrong, I'd like to try and help you. No matter what it is."

She smiled weakly. "Is it that obvious I've been crying?"

"Yes. I'm afraid it is."

She avoided my gaze, threading and unthreading her fingers together in her lap. "It's…really nothing. Just stress."

"Hmmm. I see."

There was something she wasn't telling me, but she was clammed up tight in her shell. I could tell she wasn't going to open up to me any time soon.

"If you don't want to talk about it, I'll get straight into the lesson, but if you change your mind, I'll listen to you. No one has to know that we just talked rather than doing the lesson."

She was adamant. "It's okay. Let's just get on with it."

It seemed pushing her wasn't going to get me anywhere.

"All right. Let's see…" I scanned the notes in front of me. "Last time we worked on the topic of shopping. Shall we start where we left off?"

"Okay. Oh—I did this." She rummaged in her bag and presented me with her workbook.

"Homework?" I asked, stunned.

"Yes."

My third shock of the lesson. She had never done homework before.

"Wow. You did this even though you're so busy and stressed?"

"Yes. Actually, it's less stressful to focus on homework than anything else. It's more like stress-relief."

"Can't say I've heard that before. Let's go through this first, then."

I reached for her workbook, but Jen abruptly slammed her hand down on the front cover before my fingertips could brush it.

"No," she said. "I mean, could you mark it after the lesson

then go over it with me next time? I'd rather work on something else right now."

Her request made me raise an eyebrow but I went along with it.

"Sure. If that's what you want."

"Thanks." She looked me in the eyes as she pushed the book towards me. "By the way, I've marked some parts that I'm unsure about. Please pay attention to them."

Something felt odd about this request too. Perhaps it was the strange seriousness with which she spoke, or maybe it was just my imagination and I was reading too much into it. I'd been overthinking things a lot these days. That news story from the other day was case in point. Bora and I both had our suspicions, but the suspect had not been named, and Mr. Kim was still in his job, business as usual, so it couldn't really have been about him, could it?

"I will," I replied.

I filed her workbook away in my bag, making a mental note to check it as she'd asked.

With that out of the way, we carried on with the lesson. Jen's mood seemed to lift slightly, but she was still distracted and scatterbrained.

As time went on, the evidence of her past tears faded. No one would suspect a thing unless they looked very closely.

"*Omo!*" Jen gasped when her phone started to beep. She swiped at the screen. "I've got to go. Meeting with Mr. Kim."

"With Mr. Kim?" I repeated, unable to stop the words slipping from my mouth.

"Yes."

Could that be the reason why she was so upset? Stress about her upcoming meeting with Mr. Kim?

"With Mr. Kim…" I repeated, thinking it over.

Chapter 17

Jen ignored me, grabbing her bag to leave.

"Be careful," I spluttered before she left the room.

She didn't turn back or acknowledge what I said.

I banged my fist on the table in frustration. *Shit!* This was eating me up inside. If there was even the smallest chance that my suspicions were right, I had to do something. But what?

I couldn't sit around any longer with the knowledge that something bad might happen in the back of my brain. Before I could talk myself out of it, I grabbed my things and rushed up the stairs to the fifth floor.

18

I'd sworn to myself that I'd never visit the fifth floor alone again, yet here I was.

Being after hours, the reception desk was closed. I tiptoed through the corridors, my eyes and ears tuned in for signs of movement. I was shaking and my heart was beating loud in my ears. If anyone saw me sneaking around on the fifth floor, they'd surely question my intentions, and I wouldn't be able to provide an adequate explanation for why I was there. That was why I had to be careful not to get caught.

Very few offices occupied the floor. I assumed they all belonged to the company's top executives. Even the areas of the building which were dedicated to the company's talent weren't as posh as this floor, with its designer furniture pieces, framed paintings, and fancy light fittings, all set within a rich colour scheme of gold, aubergine, and dark wood.

I had only recently learned that KAM stood for Kim, Ahn, and Moon—the three founders of the agency. Mr. Moon had retired, but Mr. Kim and Mr. Ahn remained active, though Mr. Kim was much more visible.

I silently crept towards my target. Mr. Kim's office was situated down a long, windowless corridor, quite far apart from the rest of the offices. You wouldn't go past it unless it were your destination.

My ears pricked at the clang of the elevator doors opening, then footsteps. They sounded like they were heading in my direction. Heart beating furiously in my chest, I scurried around a corner, then pressed my back flush to the wall, trying not to make a sound.

The footsteps faded, and I thought I heard the creak of a door open and close. They must have gone into their office. *Whew.* I waited to catch my breath before moving on.

Mr. Kim's door was now in sight. Fists clenched into tight balls at my sides, I approached. The door was closed, of course, and so were the blinds of the internal window.

My mind raced. *I can't believe I'm doing this. Why am I even here? What good will this do?*

Breathing fast and heavy, I leaned close and pressed my ear to the wall. His office was most likely soundproofed, but I tried to listen anyway, straining my ears for just a hint of what might be going on inside.

It was no use. I couldn't hear anything. Pulling away in defeat, my gaze fell to where a crack of light shone beneath the door. That was when another idea struck me. *Worth a shot.* I knelt down with my ear almost to the carpet to try and listen through the crack. To my surprise, I could make out a voice—Mr. Kim's voice. But I couldn't exactly hear what he was saying. It seemed to be a one-sided conversation because I couldn't hear anyone else. Maybe he was on the phone?

This isn't any good...

I stood back up. What else could I do? Knock on the door? No, that was out of the question.

Looking around again, I suddenly became aware of all the security features of the door. It seemed to have some kind of electronic lock. Maybe an eye or fingerprint scanner. I hadn't paid attention when Mr. Kim took me to his office last time, so I couldn't remember how he unlocked it. I noticed the security cameras. It felt like all of them were trained directly on me. Perhaps I was being paranoid, but could there be a screen inside his office which showed who was outside? It was possible, though I couldn't recall ever seeing one when I was inside. I started to panic. *Arrggh.* I really hadn't thought this through properly. *Maybe I should just leave.*

I heard a sound. Movement behind the door. A clunking sound like the door was about to open.

Oh shit. What do I do? Run away?

There was no time. He'd see me.

Think, Chloe, think!

The door swung open and Mr. Kim appeared, partially silhouetted, dramatic shadows filling the hollows of his face. He looked down at me and didn't seem surprised.

He knew I was out here.

"Miss Gibson," he said. "What are you doing?" Despite his politeness, there was an undertone of malice in his voice.

"I, errr, sorry, Mr. Kim, I just…I just had a lesson with Jung Jen, and she left this with me." I fished for the workbook in my bag and held it out to him. "She told me she had a meeting with you, so I thought I'd try and catch her on her way out and give it to her."

Mr. Kim's eyes narrowed. "She told you she had a meeting with me?"

"Yes. That's what she said."

"Hmm."

"Is she there? Can I give it to her?" I craned my neck trying to peer into his office through the partially open door.

"She's not here."

From what I could see, he was telling the truth. His office appeared to be empty.

"Oh. That's strange."

"Yes, it is." His eyes lowered to the workbook in my hands. "I can take that and give it to her or her manager."

I dug my fingers into the book, clutching it much tighter than necessary. "No. That's fine. I'll give it to her."

"Suit yourself."

"I'll just be going then. Sorry to interrupt you." I turned away, eager to get away from him.

Mr. Kim's hand came firmly down on my shoulder.

I froze, with a shudder emanating from the point our bodies connected.

"Miss Gibson," he said.

"Yes?"

"Don't come to my office again unless I ask you to, or you've made an appointment through my secretary. You should know better."

"Yes, sir."

He dropped his hand and I walked away, resisting the urge to break into a run to escape. I heard his door lock with a click.

It wasn't until I was safely downstairs that I considered the situation. If Jung Jen wasn't with Mr. Kim, then where was she? Was she having a secret meeting with someone else? *Hmmm*...Maybe she just got her schedule confused. *Yeah.* That was more likely. Or maybe she was meeting someone else called Kim? Another likely scenario, considering the number of Kims in Korea. *Aggghh. What an idiot!* I put myself at risk and made a complete fool of myself in front of Mr. Kim for nothing. I should never have gotten involved.

19

Another day, another English lesson, but as soon as I entered the lobby of KAM HQ, I knew something was wrong. A strange atmosphere pervaded the room. Everyone spoke in hushed tones with grave looks on their faces. I tried to listen to their conversations as I passed but couldn't hear anything except vague snatches. The words "devastating" and "tragic" stood out.

The receptionist, Minha, wore a similarly glum expression. I reached for the touch screen by the desk to sign myself in, when she stopped me.

"I don't think any of your lessons will be going ahead today," she said.

That was when I knew for sure that something serious was afoot. I was almost too scared to ask.

"Why not? Has something happened?"

She frowned. "Haven't you heard?"

"No. I just got here."

"We only found out a few minutes ago. It's terrible news. There's been a suicide."

My heart dropped and a sick taste filled my mouth.

"Who?" I asked, my throat dry.

I anticipated the answer before she said it.

"Jung Jen."

I felt faint. My head was spinning.

"No…" I choked. "Please, no. Not Jen. No."

"I'm afraid so."

"But I saw her just yesterday…"

"Yes. A lot of people saw her around the office yesterday. It's so tragic. Her manager discovered her body earlier this morning when he went to pick her up from her home. That's all I know—that's all anyone knows right now."

"Oh my God. I can't…" I pressed my hands to my temples and scrunched my eyes shut.

This wasn't happening. This was just another nightmare. *Yes. That must be it. A nightmare…*

"Are you all right?" Minha asked.

Flecks of light danced behind my eyelids. My legs felt weak. I was about to collapse.

"Whoa, there." She came out from behind the desk and rushed to provide a hand in support.

I clung to her arm, forcing myself to take slow and deep breaths until I recovered. "Thanks. I'm just so shocked."

"You should go home. Nobody will be getting much work done today."

"Yes, I will. Thank you for telling me."

"Will you be okay?"

"I think so."

No, not really, but I didn't want to cause a fuss.

She gently let me go and returned to her station.

I walked away, shivering despite the building's heating.

*Jung Jen…*The image of her in my head was so fresh and

vivid. Long middle-parted hair framing an oval face with large eyes, an elegant nose, and fine lips. She was so lovely…so *young*…and now she was dead.

I paced the floor, the reality of the situation still sinking in. *I knew something weird was going on with Jen, and now this happens.* I couldn't help feeling like I was partially to blame for this horrible outcome.

Other people entered the building with the same confusion as I did before. I wondered whether Yang Bora and Go Yoojin were aware. Surely someone had told them. How were they dealing with the news? Right on cue, my phone began to ring. Yang Bora was calling.

I picked up and cut to the chase. "Did you hear?"

"I was about to ask you the same thing. So, both of us know." Her voice sounded weak and fragile, not the usual boisterous tone.

"Where are you?"

"I'm at Actor Go's house. She's absolutely distraught. Jung Jen was a good friend to her and she had no idea that something like this would happen."

"Bora-ya…" I needed to tell her what was on my mind.

"Yes?"

"When Jung Jen came to her lesson yesterday, it was obvious she'd been crying. I tried to talk to her but she wouldn't tell me anything. I feel so guilty…"

"Don't say that. It's not your fault."

"I feel like I could have done something. If only I had tried harder to reach her…"

"Everyone close to her will be feeling that way. We all knew she was going through a difficult time."

"I suppose…" I sighed deeply. "Will you be coming home?

I don't really want to come back to an empty house right now."

"No. I need to stay with Actor-nim and keep an eye on her. You know what she's like. Who knows what she'd do, the state she's in."

"Ah. I see."

"But why don't you come over to her house?"

I perked up at her suggestion. "Would that be okay?"

"Just a sec. I'll ask."

I heard the muffled sound of her conversing with Yoojin in the background.

"Yes," she said, back on the line. "She says you can come over since you knew Jung Jen too. I'll text you the address."

"Thanks. I'll come soon."

I ended the call and made my way straight down to the carpark. The text message with the address came through and I typed it into the car's built-in GPS.

When I drove out of the carpark, the scene outside surprised me. The weather had been fine when I arrived. Now, thick grey clouds rolled across the sky and raindrops furiously pelted down, ricocheting off the asphalt. I flicked the windscreen wipers onto the highest setting.

Thoughts swirled in my head as I drove, paying attention to little else except the robotic voice of the GPS. I seemed to be catching every red traffic light, moving at a snail's pace in the heavy congestion as the relentless rain fell.

Something niggled in the back of my mind. Was it possible that Jung Jen took her life over something Mr. Kim did to her? Too many little things stacked up: Mr. Kim's behaviour towards me, the news report about a prominent entertainment industry executive, Jung Jen's reaction when I asked her about

Mr. Kim, and the fact she said she was meeting him yesterday then seemingly didn't. Coincidences? Maybe…or maybe not.

Slowly but surely, the pieces came together like a jigsaw puzzle in my head. What if Jung Jen was the whistleblower who reported the executive? What if the consequences were too much for her to handle and she committed suicide? Or worse. What if it wasn't suicide at all? Mr. Kim's face, twisted and menacing, flashed in my mind.

Someone honked at me, and I realised I was first in the queue at the intersection. Without thinking, I pressed my foot on the accelerator, speeding up to get through before the light turned red, swinging the steering wheel around a little more sharply than necessary. A sickening screech rang out as the tyres skidded on the slippery-wet asphalt. I went careening wide around the corner, shock and panic engulfing me.

20

I gripped the steering wheel, white-knuckled, heart pounding as my car hurtled towards the waiting traffic on the other side of the intersection. Time slowed down. I automatically moved my foot from the accelerator to the brake, trying not to slam down, pushing gently instead.

Please...

The car slid nearer to a collision. I braced myself, muscles tensing.

Time sped back up. It happened in a blur. My car missed the other car by a hair's breadth and emerged into the correct lane unscathed. Gulping mouthfuls of air, I regained full control and pulled over as soon as I could. Adrenaline pulsed through my body. I was shaking. I buried my face in my hands and sobbed.

Stupid. So stupid. I could have killed someone. I could have killed myself.

I never should have driven in my fragile mental state. I wasn't the best driver in the world to begin with, and I still wasn't used to the roads and traffic rules in Seoul. Add in the rain and my preoccupation with overanalysing the circumstances around Jung Jen's death and no wonder I nearly had an accident.

I didn't feel like driving the rest of the way, but I didn't really have a choice. According to the GPS, I was almost at Go Yoojin's house anyway. After taking a few more minutes to regain my composure, I pulled the seatbelt on and started the car up again, windscreen wipers reactivating with a swish and a thunk.

This time, I'd properly focus on driving, going slowly and cautiously. People could honk at me all they want.

I concentrated hard as I drove, emerging from a main shopping area onto a tree-lined street near the Han river, elegant low-rise apartment buildings tucked neatly behind fences and gates. Streetlights glowed dully through the dreariness. The rain had eased to a light drizzle.

"You have reached your destination," the pleasant female GPS voice told me.

This must be it.

To my right stood a modern five-storey building with a flat roof and balconies jutting out from its slate-grey exterior. I turned into the driveway, but a tall gate blocked the entrance. I called Bora and she opened the gate remotely. The iron bars clunked open. An outdoor light flicked on automatically as I rolled up towards the main doors of the building.

I put the car in park and turned the engine off.

Thank goodness. I made it.

I slumped forward over the steering wheel, heaving a sigh.

When I lifted my head, I saw Bora emerge from the building. I stumbled out of the car, rain spitting in my hair and on my shoulders.

"You made it," she said, coming to my side.

"Barely," I groaned.

She furrowed her brow, examining me. "It looks like you're in shock. You're pale as a ghost."

I rubbed my forehead. "I was shocked about Jung Jen, but I also nearly had a car accident on the way here. I'm still a bit shaken."

"Oh, dear. What happened?"

"My head was reeling with the news, and the rain was coming down so hard...It was my fault. I wasn't careful enough. I almost hit another car as I turned left at a traffic light."

"Thank God you're okay. I couldn't have taken any more bad news on top of all this. Come on. Let's get you inside."

She led the way through a second gate to the private entrance of Yoojin's ground-floor apartment and unlocked the door.

Spread over two levels, the actor's residence was much more extravagant and luxurious than Jinseung's old apartment. The bottom floor consisted of a large open-plan living area decorated in a glamorous, girly theme, with chandelier lighting and soft furnishings upholstered in velvet and faux fur.

"Want a hot drink?" Bora asked.

"Yes, please," I replied.

"Coffee?"

"Thanks."

"Take a seat and I'll bring it over."

I sat down on a tufted, velvety couch covered in fluffy cushions. A giant black-and-white portrait of Yoojin graced the opposite wall, her alluring pose in stark contrast to the pale and puffy-eyed figure crumpled in a heap on the chair across from me.

"Thank you for letting me come over to your house, Actor-nim," I said.

"She was my friend!" Yoojin wailed.

"I know. You must be very upset."

She sniffled and buried her head in the blanket over her lap.

I wasn't sure what else to say. She must have known Jung Jen much better than I did.

"*They* killed her," she moaned between sobs.

I straightened to attention. "They?"

"San Seung and Lee Changho's fans. The online bullying was too much. Must have driven her to it."

"Oh. I see."

"We don't know for sure that's the reason," Bora said, returning with a tray of three coffee mugs, then taking a seat beside me. "And perhaps we'll never know. She didn't leave a note, after all."

I sharply turned my head to her, surprised by this new tidbit. "Is that so? Where did you hear that?"

"Oh, I heard it from someone who heard it from Jung Jen's manager. Wait. No. Maybe I heard it from someone who *heard it from someone* who heard it from Jung Jen's manager. One of those."

"No note..." *How odd.*

Bora shook her head at me. "I know what you're thinking, but it definitely looked like a suicide. From what I heard, the police thoroughly investigated the scene and didn't find any signs of foul play. As for why she did it, well, there could have been a number of factors. Like Actor-nim said, bullying might have played a role, but she has also been under immense pressure to rebuild her career after the scandal. I wouldn't be surprised if that had something to do with it as well."

I took a sip of coffee. Upon reflection, my theory was a long shot compared to simple explanations like bullying, stress, and depression.

After finishing my drink, I took my mug to the kitchen to get a refill. Bora appeared behind me.

"What are you thinking?" she asked, looking into my eyes. "I can tell you have something on your mind."

"It's just…Well, it's silly, really."

"Nothing's silly. Tell me."

"I can't help thinking that Mr. Kim has something to do with all this."

I saw her swallow, a small lump bobbing in her throat.

"It's possible," she said.

"I recently asked her about him and she acted strangely. She was startled. She didn't end up saying anything bad about him, but still…"

"Mr. Kim was furious at her after the scandal. Everyone knows that. Yet he didn't drop her from the agency. I always found that strange."

"There was that story on the news. We both wondered if it could be about Mr. Kim. Well, what if we're right? And what if it was Jung Jen who reported him?"

Bora rubbed her chin. "I see what you mean, but there's too little information to jump to conclusions like that."

"Yesterday, Jen said she had a meeting with Mr. Kim after the lesson. I'm still not really sure why, but I went to Mr. Kim's office. To check on her, I suppose. I was afraid something might happen to her. But she wasn't there."

"She probably just got mixed up. Happens all the time."

"Yeah. That's what I thought too, but it's strange."

"I don't disagree. It seems there are a lot of unanswered questions."

We stood in silence for a minute, stewing in troubling thoughts. Then our phones made a sound at the same time.

"Huh?" I said.

Bora grabbed her phone first to check. "Oh! Here it is."

"What is it?"

"An announcement from Mr. Kim. Wait—I'll read it." She cleared her throat. "'To all KAM Entertainment staff, I have very sad news to share. Early this morning, our very own Jung Jen passed away in her home. I understand this is a difficult time for everyone who worked closely with Jung Jen. Anyone who feels they cannot work today is permitted to go home, and an on-site counsellor will be available for anyone who needs additional support. I ask that you all respect the privacy of Jung Jen's family. Do not speak to the media or speculate about the cause of death.'"

"I wonder how long it took him to get the phrasing just right," I mused.

"He's being deliberately vague, all right," Bora said.

"I don't know if I can trust a word from him anymore."

"Me too. And so much for not speculating."

I threw my head back with a sigh.

Jinseung and I talked on the phone for a long time that night.

"I feel numb," he said, voice raw.

The only time I recalled him sounding worse for wear was in the aftermath of my kidnapping.

I could hear other people in the background. Distant voices. Chatter and scattered laughter.

"Where are you right now?" I asked.

"In the lounge. It's communal, just as everywhere else is. I don't have the privacy to cry."

A vision of tears like shiny crystals on Jinseung's cheeks squeezed my heart.

"Do you *need* to cry?"

"Well, I'd like the option to without, y'know, drawing attention to myself."

"Hide somewhere."

This drew a hint of a chuckle from him.

"I will if I feel the sudden urge, but seriously, I think I'll be okay."

"Did you know Jen well?"

"We weren't particularly close or anything, but it's the shock of it. She was my colleague. My *seonbae*. Makes me think that it could have just as easily been me."

The very notion made my gut wrench.

"You've had those thoughts before?" I croaked.

He took a second to reply. "No. You wouldn't believe it, but I'm actually pretty terrified of dying."

There it was again—an air of lightheartedness despite the gravity of the situation.

"Is that a joke?"

"Sorta. Look, I recognise that I've been lucky. I've had it easy compared to others. Scandals haven't ruined me, and I've got you. So, no, I haven't thought about it."

He sounded serious now, so I believed him, relief sweeping over me.

"Just know that I'll always be there for you," I said. "You can tell me if you're feeling stressed out, or if you can't handle things, and I'll help you."

"I know. Thank you. And I'd do the same for you."

I felt a twinge of guilt again for holding back information from him, but I shook it off. Now wasn't the time.

"How are you holding up, anyway?" Jinseung asked. "You probably knew Jen even better than I did. All those one-on-one lessons…"

"We didn't talk much about our personal lives. Well, sometimes she mentioned her parents, but that's about it."

Maybe we should have talked more. Maybe I could have helped.

"Ah. Makes sense."

Buster stirred on my lap, and I stroked his snowy fur. His cuteness helped put me at ease. No wonder pets were considered a form of therapy.

"*Jagi,* I wish I could be with you right now," Jinseung said. "Talking on the phone isn't enough. I want to hug you. Kiss you better."

"Hearing you say that makes me miss you even more."

"Are you okay? Is Yang Bora with you?"

"Yes, she's here."

Go Yoojin's assistant had taken over for the night, so we were back home. Bora had already gone to bed.

"Good. Rest well, eat well—Bora too. Look after each other."

"We will."

"I love you."

"I love you too."

Then came the hardest part. I waited for him to hang up first because I couldn't do it. The end of the call was a short, sharp shock to my system. Our connection severed.

21

When Mr. Kim made his speech at Jung Jen's memorial service a few days later, I couldn't help but notice the eye rolls in the audience. He stood behind a lectern, wearing a black suit, a sombre look on his face. The wall behind him was covered with pink and purple flowers and photographs of Jung Jen along with pages of handwritten messages to her.

As per the wishes of Jen's parents, a private funeral for family members only had recently been held. Today's memorial service was for friends and colleagues, as well as a specially selected media outlet to cover the event. I sat in a row in the audience with Changsoo, Bora, and Yoojin. We watched on with scepticism as Mr. Kim continued his speech.

"The loss of Miss Jung Jen—or Jung Seoyeon, as she was known to many—has been felt deeply by the team at KAM Entertainment," he said. "In this time of great sadness, it is a reminder that we must do all that we can to promote the mental health and wellbeing of our team members."

His words were in sharp contrast to a company-wide email he sent a day ago, which basically said that the time for mourning was over, and that everyone should get back to business as usual. The free counselling service had been dismantled before hardly anyone had the chance to use it. I could feel Bora twitch with suppressed rage on the seat next to me.

Fortunately, the rest of the speeches were much more heartfelt and sincere. The sound of people sniffling and wiping their tears filled the room. Yoojin even broke down and bawled at one point. She drew everyone's attention, but no one made a fuss. Bora quietly offered her a packet of tissues.

At the end of the service, we each took turns to kneel and pray at the shrine—a simple display consisting of a photo of Jen, a memorial tablet, and a written prayer, as well as offerings of food and drink laid out in a special arrangement on the table. When it was my turn, I bent down on my knees. I silently prayed that Jen's soul was resting in peace, then dipped my head to the floor in a deep bow.

When the formalities were over, everyone stood around conversing for a while before moving to an adjacent room with low tables set out. A buffet had been prepared where guests could help themselves to food and beverages. Our group grabbed a small table to ourselves.

"What about Mr. Kim's speech, eh?" Bora said. She looked around, making sure he wasn't nearby. "What a hypocrite."

"I agree," Changsoo said. "He certainly hasn't given the staff much time to recover from this tragedy."

Not to mention what he did to me.

Bora and I exchanged covert looks, acknowledging the extra information and suspicions we held.

Yoojin squirmed. "I gotta use the bathroom. Manager-nim?"

"Sure, I'll go with you," Bora said.

Chapter 21

She got up to accompany her, leaving Changsoo and me alone at the table. Changsoo looked at me with unnerving pinpoint eyes.

"You're hiding something," he said, voice low.

"What do you mean?" I asked, unable to keep a hint of panic out of my voice.

"It's to do with Mr. Kim, isn't it? You flinch whenever anyone says his name. You can't look at him when he's in the same room."

He noticed that? Damn. The jig is up.

"Ugh. Nothing escapes you, does it?"

"Whatever it is, please tell me. Perhaps I can help."

I hesitated. *Can I trust him? What if he tells Jinseung? Worse—what if he tells Mr. Kim?*

"There's no use hiding things from me," he pressed. "I'll find out eventually. I'll ask Mr. Kim."

"No!" I stammered, accidentally raising my voice.

A quick glance around the room revealed I hadn't drawn attention to myself.

"Please don't," I said softly.

"Tell me then."

"I can't tell you *here*. In front of everyone."

"Then let's go outside and have a little talk, shall we?"

Why did I feel like a child about to get scolded?

"Fine," I said.

While Changsoo and I didn't always see eye to eye, I did know one thing for sure—he was on Jinseung's side and always would be. He wouldn't do anything that would make Jinseung hate him, and by proxy, that meant he wouldn't do anything to harm me.

I followed him outside to the carpark where he unlocked his car.

"Get in the passenger seat. No one will hear if we talk inside the car."

Unlike his work vehicle, Changsoo's personal car was messy inside and had a slight smell like stale sweat. I wanted to wind down the window but that would defeat the purpose of going in the car.

"Go on," he said, sitting in the driver seat. "Tell me what happened."

I told him about the incident in Mr. Kim's office—nothing more, nothing less. The plain truth.

Changsoo listened attentively, his mouth a straight line.

"So, that's about it," I finished.

"Mr. Kim hasn't done anything else since then?"

"No. He hasn't."

"Then let's not do anything hasty, especially since there's no proof except your word. Mr. Kim would destroy you if you came out with this. Ruthless bastard."

"I know."

"And better not tell Jinseung or he'll do something stupid."

I nodded.

"Thank you for telling me," Changsoo said. "I'll be careful about Mr. Kim from now on. Don't go meeting him on your own. If he ever requests to see you, I'll go with you."

Hearing Changsoo offer his help was actually very reassuring.

"Thanks. I'll definitely take you up on that if I need to."

"Shall we head back inside?"

"Yes. They'll be wondering where we went."

The post-ceremony celebration was in full swing by the time we returned, groups at the tables immersed in lively chatter, food and drinks flowing. To my relief, Mr. Kim was nowhere to be seen. Probably left early and went back to work. Wouldn't surprise me.

Bora and Yoojin had returned to the same table and were waiting for us. They hadn't started eating or drinking yet.

"There they are," Bora said.

"Who wants a drink?" Changsoo boomed.

Both Bora and Yoojin raised their hands enthusiastically. I followed suit.

"What was that about?" Bora asked when I had lowered myself onto the floor cushion opposite her and Changsoo was out of earshot.

"He worked out that something was going on," I explained.

"Did you tell him anything?"

"I had to."

"What did he say?"

"Not much. Just warned me not to do anything hasty. Said he can accompany me to meetings in future."

"Ah. That's okay, then."

"I think he's a bit worried."

"Unsurprising."

Go Yoojin began to get agitated from being left out of our private little whispered conversation.

"What are you two talking about?" she asked.

"It's stuff concerning Shin Jinseung," Bora improvised.

"What about him?"

Fortunately, Changsoo returned with shot glasses and bottles of soju, which took Yoojin's attention off the topic at hand. Since she would be turning twenty this year, she was legally allowed to drink with us. Changsoo poured shots for everyone around the table. Yoojin was the first to down hers.

"Don't drink too fast," Bora scolded.

Yoojin pouted. "You know how stressed I am. Barely get a moment to grieve, and I have to start filming tomorrow."

"All the more reason not to drink a lot. You won't want a hangover tomorrow."

Despite Bora's pleas, Yoojin continued to drink heavily throughout the afternoon. None of the rest of us could do anything—Bora was the only person with any semblance of control over her.

"I think you've had enough," Bora said, taking the glass from her.

"You're not the boss of me!" Yoojin screeched.

"Let's all calm down," Changsoo said, holding his hands up in gentle protest.

Yoojin got to her feet. "You didn't know Jung Jen like I did. You don't understand anything!" She turned to storm away.

People around the room gawked at her and murmured between themselves. Yoojin's behaviour was very disrespectful at such an event and unbecoming of someone with her celebrity status. Fortunately, the media crew weren't present.

"Wait!" Bora got up to follow her. "Where are you going?"

"Home!"

"Let me get you a taxi."

Yoojin left the room, Bora close behind her.

"*Aigoo*," Changsoo said, arms folded on the table. "Shin Jinseung never acted like this."

"Well, if anyone can handle her, Yang Bora can," I said.

"I agree"

Bora returned a few minutes later looking mildly exasperated.

"Is Yoojin okay?" I asked.

"She's still in a huff, but I got her safely into a taxi. If she's hungover tomorrow, she'll only have herself to blame."

"I'm going to head off now too." Changsoo said, getting up.

"Are you sure?" Bora asked.

"Yeah. Got work to do."

"All right. Guess I'll probably see you around tomorrow."

"Have a good night."

"See you," I said.

Changsoo quietly left the premises.

"Maybe we should get going soon as well," I said to Bora.

"Okay. I'll just finish this drink. Hey, since it's just the two of us now…" she leaned in close and spoke in a low voice, "have you noticed something strange?"

I paused for a second, scanning the room for a hint as to what she was talking about. "Something strange? No, I can't think of anything."

"Jung Jen's manager didn't attend today."

"Huh. That *is* strange."

"Of all the people Jung Jen worked with, he was the closest to her. He should have been here. Why wouldn't he come?"

"Too distraught?"

"It's okay to be distraught at a memorial, so that's not a good reason."

"Maybe he went to the actual funeral, so he didn't feel the need to come to the memorial."

"As far as I know, no one from work went to the funeral. It was a tiny service with only her close family members."

"Well, there's probably another simple explanation."

"Hmmm…"

"Why? What do you think it means?"

She was about to speak when Mr. Kim re-entered the room.

"Let's discuss it on the way home, shall we?" she said.

I nodded.

Outside, the sky had clouded over, causing the late afternoon to fall into premature darkness. We stood by a busy six-lane street, Bora poised to flag down the first passing taxi.

"So, what are you thinking about Jung Jen's manager?" I asked as soon as we were safely in the back seat of a cab heading home.

"Don't you think it's funny that there hasn't been a peep out of Manager Jeong since Jung Jen's death? No statement. Nothing. Everything I've heard has been second-hand information. I haven't even seen him around the office. He's the person who spent the most time with Jung Jen since her debut, and he was the one who discovered her body."

"So?"

She looked me in the eye. "What if he knows something? Something important about her death that he doesn't want anyone to know."

"Are you saying that you don't think this is a straightforward suicide case after all?"

"I don't know. I'm just conjecturing. Hey, you have Manager Jeong's number, don't you?"

"Yes."

"Try giving him a call."

"Why?"

"I suspect he won't answer."

"And if he does, what should I say?"

"Whatever you want. That you called the wrong person."

I took out my phone and scrolled through my list of contacts for his name. I wasn't quite sure what the point of this exercise was but called him anyway.

Phone pressed to my ear, I waited for him to pick up, but I was greeted by an automated message instead.

"The number you have called is not available."

22

A realisation struck me when I awoke the next morning after a deep, dreamless sleep:

The nightmares had stopped.

I hadn't had a single dream about Oh Sejung since that fateful meeting with Mr. Kim. I had barely thought about her at all. Instead, my mind had been occupied by Mr. Kim, Jung Jen, Manager Jeong, and the mysterious unnamed entertainment industry executive who may or may not be involved in all of this.

Bora had gone straight to bed when we got home after the memorial, so we hadn't had a chance to discuss our thoughts and feelings about Manager Jeong much. I was still mulling it all over as I walked Buster the next day.

The sky was clear and the sun shone bright on the quiet, suburban street, but I paid little attention to the prettiness of my surroundings, focused on the thoughts swirling in my head instead.

Two possible reasons for Manager Jeong's absence from the memorial and work in general stuck out.

A. He was too distraught to face anyone or do anything.

Or B. He was hiding.

I couldn't help but zero in on option B, considering all kinds of theories as to why he'd be hiding. By the end of the walk, I had developed a dull headache from thinking about it too much.

By habit, I checked the letterbox when I reached the gate. A single white envelope graced the metal cavity. We didn't receive much mail at our house, for privacy reasons, but occasionally there would be something.

This was an official-looking envelope addressed to me. Something from a government agency? I tore open the envelope as I walked to the door and slipped out its contents.

A gasp escaped my mouth as soon as I saw the logo in the corner of the letter—*Seoul Central District Court*. I dropped the piece of paper in my shock and it fluttered to the ground.

———

"Oh Sejung's trial will be on the fifteenth of July," I told my mother over the phone.

The letter from court had revealed the date had been brought forward. Part of me was glad the waiting would be over soon, another part was anxious about the whole ordeal.

"We'll book our flights today," Mum said. "Is it okay if we come a few days early?"

"Of course, and don't worry about accommodation—there is a spare room at my house and plenty of space."

"Thank you, darling."

"I'm so glad you're going to be here."

I meant it. While my relationship with my parents was strained at times, we were family, after all, and I missed them.

Chapter 22

"Of course we'll be there. What kind of parents would we be if we weren't there to support you?"

"Well, thank you. I know it's a long way to come, and you don't exactly love flying."

"I'd fly around the world ten times if I had to. I need to see you and make sure that vile woman gets sent to prison."

"My lawyer has been very reassuring. She said there's no reason to worry about the outcome."

"That's good to hear."

"When it's all over, maybe we could do some sightseeing?"

"I'd like that. It would be nice to see why you love that city so much."

"Let me know when you've booked the flights and what time you'll arrive. I can pick you up from the airport."

"I will. While I have you on the phone, is there anything else you want to talk about? We haven't spoken properly in a long time. What have you been up to?"

More than I could possibly tell you in one phone call.

I tried to keep my tone breezy. "Oh, you know, just life. Work. The usual. There's really not much to say."

I didn't feel bad about lying through omission. She'd overreact if I told her the truth.

"I've been following the news, you know." She sounded stern.

I shifted uncomfortably in my seat. What exactly had she found out?

"Oh yeah?"

"I saw that a girl from that KAM company died."

I cringed. So she knew that much.

"Yes, it's terrible," I said.

"Did you know her?"

"No. I didn't."

An outright lie this time.

"Oh. Well, it's not very nice, is it? So young. So much promise. I hope *you're* okay."

"I am, Mum. Don't worry about me."

"I can't help it. Bad things happened to you and I couldn't stop them."

"I'm an adult. I can't rely on you to take care of me anymore. I have to look after myself."

"I know, dear, it's just…*hard*. I think about you every day and how you're getting on. I still can't understand why you chose to go back after everything that happened."

I didn't respond. I didn't want to get into an argument and ruin what was supposed to be a constructive phone call.

"Anyway," she said after a pause and a sigh. "I can't wait to see you again."

"Me too."

"I'll let you go now then, if you've got nothing else to say. I'll be in touch soon."

"Okay. Goodnight. I mean, good morning."

"Bye, dear."

I put my phone down, feeling a confused mixture of guilt and relief. Not unlike every other phone call with my mother, I supposed.

Crunch. Crunch.

What the—?

I turned around to see Bora munching through a bag of honey butter chips.

"Was that your mother?" she asked.

"*Aigoo!* How long were you standing there? I didn't see you come in."

"You finally called her, did you?"

"I did."

"Good."

She tipped the remainder of the chips into a serving bowl so we could share them. I poured two glasses of wine.

"So, it's Yoojin's birthday in a few days," she explained.

"Is she doing anything for it?"

"Yep. Even with her busy filming schedule, she's been insistent on having a party. Frankly, I have little energy for parties right now."

"Are you going to go? Does a manager even get an invite?"

"Of course I'm invited. You know how close we are."

"So, you're going, then?"

"Yes. I think it will be a good opportunity." She fixed me with a pointed gaze.

"What do you mean?"

"I mean that a lot of the female talent from KAM have been invited. This will be one of the few times they're all together outside of headquarters and free from being constantly surrounded by staff."

I was beginning to catch her drift. *She must have a plan.*

"If any of them know something about Jung Jen, or about Mr. Kim, or anything, it could be the ideal time to get them to speak," she explained.

"You're going to play detective?"

"In a sense."

"You'd really do that?"

She nodded. "You've drawn me in and now I have to know."

23

Bora was a lump under her duvet cover.

"Hey…Are you awake?" I asked, peering in from the doorway.

The lump stirred and groaned.

"Hangover?" I asked

Another groan.

"I take that as a yes."

In all our time as friends, I had never known Bora to get a hangover before.

There's a first time for everything, I guess.

Last night had been Go Yoojin's birthday party, and I wanted to know what had happened. Did Bora manage to find anything out? Unfortunately, she was hardly in a state to tell me anything.

"Rest up," I said softly, then closed the door, leaving her in peace.

I went about my morning routine as usual: had breakfast, got dressed, walked Buster, showered. After all that, Bora still wasn't up.

Chapter 23

At eleven o'clock, I knocked softly before entering her room again, carrying a plate with peanut butter on toast and a drink I bought from the convenience store which purported to be a hangover cure.

"I brought you breakfast. Are you up to talking or shall I just leave it on the bedside table?"

Bora turned over and slowly lowered the cover off her face, squinting. Her eyes without glasses looked much smaller.

"Thank you," she said.

I sat down on the edge of her bed. "So...what happened at the party?"

"I didn't manage to find anything out, if that's what you want to know."

"So the mission was a failure, then?"

"All I managed to do was make people feel uncomfortable. No one had a negative word to say about Mr. Kim or Manager Jeong."

I hung my head. "Damn. I was so certain you'd uncover some kind of lead."

"Maybe we should look at this as a positive development. Perhaps there really is no foul play going on here."

"Perhaps..."

"Pass me that drink, will you?"

I handed her the brightly labelled bottle.

While she glugged it down, I checked my phone. I had one new work email—an email from Mr. Kim.

What's this?

I checked the message, and as soon as I realised what exactly it was, my blood turned cold.

"You okay?" Bora wiped her mouth with the sleeve of her PJ top.

"Mr. Kim wants to meet me tomorrow."

She grimaced. "Yikes."

I slipped my phone back in my pocket, unwilling to hit "accept" on the meeting invite, or even look at it a second longer. The moment I had been dreading had arrived. Soon I'd find out what Mr. Kim's true intentions really were.

Or would I?

I recalled Changsoo's offer.

"Maybe it will be okay. Manager Bong said he'd chaperone me."

Bora's forehead wrinkled in thoughtfulness. "Or…you could just go alone and see what happens."

I was so surprised, I shot up off the bed. "What? Why would I want to do that?"

"Plan A failed, so maybe it's time for Plan B." She reached for her glasses on the bedside table and put them on. That was how I knew she was about to get serious.

"Testing, testing."

I stood in an empty bathroom at KAM HQ, checking the hidden recording device attached to my bra. If it worked as it should, a recording should be saved to my phone and to the cloud.

I played back the short snippet. My voice came out through the phone's speaker loud and clear.

All right. There was no delaying it any further. The recording device that Bora set me up with worked perfectly.

Time to face Mr. Kim.

Waiting for the elevator to arrive and take me up to his office, my determination swiftly diminished. What if it went wrong? What if he worked out that I was recording him? What if I was putting myself in danger by going in alone? I didn't have any backup. Bora was on set with Yoojin. Changsoo didn't know anything about the plan—he'd definitely have talked me out of it. *Maybe he should have.*

The elevator doors opened and I hesitantly stepped inside. My throat was tight, my lips dry. I thought about backing out. It wasn't too late. I could tell him I felt sick and had to go home. The nauseous feeling in my stomach was real, after all.

The elevator climbed the levels without stopping. Two, three, four…

No. I have to do this.

So far, the most damning evidence we had against Mr. Kim was the suggestive remarks he'd made to me. If we were going to catch him out for anything, this was our best shot. If I was right about his true character, then I needed to stop him before he inevitably abused me or someone else in the future. I gritted my teeth and stepped out onto the fifth floor.

Since the meeting was within regular office hours, the receptionist was still on duty. He sat behind an arched desk, dressed in a suit and tie. Everything gleamed with immaculate cleanliness.

"I have a meeting with Mr. Kim," I reported.

"Your name, please?"

"Chloe Gibson."

He checked his computer screen before telling me to take a seat.

I twitched and fidgeted on the chair, an unsettled feeling in the pit of my stomach. How exactly was this going to play out? If nothing happened, I wouldn't catch him, but if something did happen…

"You may go through now," the receptionist said. He walked me to Mr. Kim's office despite the fact I already knew the way. The door was open, and he gestured for me to go inside. I gulped and crossed the threshold.

Mr. Kim stood by the bookcase, placing a file back on the shelf. He was dressed in a navy suit with a snazzy pineapple-patterned shirt underneath.

Before I knew it, the receptionist had disappeared, and I was alone in the office with Mr. Kim.

"Hello, Chloe. Please, sit down." Mr. Kim smiled in a way which would seem pleasant by most accounts. "This won't take long."

As I lowered my fluttery body onto the leather couch, he shut the door. My ears tuned in to hear the click of the lock. I didn't hear it, but I couldn't be certain.

To my relief, Mr. Kim didn't join me on the couch, preferring to lean casually against his desk instead. He looked totally cool and collected as usual.

"What is this meeting about?" I asked abruptly.

He didn't miss a beat. "I just wanted to address a few points I touched upon in our last meeting."

I swallowed the dry lump in my throat and croaked, "I see."

Here it comes.

"But first, how are you? Are you getting on okay while Jinseung is away? I can imagine it isn't easy for you."

"No, it's not. But I'm okay."

"Good. And has Jinseung been keeping in touch?"

"We talk most days"

"That's good to hear. Jinseung is doing well in the army, isn't he?"

"Yes, it seems so."

"I always knew he'd suit the army. He has the right personality for it. He must miss you a lot, though."

"It's the same for any couple at this age. You just have to deal with it."

"That's true."

I was beginning to wonder when we'd get down to the true subject at hand. Surely this meeting wasn't just to check in on me and exchange pleasantries.

A moment of awkward silence passed before Mr. Kim cleared his throat.

"Now, with, uh, *recent events*, I've been reminded that talent and employee wellbeing should be top priority in this agency," he said.

Hmmm. So far this was not what I expected to hear. I lifted my chin and watched him more directly, searching for clues in his unblinking eyes and relaxed demeanour.

"And upon reflection," he continued, "I realised that some of the things I said to you could be misconstrued."

What's this? An apology? An excuse?

"I don't want you to think that you owe me, or the agency, anything," he said. "Do you understand what I'm saying?"

No. Not really. I thought that was exactly what he'd meant. My expression must have looked bemused, but all I could say was, "I think so."

"I was trying to make a helpful suggestion, that's all. There *is* more work available for you to do if it suits, you just need to get in touch with HR and sort it out."

"I'll think about it."

"Good. Brilliant. You do that. Now, is there anything you'd like to say on the matter?"

"Wha…? Uh, no."

"Then you may leave and get on with your day. Thanks for your time."

"Thank—"

Wait a minute. He hadn't said anything that could be used against him. I had to get him to say something incriminating, or this whole set-up was for nothing. Drawing from the depths of my courage, I spoke up.

"Mr. Kim?"

"Yes?"

"In our last meeting, you…"

Was it just my imagination or did his eyes turn a shade darker?

"Go on," he said, daring me.

I braced myself as I let the words out. "You touched my leg."

"*Omo*." He brought a hand to his chest, frowning. "Did I do that? I cannot recall."

"You did," I pressed.

"If you think so, then I sincerely apologise. Sometimes I do break with formality—that's just my style. You're probably not used to that from Korean men. Sorry if I made you feel uncomfortable. That was never my intention."

He sounded so sincere. So genuine. Part of me wanted to accept his apology—Were my memories wrong? Had it been a completely innocent gesture after all? An accidental touch? But I held my tongue.

"Is there anything else on your mind?" Mr. Kim asked.

"That's all," I said in defeat.

I didn't think anything I could say would force a confession out of him. He was far too resolute.

He opened the door for me. It wasn't locked after all.

I left feeling both relief and disappointment. Nothing bad happened to me, I was completely fine, and yet…Nothing Mr. Kim said could fully validate my memory of what happened. Somehow the whole meeting had flipped the situation on its head and made me feel like he was the good guy, and I was the unreasonable, irrational one.

I checked the recording when I got home. Everything had been captured, just how it had occurred, and it wasn't enough to implicate Mr. Kim in any way. Even his admission to touching my leg wasn't really an admission—"If you *think* so."

Bora arrived home early in the evening. We exchanged defeated looks as soon as we saw each other, and I knew that she must have already listened to the recording.

"Either Mr. Kim truly believes he's innocent or he's even more conniving than we thought," she said. "It's possible he knew you might try to record him and used that to his advantage."

"I don't know. Seems like a stretch."

"Nothing's a stretch. He's extremely clever, that's undeniable."

She wandered to the kitchen.

"I'm guessing you haven't thought of a Plan C yet?" I asked when she returned with a glass of water.

"Plan C? I don't know if there will be one. What more can we do?"

"I suppose so. It's just so…ugh…so frustrating."

"I know."

We sat down on the couch. I flicked the TV on just to take my mind off Mr. Kim.

"How's Go Yoojin doing?" I asked, changing the subject while ads played.

"Fantastically, considering how upset she was about Jung Jen not that long ago. Her scenes have all gone great and everything's still on schedule. If you can get through filming with at least four hours sleep each night, you know things are going well."

"That's a low standard."

"Says you who only works a few hours a week."

"You should try it sometime."

"No way. That would be far too boring."

We were still talking when the ads finished and the news came on. It took me a while to notice the ticker along the bottom of the screen, but when I did, I immediately tuned back in and turned up the volume.

"A recap of our leading news story this evening," the announcer said. "The entertainment company executive accused of sexual abuse can now be named. He is Byun Gimok, CEO of Moonbeam Entertainment."

24

I decided once and for all to leave things alone. There was no conspiracy. It was all in my head. The executive under investigation was not Mr. Kim, and no evidence pointed to any misconduct except the memory in my head, which I questioned more and more each day. So I let go of my fear. If I bumped into Mr. Kim, it wouldn't matter. He hadn't done any of the bad things that I'd imagined he'd done…or so I told myself.

While I waited for Nam Sungjin to arrive, I opened my lesson notes. We'd be focusing on the future tense today.

As I tried to review my notes, something distracted me. The room was quiet except for a low buzzing noise. I hadn't noticed that sound ever before. Where was it coming from? I looked around the room, trying to locate its source. My eyes darted here and there until they landed upon a small electronic device up in the corner of the ceiling. A security camera, I realised, and it was pointing straight at me. Had that always been there? The buzzing sound was new, that was for sure. I didn't know whether I should be alarmed—how long had I been recorded in these private lessons? The thought was unsettling; then again, it wasn't unusual for companies to have a lot of security cameras in their buildings, especially in an entertainment company where the protection of the talent was paramount. I should have expected that I'd be on camera from the start.

I shrugged it off and started to turn my attention back to my notes when a memory suddenly struck me: the way Jung Jen's eyes had flicked around the room when I asked her about Mr. Kim. Had she been looking for a camera? Was that it? Was she too afraid to speak out because she knew she was being recorded? And did Mr. Kim know that I had been asking questions about him? Was that why he never acted upon his initial proposition? I ruminated on this idea for a while before reminding myself that I was done with conspiracy theories.

I'm not going to let myself get sucked into this again.

Trying to block these thoughts from my head, I returned to my notes.

Nam Sungjin arrived shortly. He was one of the new recruits at KAM. A nineteen-year-old boy, fresh out of high school, tall and skinny with floppy, blue-dyed hair and several piercings in each ear. He had a "bad boy" type image, but in reality he was attentive and hardworking, always turning up to his lessons and putting the effort in. It helped that his schedule wasn't as demanding as his *seonbaes*. It was largely made up of acting lessons and modelling work since he was too young for most major acting roles in K-dramas and movies.

"Good morning, *Seonsang-nim*," Sungjin said.

"Good morning, Actor-nim." I watched him get settled into his seat. "Do you have your workbook?"

"Yes." He fumbled in his messenger bag and retrieved it.

"Then let's get started where we left off last time—page 52"

"Oh, I already did some of that for homework."

"You did?"

None of the actors ever had time to do homework. Except…

I recalled my last lesson with Jung Jen. She'd done homework and I'd been so surprised. I never did get around to marking it. After her death, I had forgotten all about it; not that I needed to mark it now, anyway—what good would that do? But what was so strange was the way she'd acted on that day. She'd been so serious about the homework, as if it were really important. What did she say, again? *Hmmmm…*

It suddenly clicked.

Oh my God. How did I overlook this? I needed to get my hands on that homework as soon as possible.

"*Seonsang-nim?*" Sungjin asked, eyebrow raised.

I snapped back to attention. "Yes? Sorry."

"You okay?"

No. I wouldn't be able to think about anything else all lesson.

"There's something…something I need to do." My voice quavered.

Sungjin watched me with concern in his dark eyes. "Sounds serious."

I nodded.

He closed his workbook in a resolute motion. "You go do what you have to do."

I hesitated. "Are you sure?"

"Uh huh. Don't worry about it. We can reschedule."

"All right. Thank you." I didn't stick around any longer. I grabbed my things and left in a flurry.

I drove fast, throwing caution to the wind despite how

recently I'd nearly had an accident. Every time I had to stop, my foot itched to press the accelerator again.

Come on…hurry up.

The traffic light turned green.

When at last I arrived home, I fumbled with the key trying to unlock the door. I was so desperate to get inside that I forgot to deactivate the security alarm, and it started blaring after the thirty-second grace period expired. *Damn it!* I raced back to the keypad by the door and input the code.

Now, where did I put Jung Jen's workbook?

I remembered separating it from the rest of my work stuff, and I was sure I hadn't thrown it away.

It must be here somewhere…

I searched my bedroom to no avail.

Did I put it in the office? Yes. It must be there.

I zoomed to the office and started pulling each drawer out of the desk one by one until I reached the bottom. I rifled through the last drawer, pulling out loose bits of paper and throwing them aside, creating a mess on the floor. A bit farther down the pile, I glimpsed it—Jung Jen's workbook, along with an assortment of other old teaching materials. Now I clearly remembered putting it there, out of the way so it wouldn't make me think of her. A critical mistake.

My heart pounded as I opened the book and flipped to the most recently filled-out section halfway through. My hands were shaking. I wasn't quite sure what I expected to find, yet I knew there must be some kind of key. That was why she'd done the homework. That was why she'd acted the way she had.

I began at the top of the page and quickly scanned down, waiting for something to jump out at me, but nothing did. My initial certainty began to wane. Maybe I was wrong. Maybe it was just plain old homework after all.

I reached the end of her writing with no new clues.

Should I just give up?

I clenched my teeth. *No.* Perhaps I was missing something.

Think, Chloe. Think…What did she say to me when she gave me her homework?

She'd been strangely serious—I remembered that much. She had wanted me to mark it after the lesson, meaning she didn't want to be around when I read it.

What else? Something about parts she wasn't sure about…What were her exact words? "Please pay attention to them"?

I opened the workbook again, and this time I read more slowly. There was definitely something weird about her answers. There were words scattered throughout that didn't quite make sense in the context of their paragraphs, and most of them were underlined. *Why? A code?* Maybe she didn't want anyone else to pick up the workbook and be able to see her message easily, in case they destroyed the evidence. *Yes. That's got to be it!*

I flipped back to the start of the exercise and went through and wrote down all the words she'd underlined. After the first couple of words, I knew my guess was correct.

Please help.

I frantically wrote down the rest of the words which strung together to form a crude message.

Please help me Kim black mail me take important document from safe in bedroom too won nine for

The first thing I did after reading the full message was call Bora. She answered swiftly. "Yes?"

My words came out in gibberish. "Found something… big…Jung Jen…"

"Okay. Calm down and say that again properly."

I took a breath. "Evidence. I've found evidence."

Bora paused. "Hold on. Let's talk about this at home. We need to keep this conversation private."

"How long will you be?"

"I don't know, but I'll be as fast as I can. Wait for me. Don't do anything until I get there."

"Got it."

Easier said than done.

How could I just sit around with such a big revelation dangling right in front of me? Mr. Kim was blackmailing Jung Jen, and she'd asked me to take an important document from her safe. I had to get that document. As soon as possible. Too bad there were a few obstacles in my way. I had no idea where her bedroom was, no way of accessing it, and wouldn't her belongings have been cleared out by now anyway? Was it too late? *Arrgh.*

I occupied myself by taking photos of the pages in Jen's workbook, then saving them to a USB drive, my cloud storage folder, and emailing them to myself as well. If something happened to the physical evidence, then I'd have backup.

With that done, I thought about how to get to the safe—assuming that it was still there in her bedroom. Some of the staff at KAM would surely know her address. So would the police. If she had any *sasaeng* fans, they'd be bound to know too. Bora would probably have some more ideas as well.

Eventually I gave up trying to keep myself occupied and waited on a chair outside with a view of the driveway. Buster came up to me with a bone-shaped chew toy in his mouth and dropped it beside me, so I lazily threw it for him. Who knew how many rounds of fetch passed before the gate clanged open and Bora's vehicle sped up the driveway. I rushed over to her.

"Right. Show me what you've got," she said.

We went inside and I showed her the workbook, at the same time explaining to her how I came to the conclusion that Jen had left a message for me.

"What about those random words at the end?" Bora asked. "Too won nine for? Oh, wait. Ha! That's the combination for the safe. Clever."

"It took me a few seconds to work that out as well."

"What do you think the message means? She left evidence in the safe in her bedroom?"

"Yes. That's exactly what I think it means."

"Then we have to get to that safe."

"I agree. Do you know where she lived?"

"No. Only Mr. Kim and a few of the key staff on her team would know."

"Well, we can't ask Mr. Kim."

"I don't think we can ask anyone at KAM. How suspicious would that look? Word would definitely get back to Mr. Kim."

"What about Go Yoojin? Would she know? She said they were friends. Maybe she's been to her house before."

"She might know, but then we'd have to drag her into this as well. Besides, even if we knew the address, how could we get inside?"

"Break in?" I surprised myself by even suggesting it.

Bora smirked. "I didn't expect to hear you say that."

"Neither did I."

"I admire your audacity, but I don't think it would be easy to break in. Celebrities take the security of their properties very seriously, as you know, and anyway, do we really want to risk doing something like that? No. I've got a better idea."

"All right. Spill."

"We call the police."

Somehow, I didn't feel very enthusiastic about this response, and I wavered. "I don't know. As soon as we get the police involved the investigation is outside our control. Jung Jen left the message for me, not the police, and I hate to say it, but can we trust the police? Especially with a high-powered individual like Mr. Kim involved."

"All valid concerns, but you're forgetting that we already have a contact in the police, and I think we can trust him." She pulled out her purse and rifled in it, producing a business card which she handed to me. I recognised the card immediately and reading the name confirmed it.

Officer Bae Sangwook.

25

I never thought I'd have to see the inside of a police station again, yet here I was in the fluorescent-lit waiting room, a row of plastic chairs lining one end, the reception desk on the other side, and a water cooler in the corner which made a bubbling sound every so often. A few individuals waited restlessly, tapping their feet and fidgeting.

"What makes you so sure we can trust Officer Bae?" I had asked Bora when she suggested getting in touch with him.

She drew her brows together. "You're asking me that after everything he did for you?"

I shrugged. "I'm sure other police officers would have done the same."

"Actually, I bumped into Sangwook recently."

"Sangwook?"

Since when were they on given name basis?

"*Officer Bae*. We got chatting, and we've kinda kept in touch since then."

"Whoa. Why did I not know about this?"

"It's nothing, really. The odd message here and there.

Moaning about how busy we are with our jobs and so on. Anyway, I'm a good judge of character, don't ya think? Officer Bae seems trustworthy."

"I don't know about Officer Bae but I know I trust you, so I'll take your word for it."

With my approval to proceed, she called him up straight away. He told us to come to the station during his office hours and file a report, so here we were.

Bora nudged me when the receptionist approached us.

"Officer Bae will see you now," the receptionist said.

I looked down at the half-finished report on the clipboard on my lap. "I haven't finished this yet."

"That's okay. Take it in with you now, and finish it afterwards." She directed us through a door into the main office area. I spotted Sangwook immediately, sitting at the same desk where we met him on the last occasion. He looked up at us and grinned.

His appearance had changed very little since the last time I saw him. He was a big, broad guy, but he had a soft, round face and kind eyes. His hair was short and tidy, and not a trace of facial hair to be seen. I'd guess his age at around thirty.

"*Oppa*," Bora said, a slight blush creeping onto her cheeks.

My eyes snapped to her like magnets. *Oppa?* So she called him that too. Just how close were they?

"Yang Bora-ssi, Miss Gibson," Sangwook said, addressing us with more formality.

He gestured to the two chairs opposite him and we sat down.

"I didn't expect you to have to file another report so soon after the last incident," Sangwook said. "You told me briefly over the phone that you have evidence of blackmail. Care to elaborate?"

Chapter 25

I explained what had happened, starting with Mr. Kim's behaviour towards me and a plea to keep my name anonymous. Sangwook listened intently, but partway through my account, he stopped me.

"Let's go to a different room," he suggested.

We followed him down a corridor to a small, windowless room with beige walls which contained nothing apart from a small table, four chairs, and a security camera.

"I thought we'd better continue this somewhere more private," Sangwook said. "You're talking about someone who a lot of people would do anything to protect."

"Yes. This does seem wise," Bora said.

So even Bae Sangwook didn't trust other police staff.

"Please, go on," he said once we were all seated.

I continued from where I left off, through to discovering the message in Jung Jen's homework.

"And do you have this book with you?" Sangwook asked.

"I do." I retrieved it from my bag and passed it to him. I had bookmarked the relevant section with a pink sticky note.

He examined the book with interest. "I'm sure we'll be able to analyse the handwriting and prove that it belonged to her, but not the underlines—they could have been added by someone else later."

"I didn't—"

"I'm not accusing you of anything, but that's what someone could point out. It's moot anyway. The true test of the note's validity is the safe and the combination and the contents of that safe."

"Proof that Mr. Kim was blackmailing Jung Jen…"

Sangwook shook his head. "We don't know that much yet. The note only referred to 'Kim.' That could refer to half the population."

Bora scoffed. "You know as well as we do that he's the one she's referring to."

Sangwook didn't bite. "Let's get all our facts straight first. What matters most is the safe and the combination. If that checks out, then we've got a case."

"Was a safe recovered from her room after her death?" Bora asked.

"Possibly. A lot of celebrities have safes in their homes, after all. I'd have to find out." He rubbed his chin. "Though it seems strange she'd leave a safe containing an important document that she didn't want anyone to find except Chloe in her bedroom if she planned to end her life. She must have known that everything would get removed from her house."

"Maybe it's hidden somewhere secret in her room," I suggested.

"Then how would she expect you to be able to find it?"

"True."

He tapped his fingers on the table. "Her bedroom, of all places…"

"She rarely went anywhere on her own except her house," Bora pointed out, "so it makes sense in that way. Where else would she get time alone to store something in secret?"

"Hmmm. That's a good point. I wonder…Never mind. Enough speculating. The next step is to finish that report, including everything you just told me, and take it to reception—no, on second thought, you better fill it out now and give it straight to me. I wouldn't want it to mysteriously go missing. Rest assured, I'm going to personally see to it that this gets properly investigated."

"Thanks, Officer Bae," I said.

He waited with us in the room until I finished filling out the report. Bora read it over afterwards to check if I had missed anything. We didn't sign our names—neither of us were ready to go that far.

"It's finished," I said, passing the clipboard to Sangwook.

"This investigation is in my hands now," he said. "Leave it up to me and promise you won't do anything on your own. You could jeopardise the case, and at worst, you could put yourselves in serious danger."

"Yes, Officer Bae," Bora and I said in unison.

26

I envied Bora. She was so busy with filming that she probably didn't have a spare moment to let her thoughts linger on the investigation; meanwhile, it was all I could think about. When was Officer Bae Sangwook going to find the safe and the evidence which could be used to press charges against Mr. Kim?

With each day that passed, I began to worry that it wasn't going to happen. Was Sangwook really as trustworthy as Bora seemed to think?

A knock on the front door shook me out of my melancholy mood. *What the…?* I wasn't expecting any visitors, and especially not someone who could let themselves in through the gate. Was it Bora? Had she forgotten her key? Buster was going crazy, yapping at full volume, tail wagging on fast forward. He raced to the front door, and I followed him to investigate. Peering through the peep hole, my heart jumped.

I flung open the door at once.

Jinseung stood in his camouflage army fatigues, tall and commanding, dashingly handsome. Despite his clean and tidy appearance, there was a ruggedness about him that he hadn't had before. Some of the former chubbiness in his face had gone. His shoulders seemed even broader. He had only been away for a few months, but he looked much older—in a good way—a sexy, mature, masculine way.

"Sergeant Shin Jinseung reporting for duty, ma'am," he said, grinning from ear to ear at my stunned reaction.

Every cell in my body radiated with delight. Here he was, right in front of me, his body within grasp. Solid. Real. Not just a dream. Not just a voice and an image on my phone.

"Jinseung-ah!" I gasped. "How...? Why...?"

"It's my first official break. I thought I'd surprise you."

"Well, I'm definitely surprised. Come here."

Unable to restrain myself any longer, I threw my arms around him. He hugged me back with the same urgency, pulling me flush to him, wrapping me tightly in his strong embrace. He felt so good in my arms. My hands clutched fistfuls of his uniform. I inhaled his smell—sweet and earthy and subtly spicy, like cinnamon.

"*Jagi*," he breathed, lips in my hair. "It's good to be back. I'm sorry I left you."

He brought a hand to my cheek and cradled my face, staring longingly into my eyes. His other hand came next, holding the opposite side. He pressed his forehead to mine. I could feel his breath, warm and ticklish on my chin.

Meanwhile, Buster jumped up his legs trying to get attention. Though Jinseung seemed intent on kissing me, it eventually proved too much of a distraction. He broke away to bend down and scoop Buster into his arms.

"Hey there, little buddy. Don't worry, I haven't forgotten about you."

We went inside. Jinseung coddled Buster, petting him,

getting down on the hallway floor and letting him climb all over him, accepting his enthusiastic licks.

"Have you been managing okay while I've been away?" Jinseung asked me while Buster lay on his lap.

A bolt of panic shot through my spine. How much should I tell him? I didn't want to spoil the joy of this moment.

"Yes, for the most part," I said, trying not to let doubt pervade my voice.

"Any more nightmares? Panic attacks?"

"No."

Not recently, anyway.

"Thank goodness—Okay, Buster. That's enough."

He gently pushed the dog off, then led him out the back door and closed him outside. Buster stayed put on the doorstep, moaning and whimpering as if to say, "Let me back in!"

"Why'd you do that?" I asked as we crossed the hallway to the living room. "He was enjoying your attention."

"You deserve my attention too, don't you think?"

I smiled. "Well, yeah…"

He closed in on me, and suddenly I was up against the wall, trapped between his arms. Before I had time to react, his lips were on mine. He worked open my mouth and kissed me deeply, hungrily. We explored each other's mouths like new territory. It had been so long that he felt like a new lover, everything fresh and exciting.

My limbs felt weak. My mind was mush. I was so absorbed in kissing him that I didn't hear the car come up the driveway. Nor did I hear the front door open. I didn't notice anything at all until the startled "Oh!"

We broke apart. Bora stared at the scene in front of her, wide-eyed, red-cheeked.

"Bo-Bora-ssi," Jinseung stuttered.

Springing from her dumbfounded state, she sheepishly lifted a hand behind her head, grinning. "Don't mind me, guys. I'll just...make myself scarce."

"Wait—" I said, my hands thrust out in protest.

But she had already left the room. I heard her open the back door.

"Come on, Buster," she said. "Let's go for a walk. A nice, *long* walk."

"Should we try to stop her?" Jinseung asked. "I feel kinda bad. I totally forgot she lives here."

"She'll be fine. If she really wanted to stay, she'd stay."

"True."

I crossed my arms, sighing. "She certainly got an eyeful."

"Probably enjoyed it." He smirked.

"What makes you say that?"

"When she was my intern, she always used to get so excited whenever I had to shoot a kissing scene."

I laughed. "Sounds like her. I'm sure she's outgrown that by now, though."

"Does she have a boyfriend?"

An image of Bae Sangwook popped into my head. "No, but I suspect there's someone she likes."

"Oh? Interesting. I'll have to tease her about it later." He took my face in his hands. "Come on. Let's make the most of the time we have before she gets back."

He was so endearingly insistent that I couldn't do or say anything to stop him. Not that I wanted to.

We continued where we left off, kissing with all our pent-up energy from months spent apart.

But something wasn't right.

With every passing minute, the initial ecstasy of seeing

Jinseung again wore off and reality sank in. The truth was going to come out soon. I wouldn't be able to keep lying to him through omission. I was in far too deep now. I had to tell him—but the thought of his reaction terrified me. Would he be annoyed at me for keeping things from him again? Scared about what could happen to his job? Would he even believe my story? He had a longer relationship with Mr. Kim than with me, after all.

Jinseung pulled back. "What's wrong?"

"Nothing."

"Don't lie to me. I can tell that something's bothering you. Did something happen?"

That was my cue. I sucked in a breath of air. "Actually, I..."

He squeezed my shoulder, his arm around me. "Hmm? Don't worry, you can tell me."

Where should I begin?

I opened my mouth to speak when the sound of Buster's yapping filled the room. Next, Bora burst in, flustered, breathless.

Back so soon? What's going on?

"I just had a call from Officer Bae," she said.

27

Bora looked from me, to Jinseung, and back again with a strained expression on her face like she was bursting to say something but having to hold it in.

"Is something wrong?" Jinseung asked.

"Can I speak with Chloe alone?"

Jinseung opened his mouth in reaction, about to protest.

"It's okay," I cut in, exchanging a sombre glance with Bora. "I want to tell him."

No more secrets.

"Tell me what?" Jinseung asked with an edge of impatience in his tone.

"A lot has happened since you've been gone."

I felt jittery despite my resolve.

I'm really about to do this.

He softened with kindly concern. "Something *bad*?"

I nodded slowly.

"Look, I need to get this off my chest before anything else," Bora said. "The safe was empty, Chloe. He didn't find anything."

The safe was empty.

"What?" I spat. "How can that be?"

"According to Officer Bae, it had clearly been tampered with."

Now it made sense.

"Someone got to it before us."

"Exactly."

"What safe?" Jinseung asked, brow furrowed.

The moment couldn't be delayed any longer. The truth was about to come out.

"Let's sit down," I said. "I'll tell you everything."

"Me too," Bora said. "We're all involved in this."

The three of us settled around the dining room table and got down to business.

Thank goodness for Yang Bora. I didn't know how I could have managed without her there for support. She took it upon herself to do most of the explaining. She even shouldered the blame for encouraging me not to tell Jinseung what was going on.

As we recounted our story of what happened at KAM Entertainment in his absence, the expressions on his face said everything. Outrage. Confusion. Shock. Concern. Anger. His hands were clenched hard, making the veins in his arms pop out. At one point he shot up from his chair, trembling with rage.

"I'll kill him! I'll kill that bastard!"

Bora and I had to restrain him, his arm muscles bulging under our hands through his rolled-up sleeves.

"Try to stay calm," Bora said. "One reckless move could ruin everything."

"Let's leave it to the police," I said. "It's up to them now. We'll only get in the way."

Jinseung struggled against us a while longer before finally giving in, crumpling down on his seat in despair.

"I'll never forgive him for laying a finger on you," he growled, face in his hands.

Bora and I comforted him until he calmed down enough to let us engage in a rational conversation, even as he twitched with suppressed rage.

"So, the safe was empty. Now what?" I asked Bora.

"Sangwook—Officer Bae—is going to meet us and tell us what he knows face to face."

"I thought police officers weren't supposed to talk about ongoing investigations?"

"Strictly speaking. Luckily he's our friend, and a bit of begging and pleading was enough persuasion. Oh—and the promise that I'd buy him dinner."

Her admission ignited a little spark of glee, but I let it slip. There were more important things on my mind.

"When are we going to meet him?" I asked.

"He's coming here now."

"What?"

"Yep." She checked the dainty gold watch on her wrist. "He should arrive any minute now."

The intercom buzzed.

"Ah. That'll be him."

She went to open the gate.

"Bae Sangwook..." Jinseung stroked his chin. "That name sounds familiar."

"He was the main police officer involved with my case last year," I explained.

"Then we can trust him."

I nodded even though it was more of a comment than a question.

Bora re-entered the room with Bae Sangwook in tow. I noticed that his usual confident, upright demeanour had changed. He seemed battle-worn—face pallid, shoulders drooped, eyes tinged with red.

"Hello, Officer Bae," I said, getting to my feet and bowing slightly.

Jinseung did the same, reining in his residual fury to offer politeness.

"Good morning, Officer-nim."

Seeing Jinseung seemed to recharge Sangwook's battery, perking him up straight away.

"Wow. Shin Jinseung-ssi…Nice to meet you."

So, even a police officer wasn't immune to the charms of seeing a celebrity in the flesh.

"Thank you for helping Chloe. Again," Jinseung said.

"My pleasure. It's my duty, after all."

Jinseung took it upon himself to serve Sangwook a cold drink.

Sangwook spread out his notes on the table.

"I shouldn't really be doing this, you know," he said.

Bora ignored him, cutting to the chase. "First things first, how did you find the safe?"

"I'm curious about that too," I admitted.

Sangwook cleared his throat. "From the start, I suspected that Jung Jen wouldn't have really hidden important evidence —that she didn't want just anybody to find—in the bedroom at her house. That would be far too obvious. I had another idea."

"Which was?" I pressed.

"Don't we consider our childhood room at our parents' house to still be our bedroom?"

Understanding flashed on Bora's face. "Ah!"

"I interviewed her former intern and found out that Jung Jen had recently stayed at her parents' house in Daejeon, so that's where I went, and I was correct. I found the safe deep inside her wardrobe, hidden on a shelf behind her clothes."

"Why didn't she just put that in her message?" I asked. "I couldn't possibly have known…"

Sangwook shrugged. "She was probably in a fragile mental state when she wrote the message. Or maybe she expected you to work it out. Did she ever mention staying at her parents' house before?"

I skimmed through our last few meetings in my head. "Now that I think about it, perhaps she did."

"Did her parents know about the safe?" Bora asked Sangwook.

"No. They hadn't seen it before. I got the feeling that they were too heartbroken to go through her belongings. Everything looked like it was still in place exactly how she'd left it—like a shrine in her memory."

"Why didn't she simply leave the document for her parents to find instead of getting Chloe involved?" Bora asked.

"My guess is that she didn't want to endanger them for knowing too much. Or give them a heart attack—they're elderly."

"Jung Jen and I weren't that close," I mused, "but she knew that she could trust me because I had a bad experience with Mr. Kim as well—she must have worked that much out when I questioned her."

"Her lessons with you were one of the few times she had privacy from her manager and other KAM staff," Bora pointed out, "so that could be another reason as well."

"That's what I think too," Sangwook said.

While we discussed all these possibilities, Jinseung

watched on in heavy silence. I could tell he wasn't really listening. He was still processing what I told him earlier.

Bora ran a finger back and forth around the rim of her glass of water. "I have another question."

"Fire away," Sangwook said.

"It seems like you worked out the location of the safe quite quickly, but why did it take you so long to go and get it?"

"Ah," he said, frowning, "that's another thing. Ever since I decided to start this investigation, road blocks have been put in my way. My workload on other cases spiked, and I had no time to visit Daejeon."

"Coincidence?"

"No. I don't think so."

I tensed, reading between the lines.

"Does Mr. Kim have friends in the police?" I asked.

"Mr. Kim has friends in all sorts of high places," Jinseung said, finally speaking up. "They visit his office at HQ all the time. If he doesn't know someone high up in the police, he knows someone who knows someone who does."

"In the end, I had to tell my subordinate, Officer Cha, to cover for me this morning so I could secretly go to Daejeon," Sangwook explained. "He's still covering for me now. Part of the reason I agreed to come here was in case…in case I couldn't continue the investigation. I wanted you to know what I had found out so far."

Suddenly his weary demeanour made a lot more sense. The case was causing trouble for him.

"Will you be okay?" Bora asked, face etched with concern.

Sangwook lifted his chin. "Don't worry. I'll be fine. I just didn't want to leave you in the lurch if they make me stop investigating."

A lot of questions had been answered, but there was still one major point we hadn't discussed.

"Any idea who accessed the safe and how they found out?" I asked.

Sangwook nodded. "It seems unlikely that anyone else knew about the coded message. The safe had been broken into by force, not with the combination."

"Very curious," Bora muttered.

"I think whoever found the safe knew that Jung Jen might have stored evidence at her parents' house and went there to check," Sangwook said. "They came across the safe and busted it open. I asked her parents who had visited their house since her death. Many people had—as expected. They came to pay their condolences."

"And they let people go into her bedroom?" Bora asked.

"Yes. People wanted to see her bedroom to bring back memories of her and have a moment of privacy to grieve, surrounded by her things."

"Did Mr. Kim visit?" I asked.

"Yes. He visited, but he didn't go into her bedroom as far as her parents could recall. There was someone else from the agency who did, though, and this is the person whom I suspect the most."

"Who?"

He threaded his fingers together and cracked his knuckles. "Jung Jen's manager, Jeong Daeshim."

28

"Stop that!" Jinseung snapped.

His reaction to me apologising for the millionth time in three short days.

We lay in bed with a vast gulf between us. Our reunion was meant to be a happy occasion, but Jinseung had been on edge since he learned the truth.

"I can't help it," I retorted. "You're angry, and saying sorry is the only thing I can do. I want to make things better—"

"It's not you I'm angry at, it's *him*."

"I know, but—"

He closed the gap and pressed an aggressive kiss on my mouth, stopping any more words from passing my lips.

"Shhh…No more."

I obeyed, biting my tongue not to say sorry again.

He sighed and stretched his arms above his head, leaning his back against the headboard.

"As much as I hate to admit it, you were probably right not to tell me. I would have gone AWOL to confront Mr. Kim. I wouldn't have been able to control myself. I'm barely managing right now."

"Thanks for resisting. I know it's hard."

"I still want to punch him. God, I'm so mad. I don't know what I'll do if I have to see him again."

"Hopefully that won't be for a long time."

"I feel so powerless. I have to go back today. I have to leave you here to fend for yourself. You still work in the same building he does, pretending like everything's normal."

"It's a strange situation."

"I don't want anything bad to happen to you again. I want to protect you. I never want to lose you."

He cradled me in his arms. I could feel the desperation in the tightness of his embrace.

"Chloe, promise me you'll stay out of danger. You *and* Yang Bora. Stay out of danger no matter what."

"I promise."

He kissed me again, tenderly this time. We lay on our sides, our bodies close together, my hands around the back of his neck, his arms around my waist. He was warm. So warm. I sighed into his sweet kiss.

"I'm sorry I've been in a bad mood," he murmured with a voice like velvet.

I smirked. "Look at you. Now you're the one apologising."

"Let me make it up to you."

He flipped me onto my back, his perfectly flat and hard body on top of me. Our kissing became frantic, passionate.

"I forgive you," I gasped as I drew a breath.

"Don't let me off so easily," he said before crashing back to me.

When we emerged for a late breakfast, I didn't expect to find Changsoo standing in the middle of the kitchen, car keys dangling from his hand.

I stared at him, blinking drowsily. "Why are you here so early?"

"We'll need to head off shortly," he curtly replied, keys jingling.

The kettle boiled in the background. He was making an instant coffee.

Realising I was still in my dressing gown, I sheepishly pulled the tie to close the gap.

"Weren't you going to come in the afternoon?" I asked.

"It nearly is the afternoon, and I want to get a head start on the journey. I won't get back until nightfall as it is."

I crossed my arms in a huff.

Maybe I should have offered to drive Jinseung myself. Too late now.

"*Hyung*, I'll have something to eat, then we can go," Jinseung said, opening the fridge and peering at its contents. He grabbed some containers of last night's leftovers—*galbi*, seaweed salad, rice, and kimchi.

We ate at the dining table. Bora and Changsoo joined us, sipping from steaming coffee cups.

"It's so sad you have to go back today." Bora pouted at Jinseung. "I barely got to see you."

"*Ya!* The purpose of his trip was to see *me*," I lightheartedly retaliated.

"I didn't get to spend enough time with either of you," Jinseung mumbled, mouth half-full.

I ate slowly, thinking that if I stretched it out, it would delay the time Jinseung and Changsoo departed. But Jinseung finished eating before me, and he barely swallowed his last mouthful before Changsoo stood up, fumbling for his car keys again.

"Okay, guys, it's about time we get going," he said.

Jinseung rose from his chair. I clutched him protectively. Bora stuck out her bottom lip.

"Stop it," Changsoo said. "You all look like wide-eyed puppies staring at me like that."

Buster, who was lying under the table, barked at him.

"And *you* really are a wide-eyed puppy. Sorry, but we have to go."

Jinseung turned to me. "Remember what I said, okay? Keep safe."

I nodded.

He lifted a hand to my cheek and stroked it. "Goodbye, Chloe."

"Goodbye."

He softly kissed me on the lips, hugged me, then kissed me again on the cheek.

"Where's *my* goodbye hug?" Bora asked.

Jinseung grinned. "All right, you." He encircled her in a bear-like hug.

"And a kiss?" she asked, muffled by his chest.

I was sure she was only kidding, but Jinseung didn't object. He kissed her on the cheek, causing her to squeak like a startled mouse. If that had happened two years ago, she probably would have dropped dead.

"Look after Chloe for me," he said.

"I will."

He ruffled Buster's fur. "Bye, buddy."

"Right. Let's go," Changsoo said, standing in the doorway with his arms crossed, itching to get away.

Jinseung grabbed the backpack he'd packed the night before and tossed it over his shoulders. He squeezed my hand.

"See you on my next break. I'll give you a warning next time, promise."

"Love you," I said.

"Love you too."

The number of times we'd had to part for long periods like this was starting to rack up, but that didn't make it any easier. My stomach lurched as he turned to leave. I followed him as far as the front door, Buster at my heels. Jinseung stepped outside and kissed me one more time across the threshold before Changsoo closed the door behind them. I stood watching from the window until Changsoo's car disappeared out the gate.

"He's gone," I said, the familiar bitter emptiness in my heart from his absence.

"I'm sure he'll be back before you know it," Bora said, placing a comforting hand on my shoulder.

"More likely the days will drag on."

"Hey, it's not all bad. You have me."

"I s'pose."

"That was half-hearted," she goaded. "Maybe this will cheer you up—I'm free this evening. Let's go out, have a drink, chat like old times—nothing about all the crazy stuff going on."

I appreciated her effort, and it didn't sound like a bad idea at all.

"You know what? I think that *would* cheer me up."

She lightly slapped my back. "That's the spirit!"

The bar's interior was all shiny black and purple neon. R&B music played at low volume lending a relaxed vibe and the ability to have a proper conversation without having to shout or strain your ears. A small handful of other patrons occupied the bar and the booths, quietly drinking and chatting.

As Bora's *unnie,* I ordered and paid for our drinks—two soju-based cocktails—and brought them back to our booth.

"Mmm. Looks delish!" Bora said, accepting her watermelon-infused drink.

"It has been a while since we went out like this, hasn't it?" I said.

"Yeah. I've been too busy to go out much ever since I became Actor Go's manager."

I rested my head in my hand, elbow on the table. "It's a shame that Shin Jina isn't here…"

"You're right. We should have invited her."

"Never mind. Next time. Whenever that will be."

"Hopefully soon."

We sipped our drinks.

"So, Jinseung looked well," Bora said after a pause. "Apart from how he took the news, I mean."

"Yeah. He hasn't had it that bad in the army, to my relief."

"If you're tough enough to excel in the entertainment industry, you're tough enough to excel in the army."

"That seems to be the case."

"He missed you, though. That was obvious." She smirked.

I recalled her walking in on us and blushed. "Sorry about, uh…"

"Don't worry about it. You two are just so cute! I wish someone would ravish me like that. *Aigoo.* I haven't had a boyfriend in years. What's it like?"

"With the amount of time we spend apart I'm starting to ask myself the same question."

"Pfft. You're so dramatic."

Talking about boyfriends piqued my interest and I couldn't help myself.

"About Bae Sangwook…"

Bora glared at me. "We promised we wouldn't talk about all that."

"I don't mean *that*. Do you like him?"

"I…*what?*"

"Come on. Don't deny it. I can tell."

She dismissed me. "I'm too busy to have a relationship."

"That didn't answer my question. Do you *like* him?"

"Well…" She turned the base of her cocktail glass in her fingers. "He's attractive, don't you think? Manly, fit, direct, and yet sensible and hardworking and smart. Y'know?"

"So you *do* like him."

She threw her hands up in the air. "I don't know. Yeah. I guess you could say that. *I like him*. Doesn't mean we have to date. I don't even know if he feels the same way about me."

"It's not like you to be shy about what you want."

"Who's shy? I don't know what I want."

"Hmm. If you say so."

Bora's phone started to ring and she grabbed it from her bag.

"Who's calling? Sangwook *Oppa*?" I chided.

She jabbed my shoulder. "Shut it, you. It's an unknown number. Better take it. Might be work-related." She answered the phone. "Oh, Sangwook-ssi, why are you calling from a different number?"

I was about to poke fun at her since it was Bae Sangwook after all, but her expression had turned dark.

"Understood," she said. "Just a minute."

She got up from the table, beckoning me to come with her. Leaving our half-finished drinks behind, I followed her towards the bathrooms. Bora scanned the area, making sure we were alone, before tugging me inside the disabled bathroom—a completely separate room unshared by other cubicles. She turned the lock.

"Chloe's with me too. I'm going to turn video on," she told Sangwook. "I don't think anyone will be able to hear through the door."

She pressed a button on the screen then put her phone down on the closed toilet lid. We crouched and huddled around it. Thankfully the room was nice and clean.

Sangwook appeared on the screen in what looked like a small, lamp-lit room with a whiteboard behind him which was covered with notes and pictures I suspected were related to Mr. Kim and Manager Jeong. He wore a serious expression on his tired face.

"Okay, I can see you," Bora said.

"I have an update," Sangwook said.

I prickled at the gravity of his voice.

"I have managed to locate Jeong Daeshim," he continued.

Bora and I looked at each other with a mixture of triumph and confusion.

"That's good news, isn't it?" I asked doubtfully.

"But I can't go. I'm positive now that someone's trying to stop this investigation."

"What happened?" Bora asked.

"I've been sent away to participate in a three-day conference."

"After the conference—"

"I have reason to believe that Jeong Daeshim is about to try to leave the country, and once that happens, it'll be much more difficult to track him down."

"Could you ask another police officer to go?" I asked.

"That would be the obvious solution, but the problem is that I don't know who I can trust to carry out the task, and anyone who tries will probably get stopped too."

"Officer Cha?"

"He's going to the conference as well."

"Then what can we do?"

"I'm sorry, but I think the best thing to do at this point is drop this lead and let it go—"

"No," Bora said. "I have an idea. Tell me where Jeong Daeshim is."

"Cheong—wait, you're not planning to go there yourself, are you?"

"…No."

"You are, aren't you? Please don't go. We have to drop this. We'll get another chance—"

"Tell me exactly where he's staying."

"No. Absolutely not."

"Then think of a way to catch him. We can't just let him go."

Sangwook drew a deep breath. "All right. I'll do what I can."

"Good."

Bora ended the call. She turned to me. "How do you feel about a trip to Cheongsando?"

29

"I'm going. With or without you," Bora said, midway through packing her duffel bag. "Now, do you still have that recording stuff I lent you?"

"Please," I begged. "I promised Jinseung that we wouldn't put ourselves in any danger—"

"*You* promised Jinseung. *I* don't recall saying anything."

"And Bae Sangwook?"

"If he cared about me at all, he'd put up more of a fight to stop me from going. Can't he get out of that conference somehow? Will he be under surveillance nonstop?"

"He must have his reasons."

"Regardless, I'm going, and that's the end of it."

"You're being reckless—"

"So what? You don't have to come."

"But I can't let you go on your own!"

Bora zipped up her bag. "I'm leaving first thing tomorrow morning."

By the resolve in her voice, I knew that nothing I could say or do would stop her.

"Why are you so hung up on this?" I asked. "It's not like Mr. Kim did anything to *you*. It's not like Jung Jen asked for *your* help."

"I just...I have to do this."

"Why? What reason could you possibly have to do something as dangerous as this?"

She placed her packed duffel bag at the foot of the bed, ignoring me, but I wasn't going to leave her room until I had answers.

"Why?" I asked again.

"Leave me alone," she replied, a hitch in her voice. Her face was red. She turned her back to me, avoiding my eyes.

This was clearly a touchy subject. Now I was certain she was keeping something from me, and whatever it was, I had to know.

"There's something you haven't told me, isn't there?" I asked.

No response.

"I'm right, aren't I?" I pressed.

A stifled whimper.

I took her shoulders and turned her to face me. Tears were spilling from her eyes and rolling down her cheeks. My heart cracked like it was made of glass.

"What's wrong?" I asked, softening my tone. "Please, tell me."

"You might hate me if I tell you," she choked.

"I won't. I promise I won't. Come on, let's sit down. Tell me what happened. Did Mr. Kim do something to you as well?"

Bora shook her head. "No. Worse than that."

I wondered how it could possibly be worse.

I sat on the side of her bed and patted the space next to me on her cream duvet cover. Bora stared at the space for a few seconds, as if still weighing up whether she would tell me or not. At last, I felt the bed dip as she settled down.

"Have you ever wondered how I got my job as intern?" she asked, staring sombrely ahead at the wall.

"No, I can't say I have."

"A paid internship at an entertainment agency is a coveted position. There were hundreds of applicants—no, most likely thousands."

"You're so bright. I never would have thought to question it."

"Well, I didn't get the job just for being bright. There would have been so many others just like me, or better than me. I'm far from perfect."

"No one's perfect."

"You have to be pretty close to it."

"So, you didn't get the job on merit alone, is that what you're saying?"

She nodded, tears gathering in her eyes again. She brushed them away and took a moment to recover before continuing.

"The interviews were held over several days. I took mine in a group with two other applicants in front of a panel of three interviewers. I was so nervous. Long story short, it didn't go well for me. I was so sure I'd blown it. That's why after the interview I took the opportunity to sneak away and explore the building. I wouldn't get the internship, but at least I might get to see a celebrity. That was my thinking."

"You were pretty cheeky."

She cracked a faint smile. "Yeah, I was bold."

"And did you run into any celebrities?"

Her smile disappeared. "I did."

"Who?" I asked, even though I thought I might know the answer.

"Jung Jen."

"I see."

"I was lost in an area of the building that was like a maze, and no one was around," she explained. "But then I heard voices. Raised voices. Yelling. I was curious and followed the sound. I saw Jung Jen. She was still at the height of her fame back then. I would have been so excited if I had seen her in any other situation. She was in a room with Mr. Kim."

My stomach lurched.

"By the time I got there, they had stopped arguing." Her voice became strained.

"Take your time."

"He...Mr. Kim was..."

My heart was throbbing in my dry throat as I waited for her to gather her words.

"He was forcing himself on her," she said, unable to stifle a sob. "Kissing her. His hands up her skirt. I was frozen in the doorway, watching, not knowing what to do."

I winced.

"Jung Jen's back was to me," she continued, "but Mr. Kim saw. He locked eyes with me for a second, then he pushed the door closed and I ran away."

I felt numb, unable to process the full extent of what she had just admitted to me. She knew about Mr. Kim's true character all along and kept it hidden from me, from everyone.

"Shortly after the incident, maybe a day or two, I got a call. I was asked to attend a second interview. I didn't expect to make it to the next round, so it took me by surprise. I turned up and found out that it was a one-on-one interview with the same man I saw with Jung Jen—Mr. Kim."

"What happened?" I croaked.

"To anyone listening, it was a totally normal job interview, but I knew differently. It was a test. Without saying anything aloud, he was checking to see if I'd bring up what I'd seen, or if I'd stay silent."

"You stayed silent."

"Yes."

"And you got the internship."

She looked down at the floor, her shame clearly displayed on wet hot cheeks and puffy eyes. "Yes."

"You knew all along."

"It's no excuse, but I made myself believe that what I saw was consensual—they were having an affair and it was none of my business. I convinced myself that was reality. It was the only way I could be happy working in my dream job, and I never witnessed or heard anything like that ever again, except—"

"When I told you what he did to me."

"I was in denial."

My fingers dug into the mattress. I was angry, and yet... What would I have done in the same situation? I knew exactly how hard, how *futile*, it was to speak up and do something, and then it was too late...

"I get it now—why you want to go and confront Manager Jeong," I said.

"I can't make up for what I've done, but I can at least do this."

"So there's no way I can stop you?"

She shook her head.

"Then I guess I'll have to go with you."

"You don't have to."

"No, I do. I'm coming."

"Then we'll leave tomorrow morning. Goodnight, Chloe."

"Wait, just answer me one question. How do you expect to find Manager Jeong? You only know the name of the town he's in and even that's a guess."

"Oh, I know where he is."

"How?"

"There were coordinates written on the whiteboard behind Officer Bae. I recorded the video and zoomed in a little."

Damn. Did those glasses give her superhuman eyesight or something? Still, I wasn't convinced.

"What will you do when you get there? Confront him head-on?"

"I'll make up some kind of story—a reason for being there."

"Hmmm."

Can she really pull this off?

I didn't like it, not one bit, but I simply couldn't let her do this without my help.

"I will go with you, but we're bringing backup."

"Who?"

The other member of our trio, Shin Jina, was the first person to come to mind—but no, I couldn't drag her into this. Jinseung would never forgive me for putting her in danger, as well as myself. I'd need someone else. Someone tough. Someone we could trust. Who else did I know? I racked my brain.

Yes...He'd be perfect.

"What about Jinseung's friend, Young Jae?" I suggested. "He'd make a good bodyguard, wouldn't he?"

I thought she'd protest, but she didn't.

"Do you think he'd agree to go with us?" she asked.

"He cares about Jinseung enough that he'd want to protect me, and he said to call him if I ever needed help while Jinseung's away."

She nodded. "All right. Call him."

30

"You're crazy, you know that? Batshit crazy," Young Jae said the moment I opened the door.

It was five o'clock in the morning and Young Jae arrived just like he'd promised over the phone. He was wearing what I assumed was his old army uniform—a long-sleeve shirt and trousers in green-brown camouflage print. Appropriate clothing for the mission that lay ahead.

"Are you sure you still want to go ahead with this?" he asked, eyebrow cocked.

"Yes," Bora said, pulling her duffel bag over her shoulder beside me.

"Then am I right to believe that you have some kind of plan?"

"Of course."

I was much less confident, but I knew Bora wouldn't back down, so I had to forge ahead.

"Thank you for doing this," I said to Young Jae. "I know it's a lot to ask."

"I still haven't wrapped my head around what you told me

last night. I just know that Jinseung would kill me if I let anything happen to you, so I gotta go along with it."

"Let's get a move on," Bora said. "We don't have time to lose."

"Need me to drive?" Young Jae asked.

"I was going to drive," I said, "but that's not a bad idea. Let's take your car. It will be less recognisable than Jinseung's."

"No problem."

We had already packed for the journey, including extra clothing in case we had to stay overnight. Young Jae carried our stuff to his car like it was weightless, and I felt relieved to have a guy that big and strong at our disposal.

I hopped in the front with Young Jae. Bora got in the back.

"Weren't you meant to be working today?" I asked Bora, suddenly remembering that this wasn't her day off. "How were you planning to get around that?"

"I asked Actor Go and the intern to cover for me," she replied. "They'll lie and say I'm out on set with them if asked."

"Wow. They've really got your back."

"Actor Go knows I wouldn't skip work unless I had an important reason."

"And you, Young Jae-ssi? Were you supposed to be working today?"

"Yeah. I'll just say I'm sick."

"Easy peasy."

The four-hour car ride was plenty of time to discuss our plan of attack. Bora was going to approach Manager Jeong, telling him that Mr. Kim had sent her. That would hopefully pique his interest enough to make him want to talk to her. Bora would try to gain his trust by saying that she was involved too —that Mr. Kim was also blackmailing Go Yoojin. From there she'd try to extract information from him. Anything that could be recorded and used against him. If she could find out what happened to Jung Jen's evidence, even better. Bora had nerves of steel, and I was confident that she'd be good enough at improvising to come up with a convincing act. Young Jae and I would be on standby, listening in, ready to come to her aid if she had any difficulties. Hopefully it wouldn't come to that.

The weather was patchy during the drive—pockets of heavy rain amidst long stretches of sunshine. I saw parts of South Korea I'd never seen before, but I was too focused on the mission ahead of us to properly take in the scenery. We didn't stop except for one toilet break halfway.

The final stretch of the journey to Cheongsando was aboard a passenger ferry from Wando. Once we'd parked the car below deck, we went up to the seating area. We didn't speak of our plan in front of the other passengers.

Fifty minutes later, we arrived at Cheongsando port. If I had come here under any other circumstances, I'd be excited to explore such a beautiful destination. The island was a tourist spot, known for its natural beauty and the slow way of living. I knew a couple of K-dramas that had been filmed in the area. I would have liked to do some sightseeing.

The atmosphere was tense in the car as we followed the directions on the GPS to Manager Jeong's hideout.

"How are you feeling?" I asked Bora, turning my head to the back seat.

"A bit nervous," she confessed.

"We don't have to go through with it if you're having second thoughts. We can cancel and turn back now. I wouldn't be mad at all."

"Oh, don't worry. I'm not having second thoughts."

But I am worried.

Chapter 30

As we wound through quiet countryside dirt roads, steadily approaching our target destination, I secretly wished that it would be too late. Manager Jeong could have fled by now. He had already had a decent window of opportunity. I clung to this hope. If he had gone, we wouldn't need to put ourselves at risk.

"This must be it," Young Jae said as we passed a dilapidated two-storey house with peeling white paint on its exterior. A gated wooden fence sealed the perimeter, surrounded by an overgrown field scattered with colourful wildflowers. I would have found it pretty if not for the prospect that a dangerous man could be lurking inside.

Young Jae parked on a road a little farther away, out of sight from the house.

"Shall we go over the plan one more time?" he asked.

"It's simple, really," Bora said. "I'll approach the house and try to talk to Manager Jeong, secretly recording him. You two hide nearby and listen in on the audio stream. If the situation takes a turn for the worse, well, that's when you, Young Jae, might have to intervene."

"Understood."

"Let's check the equipment one more time," I suggested. "Is there a good signal out here?"

Bora attached the small microphone under her top, and we did a test run, Young Jae and me listening through earbuds. It worked perfectly.

"Have you got your self-defence kit?" I asked.

"Yes."

"All set, then?" Young Jae asked.

She nodded.

It wasn't cold but my teeth chattered uncontrollably as we left the car. Young Jae and I separated from Bora before the house came back into view. Bora walked along the side of the dusty road, while Young Jae and I crept up to the fence, crouching in the long grass. We watched from through the cracks in the splintered wooden fence as she unlatched the gate and approached the doorstep. Through our earbuds, we heard her quietly tell herself, "All right, here goes." She knocked on the door.

31

I held my breath as I waited for someone to answer Bora's knock. Was he there? Would he answer? I pleaded to God the answer was no. As far as I was concerned, nothing we could possibly gain from this would be worth the risk.

Young Jae lay beside me in the tall, dry weeds, propped up by his elbows and forearms. He wore a serious expression, his eyes narrowed with intense focus.

No one answered the door.

Well, that's that. We came here for nothing. Let's go home—

Bora knocked again, louder this time.

The door opened straight away. I flinched in reaction to the sound, loud and clear through my headphones. Young Jae placed a hand on my back to still me.

"Manager Yang? What are you doing here?" He was out of view, but the voice was unmistakably Manager Jeong's. He had a distinct voice: monotone and a little bit nasal.

"Mr. Kim sent me," Bora confidently announced. "Can I come in?"

Manager Jeong paused, hesitant. "Why would he send *you*?"

"I think it's better if we discuss this inside."

"...All right. Come in."

They entered the house, door closing behind them. I heard rustling as Bora took off her shoes, then their light footsteps through the house, ending when they must have sat down in a nearby room. I couldn't see anything through the dusty window.

"Why did Mr. Kim send you?" Manager Jeong asked.

I clenched my muscles, anxious as to how Bora would proceed.

"He wanted me to get something from you," she explained. "He wouldn't tell me *what* exactly, but he believes you have some kind of document in your possession. Something he doesn't want anyone to get hold of."

Please work...please...

"And why should I trust you?" he asked.

"Because I'm involved in this too. I know what Mr. Kim has been doing to Actor Go, and I let him get away with it. If anything gets out, I don't know what I'd do."

"Go Yoojin?" He sounded shocked. "I didn't know..."

"This document that Mr. Kim wants—"

"I destroyed it."

"But you made copies, didn't you?"

I felt something crawling on my arm and looked down. A huge black beetle. I slammed a hand over my mouth to stifle a shriek. Young Jae calmly flicked the bug away.

"I can't believe Mr. Kim sent you of all people," Manager Jeong said.

I heard footsteps again and imagined him pacing the room, matching the rhythmic back and forth sound.

Chapter 31

"You know very well that he can't come here himself," Bora said. "Who else would he send?"

Manager Jeong didn't comment.

"Where have you hidden the document?" Bora pressed. "Mr. Kim wants reassurance."

"I'll be out of the country tomorrow. That's all the reassurance I can give him."

"That's not good enough."

"How does he know about the document, anyway? I never told him about it."

"He's not stupid. So, where is it?"

"Like I said, I've destroyed it."

"And all the copies? I don't think he'd believe that. You must have them somewhere."

"As if I'd tell you." He had venom in his voice. "He should have sent someone else. I didn't even know you were a part of this."

"I know everything."

"And Mr. Kim is okay with that?"

"He trusts me."

"He has something on you?"

"You don't need to know the details."

A short silence, then Manager Jeong spoke. "You might as well leave. You're not going to get anything out of me."

"Mr. Kim won't rest until he knows those documents are destroyed. Even if you leave the country, he'll come after you."

"Hmmm."

"What's in them? Evidence? Testimony from Jung Jen about what exactly happened?"

"I'm not saying anything. Now leave."

"It must be evidence. That's why Mr. Kim doesn't want any chance of them being leaked. That's right, isn't it? Evidence that Jung Jen was being abused? And that's the reason she killed herself?"

Crap. She's really done it now.

Manager Jeong exploded. "That's enough! Get out of my house. Leave this island."

She had tested the limits of his patience to the brink. She was treading dangerous waters now. I wished she'd back down and get out of there. Young Jae shifted beside me, poised to rush in to her rescue if things went further south.

"All right," Bora said calmly. "I'll leave. But first, what should I tell Mr. Kim? I can't go back to him empty-handed."

Manager Jeong seemed to consider her point, then replied, "Tell him that the evidence has been destroyed."

"Fine. I will. He won't believe you, but that's what I'll tell him. I'll go—"

"Wait a minute."

My breath caught. Manager Jeong's tone of voice had changed. He sounded suspicious of her now.

"How did you get here?" he asked. "Where's your car?"

Bora hesitated. For the first time she seemed caught off-guard. "I-I was dropped off."

"By whom?"

"Local taxi driver."

"You didn't ask them to wait for you?"

"Wasn't sure how long this would take."

"Hmmm…"

He was thinking about this more clearly now. Bora had to get out before he deduced what was really going on.

"I'll just—be leaving now." Her voice wavered with a subtle note of panic.

Manager Jeong must have realised by now that something

wasn't quite right. "How can I be so sure that Mr. Kim sent you? He didn't tell me anything."

Bora started to reply. "He-"

The sound cut out. I wondered if it was just me, but Young Jae looked at me like the same thing had happened to him.

"What should we do now?" I whispered.

"You stay here. I'm going to try and get closer to check everything's okay."

"And leave me here by myself?"

"It's the safest place."

I grabbed on to his shirt as he made to move away. "Be careful."

He nodded and I released him. He crawled on his hands and knees towards the gate. It had been left open, swinging slightly in the breeze. Bora must have left it unlatched on purpose.

I watched Young Jae through a gap in the fence as he stealthily approached the house, steering clear of windows. He pressed his back to the exterior wall and slowly moved around the outside.

Everything was quiet except for the sound of cicadas crying in the distance and my heavy breathing.

Young Jae crouched below a window, his face screwed up in concentration.

I didn't need the headphones to hear Bora's scream.

32

Without thinking, I leapt from my hiding spot into plain view. I wanted to call her name at the top of my lungs. *Bora-ya! I'm coming!* The words were poised on the tip of my tongue, but Young Jae saw and shot me a warning glare in time to stop me. I ducked back under cover.

Young Jae silently approached the front door and tugged at the handle, but it wouldn't open. He gave up and crept around the exterior of the house again, leaving my field of vision.

I was wondering whether to move so I could get a better view when all of a sudden the front door swung open and Manager Jeong stepped onto the doorstep. He was sloppily dressed in baggy sweatpants and a threadbare t-shirt. Unshaven. A drastic change from his stylish work attire. His shifty eyes surveyed his surroundings.

Did he hear something? Is he onto us? Where is Bora?

He took one step down.

Then another.

Please, don't come towards me.

He reached the ground. Something piqued his attention,

and he followed the direction Young Jae went, disappearing around the corner of the house.

I watched on, trembling uncontrollably in the tall grass. My heart was pounding so loud I thought he might be able to hear it.

If Manager Jeong caught Young Jae, what was I going to do? My instruction had been to run, take the car, and drive away to find help. But by then, would it be too late? What was Manager Jeong capable of?

Get a grip. Young Jae's got this.

Out of the two of them, Young Jae was bigger and stronger. He could take him on, no problem.

Young Jae emerged from the other side of the house, alone. His gaze was fixed on the front door, which Manager Jeong had left slightly ajar. He sneaked towards it, quickly, quietly. He barely made it inside before Manager Jeong reappeared.

Manager Jeong returned to the doorstep, where he stood and craned his neck from side to side, doing a final check. He appeared satisfied and turned to re-enter the house.

That was when I noticed it.

There was something sticking out of his back pocket. Something black, angular, possibly metal. *A gun?*

My blood ran cold.

Young Jae and Bora were still inside, and they couldn't possibly fight Manager Jeong if he had a gun. They needed more time to escape.

I had to do something. Something quick. Distract him. Create a diversion. Make a noise. Throw something.

Yes. That's what I'll do.

I scrounged on the ground until my fingertips brushed cool, jagged stone. I grasped the rock and crawled into position.

In one adrenaline-fuelled motion, I stuck my hand above the fence and flung the rock as hard as I could. It ricocheted off the side of the house and caused enough of a sound that it would have surely caught Manager Jeong's attention.

He came back out.

"Who's there?" he called, sneering.

I lay flat on the ground, unmoving. Not even breathing.

I thought he'd check the area where the rock had landed, but I was wrong. He walked straight towards the gate.

Oh, shit.

I hadn't thought this through. I had drawn too much attention to myself. If Young Jae and Bora didn't hurry up and come to my aid…

He was on the other side of the fence now, just metres from me.

Please, God, please…

I could no longer see him or hear his footsteps on the soft field.

I didn't know what to do. Stay put, hoping that Young Jae or Bora would come out and get his attention before he found me, or get up and make a run for it.

I stayed glued to the spot, mostly from indecision. I had to bite my tongue to stop my teeth from chattering.

No sign of Young Jae or Bora.

Manager Jeong was probably making his way around the outside of the fence, and any second now, he'd spot me.

This was it. I couldn't just lie there and wait for him to catch me. I had to run. If I could reach the car, I could get away from him. *As long as he doesn't shoot.* I got to my feet.

"*Ya!*" Manager Jeong called, spotting me instantly.

I kept my eyes ahead and ran for dear life, my feet thudding on soft earth.

Chapter 32

Just…a bit…farther….

I tripped. My ankle rolled. A spike of pain shot up my leg and I screamed.

I didn't stop to recover, but I couldn't match his pace. I was limping. He was close now. I could hear his breath.

He reached out and grabbed me by the arm, his grip tight.

I should have been scared for my life, and yet…

Why does this feel so familiar?

Before I even registered what I was doing, I tore through the sequence of movements I learned in self-defence class and broke his grip.

Manager Jeong stumbled back, a stunned look on his face, and in his moment of confusion, I hurled a kick to his groin, released the can of pepper spray from my keychain, and sprayed it straight in his face.

I didn't anticipate the slight blowback.

As Manager Jeong buckled, shrieked, and wept in pain, my own eyes stung and watered. I gritted my teeth and endured the pain to keep my blurry eyes open a crack.

Now's my chance. I can make it to the car—

"Chloeeee!"

Bora's voice. She was close by. So was Young Jae. I stopped in my tracks. We came together in a triangle around Manager Jeong, who was still incapacitated on the ground.

"Thank God, you're safe," I said.

"Could say the same about you," Bora said.

Young Jae interrupted our reunion. "No time for chitchat. Let's get outta here."

"Not so fast!" Manager Jeong growled. He pulled his gun even as he writhed in pain, his slitted red eyes streaming moisture.

Young Jae gasped. Bora whimpered.

"Stay back," he warned, shakily getting to his feet. "Cooperate or I'll shoot."

There was no way he could aim properly in his condition, but even a random shot could be deadly.

I was numb. Unable to move. Unable to think properly. Even with my impaired vision, I registered the helplessness on Bora and Young Jae's pale, panic-stricken faces.

I shook myself out of my stupor.

There's got to be something we can do. It's three against one and he can barely open his eyes.

Bora must have been thinking the same thing, because she suddenly made a move. She ducked and lunged at Manager Jeong with full force, knocking him back to the ground.

A shot fired, cracking through the atmosphere.

33

The acrid, burnt smell of gunpowder assaulted my nostrils.

I screamed. "Bora! Nooo!"

Nothing mattered now except saving her. Pulsing with adrenaline, I pounced at Manager Jeong. So did Young Jae. Together, we pinned him down and knocked the gun from his grasp.

In the flurry of it all, I couldn't tell if Bora was hurt.

A distant rumble grew louder. Tyres screeched, smelling of hot rubber. Dust filled the air.

Car doors flung open, and two men ran towards us through the field, silhouetted by bright sunlight behind them. Friends or foes? I didn't know. Either way, it would all be over soon.

"Weapons down!" one of the men shouted.

That was when I knew the balance had tipped dramatically in our favour. The voice was Officer Bae Sangwook's.

I heard Bora gasp beside me. So, she was conscious enough to know what was going on. *Thank goodness.*

Everything happened quickly from that point forward.

Sangwook instructed us to stand up, hands in the air. The other man, whom I recognised as Officer Cha, retrieved Manager Jeong's gun from the ground.

Manager Jeong had no chance to bolt. Sangwook was armed and ready to shoot if he did.

Bora, to my relief, looked okay. Shaken, but okay. Not a trace of blood to be seen. The gunshot must have missed her entirely.

"Jeong Daeshim-ssi, you're under arrest for withholding crucial evidence from the police," Sangwook said.

Manager Jeong's face twisted in disdain as Officer Cha handcuffed him.

"The rest of you, hands down. You're safe now," Sangwook said.

Tears streamed down Bora's cheeks. She ran towards Sangwook and flung her arms around him.

"Thank you. Thank you," she said between sobs.

Sangwook awkwardly patted her back.

Meanwhile, Officer Cha attended to Manager Jeong.

"You can work with us or against us now. I'd strongly suggest you cooperate if you want to get let off lightly."

"You can't do this! I haven't done anything!" Manager Jeong spluttered.

Bora broke away from Sangwook and stepped towards Manager Jeong, hands fisted at her sides.

"What you said in the house proves otherwise," she said. "You as good as admitted that you had seen evidence about what happened to Jung Jen!"

"You can't prove anything!"

I took my phone out of my pocket and played the recording on the highest volume, skipping to the part where

Manager Jeong said, "Tell him that the evidence has been destroyed."

"Everything you said inside, everything you did, was recorded," I explained.

He didn't need to know that the recording cut out at one point. I stopped playing it before then.

Manager Jeong's face turned beetroot red. He flailed and growled, helpless against Officer Cha's restraint.

"Now, what can you tell us about Jung Jen's document?" Sangwook asked. "Where is it?"

"I'm not saying anything."

"Suit yourself. With or without it, the recording is enough to implicate you in this, and continuing to withhold information will ensure a much harsher sentence. Officer Cha, search the house."

Manager Jeong's flustered reaction was enough to reveal that he was, indeed, hiding something in there.

"You can't! You need a warrant."

Sangwook sniggered. "Do I? I've broken a lot of rules to come here. I'm okay with breaking more. Getting that evidence is more important. Officer Cha, proceed. I'll take care of Daeshim from here."

Officer Cha nodded. He made a stopover at the car before heading towards the gate, lugging a large case of what I assumed was equipment to aid the search.

Sangwook held on to Manager Jeong. "You're coming with me to the station."

"Wait! This is all a big mistake!"

"This is your last chance. Tell us where you've hidden the evidence and I'm sure the court will consider it in your favour."

"I...I..."

"Officer Cha will conduct a thorough search and find it regardless. Face it, there's no escaping your fate now, so you'd better fess up."

"..."

Sangwook yanked him towards the vehicle.

"I want immunity!" Manager Jeong spluttered.

Sangwook scoffed. "If you'd cooperated from the start that might have been an option. Too late now."

"...But they'll be lenient, right?"

"Yes, telling the truth is your best shot at leniency. Now, I'll ask you one more time. Where's the evidence?"

Manager Jeong dropped his head low. The tips of his ears were tinged red. He must have realised he was done for and had no choice but to relent.

"There's a USB drive taped inside a light fitting," he mumbled.

"All right. Lead us there. And don't even think about trying to run. There are other officers on standby around the island in case you attempt to flee." Sangwook let go of Manager Jeong's arm and jabbed him in the back towards the direction of the house.

Closely flanked by Sangwook and Young Jae, Manager Jeong silently proceeded through the gate and towards the front door of the house. Bora and I followed behind them, clinging to each other for physical and moral support.

"You're limping," Bora said. "And your eyes are red."

"I twisted my ankle and a little bit of pepper spray got in my eyes."

"*Omo*. Lean on me. You can close your eyes too. I'll guide you."

I wasn't in too much pain anymore, but I still took up her offer, relaxing my eyes and left foot.

"What about you?" I asked. "Are you okay? Did he hurt you?"

"I'm fine, just overwhelmed. My nerves are wrecked."

"I don't know what I would have done if you got injured—or worse."

"I took a calculated risk. One of us had to take action before the pepper spray wore off."

"You were extremely brave. What happened in the house? The sound cut out, then we heard you scream."

"I thought he was going to attack me, so I screamed to get your attention. Then he showed me his gun and told me to be quiet. I was powerless after that. He led me to a room where he locked me inside."

"So that's what happened. How did you get out?"

"Young Jae managed to pick the lock using one of the tools on his Swiss army knife."

"Clever."

"But time consuming. I was dreading what would happen if we got caught. Or if *you* got caught. I didn't know what was going on outside, but I knew there was a strong chance he'd find you."

"He did."

"But you managed to fight him off."

"I still can't believe it myself."

Bora sniffed back a fresh wave of tears. "I'm so sorry."

"For what?"

"Dragging you into this."

"We're equally responsible."

"You tried to talk me out of it. I didn't listen."

"Shhhh. What's done is done."

I opened my eyes again when we entered the house. The interior was dated, with scuffed floorboards, faded walls, and gaps in the window frames. A constant draft circulated. We entered the living room, large and high-ceilinged, sparsely furnished except for an empty bookcase, two worn-out couches, and a dusty floor lamp. Thick cobwebs occupied every corner. It seemed like the house had been vacant for a long time before Manager Jeong took refuge there, and he had done little to amend its state of disrepair.

Officer Cha was busy tearing into the couch cushions with a knife when Sangwook interrupted him. "Officer Cha, stop the search. Jeong Daeshim has agreed to lead us to the evidence."

"Yes, sir."

"Which light fitting is it?" Sangwook asked Manager Jeong.

"In the cupboard."

He led the way and opened the door to a dark and narrow utility closet with shelves full of old junk covered in a thick layer of dust.

Sangwook flicked the light switch but it didn't work. Officer Cha shone a flashlight inside.

"Is that it?" Officer Cha asked. He directed the flashlight at a bulb high up on the wall above the door.

"Yes," Manager Jeong said. "There's a stepladder in here."

Sangwook retrieved the ladder and positioned it under the bulb. He climbed up and twisted the bulb from its socket, then felt around inside the small cavity. I heard the sound of stubborn tape being peeled off in a quick motion, like a wax strip.

"Found it," he said, coming down the stepladder with the USB drive and the piece of black duct tape in his hand. "Officer Cha, go get the laptop."

We waited in strained anticipation for Officer Cha to return with the laptop so we could view the contents of the drive. My heart was racing. My mouth was dry. What were we about to

Chapter 33

see? What was so bad that Jung Jen died because of it? I was desperate to know, yet terrified of the answer.

Officer Cha came back and set up the laptop on the dining table. We all huddled around, except for Manager Jeong who stood apart, looking down at the floor. He seemed deeply ashamed of whatever was on there.

I held my breath as Officer Cha plugged the drive in and opened it up. An error sound played and a pop-up asked for a password.

"What's the password?" Sangwook asked.

Manager Jeong said nothing. He just shuffled on his feet.

"Tell us the password, or the digital forensics team will work it out, and you won't get any brownie points for helping."

"Three, two, nine, six, space, capital B."

Officer Cha typed the password in and pressed enter. I expected to hear another error sound, but none came. He had successfully opened the drive. I saw two lone files in the window—an MP4 and a PDF.

"A video?" Sangwook said, peering closely.

Before doing anything else, Officer Cha copied the files and made backups. With that taken care of, he double-clicked the icon of the MP4 file.

I shook to the rhythm of my hammering heart and fluttering stomach as the video loaded in the media player. This was it. The moment of truth.

Jung Jen appeared on the screen in a grainy video.

"If you're watching this, I'm probably dead by now," she began.

34

Jung Jen was pale and hollow-eyed, a husk of her former self. She appeared to be sitting on a bed, but the low light conditions made it hard to tell. *Her bedroom at her parents' house?*

The five of us watched the screen with bated breath.

"Before I go, I have to explain what happened to me so that the people involved can be held responsible," Jen said, eyes downcast.

Her voice was so soft that Officer Cha had to turn the volume up full.

"This all started after my involvement with San Seung and Lee Changho," she said. "No—before then."

I remembered what Bora had told me—how she had witnessed Mr. Kim assault Jung Jen. If I had the timeline correct, that would have been quite a while before the scandal broke.

"I didn't realise it at the time, but I can see clearly now. Mr. Kim was grooming me from the very beginning, testing my boundaries, how far I would allow him to go without complaining."

I thought of Mr. Kim's hand on my leg and shivered with repulsion. Had he been testing my boundaries too?

"You have to understand that I come from a poor background," Jen explained. "Acting was my dream. I wasn't going to let anything stand in my way, not even a bit of sleazy behaviour. In fact, I considered it the norm. At least, that's what Mr. Kim made me think." She lowered her head. "Things took a turn for the worse after the scandal. I'm sure you've heard the story. My popularity plunged and I couldn't get big roles anymore, couldn't earn what I used to earn. That was a problem for me. My spending was out of control at the time. I had debt, and my parents had debt too —and expensive health issues. They were relying on me. I was in a lot of trouble financially…until Mr. Kim offered me a solution."

Bora and I exchanged wide-eyed glances of dread.

Jen continued. "All I had to do…" She stopped and sniffed and brushed the tears from her eyes. "I'm sorry. This is difficult. Just repeating it makes me feel sick." She took a deep breath. "All I had to do was have dinner with Jang Hojin, the CEO of Z-Tank Corp. Easy, right? He was a big fan and willing to pay handsomely for the pleasure of meeting me. So, I agreed." She shook her head and covered her eyes with her hands. "I was so stupid."

I braced myself for what she might say next, fending off the tightening grip of nausea around my stomach.

"Jang Hojin seemed like a nice man," she said. "Young and attractive. Rich beyond belief. He wouldn't have been short of female admirers. It pains me to admit it, but in a way, I was actually quite flattered. He chose me of all people.

"He was staying at a hotel in Gangnam, and he had booked

a table in the hotel's restaurant. Only, when we got to the restaurant, we were told they had lost our booking—or they had never received it in the first place, more likely. They were fully booked all night and couldn't accommodate us. Hojin suggested we eat in his hotel room instead. I'm sure you know where this is going."

My hands clenched into fists. Bora held my arm tight.

Officer Cha paused the video.

"I can stop this now if you're uncomfortable," he said. "Officer Bae and I will review it at the station."

"No," I said. "We've come this far for the sake of finding out the truth, and now it's within our grasp."

"I agree," Bora said. "We've got to know, no matter how difficult it is."

"All right," Officer Cha said, "but if you change your mind, just give me the word."

He pressed play and the video continued.

"Jang Hojin is a very charming and charismatic man, and I was a little bit drunk" Jen said. "I didn't consider what happened to be rape at the time, but looking back, I do feel like I was pressured into it.

"Mr. Kim gave me the money the next day, and at that point it clicked that maybe sex had been the whole point all along, and I had basically just engaged in prostitution. I felt terrible." She stopped for another deep breath and to wipe her eyes. "Only a few days passed before Mr. Kim came to me with another *assignment* like the last one. I told him no. He said I had to, but I resisted—even if I lost my contract I wouldn't go through with it. That's when he showed me the video."

I felt a collective flinch travel through the room. All of us must have realised what she was going to say next. We already knew blackmail was involved, after all.

"I had no idea that I had been recorded that night in the hotel room," she explained between sobs. "Mr. Kim said he'd release the video if I didn't go along with what he wanted. I panicked. I was so scared of the video being leaked that I didn't dare tell anyone what was going on. I felt like I had no other option."

My heart broke for her. *What an unthinkable situation to be in.* My head reeled just trying to imagine what I'd do in her place.

"At first the men that Mr. Kim set me up with could be considered good-looking," Jen said. "Smart, successful, young...Obviously they weren't *good* guys, but they were palatable in some respects. I met them in fancy hotel rooms, ate at expensive restaurants. Some of them bought me extravagant gifts. But that didn't last long. Soon I was seeing much older men, men that most other women wouldn't go near with a barge pole. Cruel men. Powerful men. I was repulsed by them. No more fancy hotel suites either. Most of the encounters actually took place at KAM Headquarters itself."

Bora and I both gasped. *How could that be?*

"There's a secret room accessible from Mr. Kim's office, behind the bookcase," Jen explained. "I don't know if it was set up just for me, or if it has been used before for similar deeds."

I couldn't believe what I was hearing. This was the sort of thing that happened in TV dramas, not real life. Yet I clung to her words, and I knew they were the truth. I watched on, riveted and disturbed.

"At first my manager didn't know what was going on," Jen said, "but he found out pretty quickly and did little to stop it from happening. After a while, he actually started to help facilitate the abuse."

I heard a sputtering whimper from Manager Jeong, then he started to bawl his eyes out.

"I'm sorry, Actor-nim! I'm so sorry," he cried.

"Mr. Kim continued to pay me for what I was doing," Jen said. "I thought that if I could save up enough, I could run away and hide. Escape from everything and everyone. The only problem was my compulsive spending, and the stress of what was going on made it worse. It was a vicious cycle. He gave me money, I spent it, I needed more money. Mr. Kim knew I was fully dependent on him, and that's the way he liked it. Complete control."

"Bastard," Young Jae growled under his breath.

"That's it," Jen said, looking almost relieved. "That's what happened."

Finally having a chance to explain what happened to her must have been a weight off her shoulders.

"I've had enough," she said with a vague, defeated smile. "I can't go on like this and I can't live with that video out in the open. I just want to end it all. But before I do, I wanted to leave this message—secretly, so no one will be able to destroy it before it gets out."

She looked directly at me, a ghost behind a screen. Her gaze was so eerie I got chills.

"You're the one I've chosen, *Seonsaeng-nim*, because you seem to know that Mr. Kim is up to something. Maybe he's abusing you too. All I know is that I think I can trust you to bring this message to light. Please hurry, but be careful. Your life could be in danger if anyone knows you have this."

An indistinguishable noise in the background of the video caught her attention and she turned her head towards its source. Visibly startled, she reached out towards the camera, then the video cut out.

Chapter 34

None of us said anything for a few minutes. We were all too shocked to speak. The only sound was Manager Jeong quietly sobbing in the corner behind us.

"That was...worse than I thought," I choked out at last. "I thought Mr. Kim was sexually abusing Jung Jen, but I had no idea he was pimping her out to other men."

"That creep," Bora uttered in plain disgust. "*Those* creeps."

"What about the other file?" Sangwook asked.

I had forgotten there was more. Officer Cha opened the PDF. A scanned document—a handwritten note. Names. Lots of names. They were separated into two categories labelled abusers and helpers. I understood those to mean people who directly participated in the abuse and those who helped to facilitate it.

"A list of all the people involved," Officer Cha muttered. "*Aigoo*...There are some high-up men on this."

"Wait—" Sangwook said. "Stop scrolling. There. Zoom in. Is that what I think it says?"

"You're right," Officer Cha said. He swallowed dryly. "That's him."

"Who?" I asked.

"Police Commissioner Ma Sungil," Sangwook said. "No wonder there were efforts to stop us from investigating this."

"This is big. Monumental," Officer Cha said. His hand was trembling over the mouse.

We descended into another long silence before Sangwook unplugged the drive and dropped it into a clear plastic bag.

"What will happen now?" Young Jae asked.

"We'll hand Jeong Daeshim over to the local police station," Sangwook said. "You three have your own vehicle, right? Follow us there. You're all involved in this, so we'll need your testimony as well."

"Come on, Daeshim-ssi, you're coming with us," Officer Cha said, grabbing his arm.

Manager Jeong didn't resist.

Bora, Young Jae, and I didn't say much as we drove to the station.

We followed all the necessary procedures with the police, filling in reports, stating everything that had happened. Not even the commissioner would be able to stop the course of events now. Manager Jeong was willing to speak and Jung Jen's video and note were far too compelling to ignore. Officer Cha had sent the files far and wide within the police force and prosecution offices so they couldn't be covered up anymore.

After a long day at the station, we sat down with Sangwook and Officer Cha at a small restaurant with plastic tables and chairs, peeling green wallpaper, and a drinks refrigerator that continually buzzed. We hadn't had the chance to eat all day, yet none of us could stomach much. The downtime served as an opportunity to discuss our unanswered questions, at least.

"How did you know we'd come here?" I asked Sangwook while I picked at the spicy pork-and-rice dish in front of me.

"I twigged pretty quickly," he said. "The coordinates were written on the board behind me during our call. I shouldn't have been so careless."

"It took you long enough to get here," Bora said, pouting. "I nearly thought you weren't going to."

I shot her a pointed look. "Wait—were you *expecting* Officer Bae to come?"

"I knew—I *hoped* he'd find a way to get out of the conference."

"Was that your plan all along?"

She shrugged. "More or less."

"You should have told us!"

"I didn't want us to rely on him coming, just in case he didn't actually show up. I was beginning to get doubtful myself."

"You put your life at risk hoping he'd come save you like some scene out of a drama?" Young Jae asked, incredulous.

"Well, I wouldn't quite put it that way."

"You were foolish and reckless," Sangwook scolded. "I'm disappointed in you."

"If we hadn't gone through with it then Jeong Daeshim might have gotten away," she snapped back. "We might never have found the evidence—"

"I've probably lost my job over this," Sangwook grumbled. "Going AWOL from the conference, arresting Jeong Daeshim, and searching the house without a warrant..."

"Surely not," Bora retorted. "If you manage to put Mr. Kim and the others behind bars, you should be rewarded, not fired."

"That may be so, but we're not quite out of the woods yet. No doubt the defence will say that Jung Jen was lying."

This dose of reality went down like a bucket of cold water being poured over us.

"But there's still more we can do," Officer Cha piped up. "There are a few missing pieces in the puzzle we should hopefully be able to recover."

"What missing pieces?" I asked.

"The secret room at KAM headquarters and the video which was used to blackmail Jung Jen," he explained. "With those two pieces, we can corroborate Jung Jen's testimony. With those two pieces, Mr. Kim won't stand a chance."

"Can I sleep in your room?" Bora asked, standing outside my door, eyes downcast and cheeks blazing. "I don't want to be alone tonight."

"Of course you can," I replied. "Come in."

To be honest, I felt the same way she did. Even with Bae Sangwook and Officer Cha staying on the same floor of the hotel, I was on high alert. My racing heart hadn't slowed since the confrontation in the field, and I kept seeing the grainy image of Jung Jen in my mind. I didn't think I'd be able to sleep.

Bora's slippered feet crossed the threshold. She was dressed in her blue gingham-print pyjama set and hotel robe. Her eyes looked significantly smaller lacking the usual addition of glasses.

"Huh? Your room's big," she noted.

"It is? Luck of the draw, I guess."

"Sorry. I wasn't complaining or anything."

The room *was* spacious—but basic. Everything was clean and white. I opened a cupboard containing a mini fridge and an electric kettle and boiled some water.

"Chamomile tea?" I asked. "It might help you relax."

"Yes, please."

She sat on the end of the bed, leaving the single chair at its foot available for me. She twiddled her thumbs, oddly quiet while I made the tea.

"How's your ankle?" she asked when I sat down.

"A little sore."

"Let me take a look."

I lifted my pyjama leg an inch then paused. "Really? You're not one of those people who are grossed out by feet?"

"Not at all."

"Okay, then."

Chapter 34

I removed my slipper and raised my bare foot.

She took her glasses out of her robe's pocket and put them on to inspect the damage, peering closely, with a small crease between her brows.

"It looks fine. Slightly swollen, maybe."

I was about to lower my foot when she suddenly took it in her hands and began to massage my ankle.

"How does that feel?" she asked.

"Good. That's helping."

"Chloe…"

"Yes?"

"I'm sorry about today."

My usual instinct would be to respond, "It's okay," or, "It's not your fault," but this time, I stayed silent. A big part of me did blame her, after all.

"You already survived one life-threatening situation and I made you put your life in danger again," she said.

I wrenched my foot from her gentle grasp. "What's done is done. We came out alive and helped spur major progress in the investigation."

"It wasn't worth it. I'm okay with sacrificing myself, but not you. Not after everything you've already been through. I should have gone by myself."

"No, you shouldn't have. You couldn't have done this on your own, and I wouldn't have let you."

She started to cry. Big, fat, juicy tears rolled down her cheeks and sploshed off her chin.

"I was scared," she spluttered. "Terrified."

Her tears sparked my tears. I moved to sit beside her on the bed and let her weep on my shoulder.

We stayed like that for a while, forgetting the cups of tea which sat cooling on the ledge by the TV.

"Are you going to tell Jinseung what happened?" Bora asked when she recovered from her crying enough to string a proper sentence together.

I nodded. "There's no way I could keep something like this a secret, and Young Jae will definitely tell him if I don't. But not tonight. I'm too tired. Tomorrow night when we're back home. I'll explain everything."

"Please, blame me all you want. Make sure he knows it was all my fault."

"I will. Can't have him thinking this was my idea."

She cracked a little smile.

35

I looked around the busy ground floor of KAM HQ—staff members and visitors chatting, laughing, totally carefree except for the usual stress of their jobs.

All these people have absolutely no idea that all hell is about to break loose.

It felt strange, to say the least, going in to work and pretending as if nothing out of the ordinary had happened and that the police weren't going to bust in and perform a raid at any minute.

Throughout my lesson with Nam Sungjin I had my ears tuned in to catch a commotion from the corridors as police officers descended on the building—but nothing happened.

I went back down to the lobby at the end of the lesson. Nothing had changed. No sign of the police. What was going on?

Don't tell me that they still haven't got the warrants they need.

Even with all the evidence we had gathered, could red tape be holding up the process?

I signed out and made my way to the elevator.

Oh well. It'll be easier if I'm not here when it happens. I've already dealt with enough.

The elevator doors opened and I was about to step inside when I heard what sounded like a stampede, followed by a series of gasps and murmurs.

"What's going on?"

"Why are the police here?"

"Has something happened?"

And so it begins.

I stood and watched as the police swarmed the building and proceeded to block all exits. No one was allowed to leave while they searched the premises for more evidence and arrested all the suspects.

Some of the staff members around me asked if I knew what was going on. I shrugged and pretended like I didn't know. How could I possibly explain everything?

The first arrest was Mr. Kim's secretary. He went with the police, his head bowed in shame and his hands cuffed behind his back as they led him to a police car waiting outside the building. Onlookers stared at the spectacle, pointing, whispering, wide-eyed and mouths agape. A few others shuffled on their feet and fidgeted with their hands, eyes darting anxiously around the room, guilt written on their faces—whether over this or some other unknown crime.

The second arrest was the fifth-floor receptionist. A handful of other arrests followed, but notably, Mr. Kim was not one of them. Perhaps he wasn't in the building. Did he know this was going to happen? Had he already enacted an escape plan?

When we were finally allowed to leave, we were greeted by a chaotic scene outside—reporters, cameras, microphones. Police officers had to direct cars and foot traffic safely through the crowds of media and journalists.

Chapter 35

The tinted windows of Jinseung's car ensured my privacy as I drove out of the carpark. Now, to the secret rendezvous.

This can't be right, can it?

I stood outside a graffiti-covered metal door in a back alley, too afraid to knock. I fumbled in my bag, retrieved my phone, and scrutinised the email's directions.

Hmmm...Seems accurate.

I tentatively reached out and knocked, then deciding I had done it too softly, knocked again with more force, hurting my knuckles on the cold, hard, metal surface.

The door creaked open and a head popped out. To my relief, it was Young Jae. He wore a beanie and a pair of gold earrings. He smelled like cigarettes. If I didn't know him, I'd find him intimidating.

"Come in," he said.

"The entrance is a bit uninviting," I grumbled as he shut the door behind me and bolted it.

He smirked. "It's the back entry. Besides, it's my private studio. It doesn't need to look inviting. This way."

He guided me down the dimly lit hallway to a cramped, windowless room full of sound equipment and a microphone stand amidst a jumble of power cords on the floor. Four mismatched chairs were arranged in front of a guitar rack and a tower of amps. Bora was seated on one of them, legs crossed and arms folded.

"Officer Bae isn't coming," she said.

"Why not?" I asked, unable to mask my disappointment.

I desperately wanted to know how the case was progressing. After everything we had contributed, weren't we owed that much at least?

"He's tied down at the station. Must be pretty hectic."

"I heard some pretty serious shit went down at KAM HQ today," Young Jae said, taking a seat.

I nodded. "Yep. I was there. I'll tell you what happened."

"I have information too," Bora said. "Officer Bae might not be coming, but we've been talking through encrypted email. This meeting won't be for nothing. *Unnie*, you go first."

I shared my story, recounting every detail I could recall from the raid.

"Must have been pretty scary for everyone who had no idea what was going on," Bora said, biting her lip.

"There was a lot of panic and confusion."

"Imagine seeing five of your colleagues get arrested right in front of you," Young Jae said, "and more brought to the police station for questioning, wondering if you'll be next. That's pretty effed up."

"But not Mr. Kim," I pointed out.

"Why am I not surprised?" Bora said. "Clever bastard either worked it out on his own or someone tipped him off."

"What did you find out from Officer Bae?" I asked.

"Remember how Jung Jen described a secret room at KAM HQ?"

"Of course. How could I forget?"

"She wasn't lying. The police found it during the raid."

I swallowed the bile which suddenly rose in my throat.

"It was empty," Bora explained. "Whatever was in there had already been removed."

"Further evidence that Mr. Kim knew this was going to happen." I sighed.

"And what about the sex video?" Young Jae asked. "Have you heard anything about that?"

"It hasn't been recovered yet," Bora replied.

"Ah."

"Have there been any more arrests?" I asked. "Anyone out of the men on Jung Jen's list?"

Bora shook her head. "Not that I know of. I imagine the police are still gathering evidence."

We sat in silence for a moment. No doubt the others were sifting through their thoughts and feelings just like I was.

A blaring alarm intercepted the thoughtful quiet.

I winced. "What the—?"

The sound emanated from the vicinity of Bora.

"Sorry," she said. "It's my phone."

Not a ring tone or notification ping I was familiar with.

She fumbled in her pockets, grabbed her phone, then turned off the alarm.

"I set up an alert," she explained. "Any news articles mentioning KAM Entertainment and my phone rings and vibrates like crazy."

"Does this mean there's been a new development?" I asked.

"Let me see." She adjusted her glasses and peered closely at the screen.

36

"What is it?" Young Jae asked. "What does it say?"

Both of us hunched over Bora's shoulders, trying to read her screen.

"There's been another arrest," she said.

"Who?" I asked.

"It doesn't say. But it's in connection to KAM Entertainment. They were arrested at Incheon Airport this morning, attempting to board a flight to Xiamen."

"My money's on Mr. Kim," Young Jae said.

"Mine too," I agreed. "Who else would try to escape the country?"

"I'm sure Sangwook can confirm one way or another," Bora said, "but I have a feeling you're both right."

I flopped onto my chair. "Thank goodness. I might actually be able to sleep tonight."

"It's over," Young Jae said.

Bora shook her head. "For us, maybe, but there's still so much more that needs to happen. We'll have to wait and see

Chapter 36

how things play out over the following weeks, months, maybe even years. Who knows how deep this corruption goes? There could be more victims, other entertainment agencies involved, a connection to Byun Gimok…"

"True," I said. "But the three of us have done all we can. The rest is up to the police."

"Back to normal life," Young Jae said with a tiny hint of regret.

"As normal as can be, given the circumstances," Bora said. "What's gonna happen to KAM Entertainment? What will happen to all the talent and staff who worked for Mr. Kim, including me and Chloe, Jinseung and Yoojin?"

Of course I was worried about that, but I wasn't thinking about myself, only Jinseung. What impact would this have on his career? Even if the agency survived, its reputation would be tarnished.

"Hopefully someone will step in to fill Mr. Kim's role," Young Jae suggested. "KAM Entertainment is a resilient beast. It won't crumble and fall that easily."

"I suppose we'll just have to wait for the CEO to release a statement," Bora said, folding her arms.

We didn't have much left to say. Bora and I thanked Young Jae for his contribution once again, then left the studio.

Night had fallen in the meantime, blanketing the sky in darkness. We walked to where I had parked the car. Yawning, I opened the door to the driver side.

"Sleepy?" Bora asked. "Want me to drive?"

I shook my head. "It's just…been a long day. I'll be fine." I took the seat at the wheel and dropped my phone into the cup holder.

"Your phone's flashing," Bora said, pulling her seatbelt on.

I didn't pick it up since I had already started to back out of the carpark. "Want to check it for me?"

She swiped away the screensaver. "*Aigoo*. You have, like, ten missed calls."

I winced. "Oops. I had my phone on silent during the meeting. Is it Jinseung?"

"Yep."

Jinseung already knew what happened. I told him everything once we returned to Seoul. He was shaken, angry, but most of all, he was relieved that I was okay. He was probably calling now because he'd heard the news of what went down at KAM Entertainment and the arrests.

"Shall I call him back?" Bora asked. "I'll put it through the Bluetooth."

"Yes, please."

She connected my phone to the car speaker and made the call. Jinseung answered straight away.

"You finally pick up," he said.

"I'm so sorry! I was having a debrief with Bora and Young Jae and didn't notice you were calling."

"It's okay. What are you doing now?"

"Driving home with Bora."

"Am I on speaker?"

"Yep."

"Bora-ya, make sure Chloe gets home safe."

"Yes, sir!" Bora said. "I won't let you down."

"Good."

After taking full responsibility for what occurred in Cheongsando, Bora had promised Jinseung to be on her best behaviour.

"Changsoo told me what happened," Jinseung said. "The raid, the arrests...He didn't know if Mr. Kim had been apprehended or not, but he couldn't get through to him when he tried to call. In custody or in hiding, my guess."

"In custody," Bora said, looking at her phone. "Bae Sangwook has just sent through confirmation."

I heard Jinseung exhale. "That's a relief. I thought he might have got away."

"He did try to leave the country, but border security caught him."

Jinseung sighed. "What a weird feeling. I've known Mr. Kim for so many years and never imagined him capable of something like this. I'll probably never see him again."

"We'll see him at his trial," Bora reminded us.

His trial.

Her words echoed in my brain until it clicked and I gasped so hard I made the car wobble. Bora stuck out her hand to stabilise the steering wheel.

"*Omo!*" I cried. "Oh Sejung's trial. It's soon, isn't it? What's today's date?"

"The twenty-fourth of June," Bora said.

"So…it's in three weeks, then. I'm not prepared. I've been so preoccupied by the situation—"

"Calm down," Jinseung said. "I've been in touch with your lawyer. She has everything under control, and you still have time to meet her again."

"Yes. You're right. Thank you for doing that."

"She's one of the best lawyers in the entertainment industry. Everything's going to be fine."

My hands tightened around the steering wheel. "Oh Sejung…"

"Are you scared about seeing her again?"

"I don't know. I haven't been thinking about it."

"Well, you'll have plenty of support. Your parents are coming, aren't they?"

"Yes. They are. And Han Seri and her parents too."

"And you'll have me. I've already arranged my leave."

"So…I'll see you again soon?"

"You will. Stay strong in the meantime, okay? I know you'll get through this."

37

Three weeks later

The riot of butterflies inside my stomach intensified throughout the drive to court.

Today was the first day of the trial, the day I'd have to see Oh Sejung again.

The leather upholstery squeaked as I squirmed in the back of the taxi between my parents. Mum took my hand in hers.

"It's going to be okay," she cooed.

My lawyer, Ms. Yoon, sat in the front passenger seat. The elegant older woman wore a beautifully tailored suit, her grey hair pulled back in a strict bun and her lips painted red. An Hermès handbag rested on her lap and a fat leather briefcase by her feet.

The car slowed down. A nearby sign said Seoul Central District Court. We stopped.

Here we are. This is it.

I wound a lightweight silk scarf around my neck and

pulled it up to cover the lower half of my face, then popped on a pair of oversized sunglasses.

So far, we had managed to keep the case a secret from the media, but Ms. Yoon had warned me of reporters lurking in and around the building. It was only a matter of time before someone scooped the story, especially once Jinseung arrived. Still, I wanted to protect my privacy as much as possible.

We emerged from the car and walked up a wide pathway surrounded by manicured lawns and leafy green trees to the stately building's arched entrance.

A security guard greeted us in the foyer. He motioned to me to lower my scarf and remove my sunglasses.

"ID?" he asked.

Once I had shown him my passport, he let me cover my face again.

He IDed Ms. Yoon and my parents as well, then we walked single file through a metal detector and received pat downs from the guard on the other side.

Mum assaulted Ms. Yoon with a barrage of questions as we navigated the large building. Ms. Yoon patiently reassured her, speaking in flawless English. Dad just listened and nodded along.

My nerves picked up again as we approached the designated courtroom. Soon I would come face to face with Oh Sejung once again. My stomach twisted so tight I thought it might pop.

"You two head through," Ms. Yoon told my parents. "I want to have a final word with Chloe in private."

Mum looked like she was about to protest, but Dad put a hand on her shoulder and guided her through the door into the courtroom.

I had no idea what Ms. Yoon wanted to tell me in private,

but I followed her wordlessly down the corridor to a pair of closed double doors where another guard stood. He checked our IDs again then let us through.

"This is a VIP area," Ms. Yoon explained, "for high-profile court attendees such as yourself and Shin Jinseung."

My heart skipped a beat. "You mean…?"

She pushed a door open.

Jinseung rose to his feet in the plush waiting room. I ran to him with open arms.

"*Oppa!*"

"*Jagi,*" he returned, welcoming me to his warm, hard chest.

"I'll just be outside," Ms. Yoon said. "I'll knock when it's time to go."

The door clicked shut.

Jinseung was dressed in formal military attire: a dark teal suit with gold buttons and a badge displaying his rank of sergeant. He looked as dashing and regal as a prince. *My* prince. Tall, lean, groomed to perfection. He smelled of soap and fresh laundry, with a hint of his own sweet spiciness underneath.

"How are you holding up?" he asked.

"Let's put it this way, I couldn't eat breakfast because I didn't think I'd be able to keep it down."

"You'll have your appetite back by lunchtime. I'll buy you something to eat."

"When did you get here?"

"Just a minute ago."

"You sure cut it fine."

"Sorry for the hold-up. I would've come last night if I could, but, you know, slight mix up. Their end, not mine."

"Never mind. Did you make it here without anyone seeing you?"

"I think so."

"Good."

A knock came from the other side of the door.

"Already?" I grumbled.

"*Jagi*, just one thing."

Jinseung grasped my chin, tilted my head up, and pressed his lips to mine.

"I'm so glad you're all right," he said.

He continued to hold my chin and gazed into my eyes so intently I blushed. After all this time, he still had the power to turn me to mush with little more than eye contact.

Another knock. Ms. Yoon peeked her head inside.

"It's time," she said.

I let out a shaky sigh before leaving the room, hand in hand with Jinseung, not caring who saw us at that point.

"Do you remember what you're going to say?" Ms. Yoon asked me on the short walk down the corridor.

"I think so."

"Just do your best. Be honest and give as much detail as possible."

I nodded.

"Here we are."

I gulped a quick breath of air before entering.

For some reason I expected to see Oh Sejung as soon as I walked in, but I only saw friendly faces. Yang Bora, Young Jae, Bae Sangwook, and Shin Jina sat together in a row near the front of the gallery. Behind them, Han Seri, her parents, and a young Caucasian man whom I recognised as her boyfriend, Adrian. Bong Changsoo sat farther back by himself. Jinseung's parents were there too, right up front near my own parents.

My heart instantly filled up and overflowed as tears in my

eyes. All these people had come to support me. I couldn't be more grateful.

But there was no time for greetings and thank-yous.

Ms. Yoon walked me down the gently sloping wooden floor to our designated table positioned between the judge and jury areas.

The jury seats filled up.

On the defendant side, the seats remained largely empty, with just a couple of people occupying separate spaces. Friends or family of Oh Sejung, I didn't know.

My eyes wandered while I waited, tense with apprehension. The courtroom reminded me of a small lecture theatre, with white walls, dark wooden tables, and black chairs on a slanted floor. A Korean flag hung limply by the empty judge's table at the front.

I snapped my head around when I heard the door at the back of the room creak open. This was it. The moment I'd been dreading. Oh Sejung entered the room, flanked by a police officer and a suited man whom I assumed was her lawyer. She was pale and bony, wearing an orange jumpsuit, hands cuffed behind her back. Her hair had been chopped short. Her eyes were the same as I remembered—two bottomless black pits which could strike terror directly to the root of your soul. She didn't look at me, choosing to leer at Jinseung instead. He didn't give her the satisfaction of looking back.

"All rise," the clerk said.

We stood as the judge entered and took up residence at her table. It seemed like the trial was about to start, when two last stragglers entered the room—a young woman, her identity obscured by a headscarf and sunglasses, and a young man I didn't recognise. I couldn't work out who the woman was until she removed her glasses, revealing herself as Go Yoojin.

The young man must have been her assistant or intern. I gave her a nod of acknowledgement and a thankful smile as she sat down near Changsoo.

The judge began the trial with a list of the charges brought towards Oh Sejung, including kidnapping, attempted murder, drugging, assault, stalking, harassment, and so many more I lost count. Next, the prosecutor made an opening statement, followed by the defence.

My moment had come. The judge called me forward to give my statement. A hush fell as I walked up to the stand. I could feel everyone's stares like hot lasers on my face.

For a moment, I just froze, completely overwhelmed.

Come on, Chloe. Get a grip. You can do this.

I reminded myself why I was there. Oh Sejung was going to get punished for what she did to me. Drumming up as much audacity as I could, I locked eyes with her, daring her to put up her best fight.

You're going down.

38

The waiting felt like an eternity. As the hours crawled forward, doubt began to creep into the back of my mind. Had I done everything I could to convince the jury of Oh Sejung's guilt? What if she got a much lighter sentence than I felt she deserved? What if she didn't go to jail at all?

No. Now I'm just being silly.

Ms. Yoon must have sensed my unease.

"The verdict will be in our favour," she reassured. "We have too much evidence and witness testimony on our side to ignore. Just hold tight and you'll see."

The trial was in its fifth day, and the jury had been deliberating for four hours now. The courtroom was jam-packed. Word must have spread via the court reporters to the media at large, who flocked to view the spectacle—*Shin Jinseung's girlfriend versus the sasaeng fan*. They weren't allowed to take pictures, or even to name names, but I expected a lot of details would still leak out. It bugged me—though much less than my concerns about the outcome of the trial.

Everyone hushed when a man emerged from the jury room

and conferred with the judge. I couldn't hear what they were saying, but the judge nodded and cleared her throat. He passed her something—*an envelope?* Then he went back to the jury room and quickly returned, followed by the entire jury. They took their seats.

The judge hit her gavel.

"I would like to announce that a verdict has been reached," she said.

A buzz of anticipation rippled through the room. I held my breath, knuckles white as I clamped the edge of my chair.

Please…please…

Her voice rang out. "Oh Sejung-ssi, you have been found guilty on all charges. Sentencing will occur on the twentieth of August. Until then, you will be remanded in custody."

The weight lifted from my shoulders immediately. I felt so light I could've floated to the ceiling like a helium balloon.

As the police took a groaning, howling Sejung away, Ms. Yoon patted my back.

"Congratulations, Chloe," she said. "You won."

I won…I really won!

My friends and family swarmed to me with a whirlwind of hugs and congratulations.

"Well done," Han Seri said, hands on my shoulders. "You were so brave!"

Bora gave me a fist bump. "You nailed it!"

Jina took both my hands in hers. "That was epic. Congratulations!"

Changsoo simply smiled and nodded at me, though I detected the faint glimmer of a tear in one eye. My parents, on the other hand, were crying outright. They couldn't understand Korean, but they knew a guilty verdict when they saw it.

Ms. Yoon had translated a lot for them during the breaks as well.

My attention turned to Jinseung, who stood alone in the aisle, shaking, on the verge of tears. The trial had been tough for him, reminding him of all the terrible things I went through that he couldn't protect me from. I approached him.

"It's okay. It's over now."

Ironic that I should be comforting him instead of the other way around.

"I'm sorry," he said over and over. "I'm so sorry. I'll never, ever, let something like that happen to you again. Even when I'm away in the army, I'll do everything I can to protect you."

"I know you will. Thank you. And thanks for hiring Ms. Yoon. She was fantastic, a total lifesaver."

Mrs. Woo stood up on a chair next to her worried-looking husband who held his arms out in case she fell. She waved her hand in the air to get everyone's attention.

"We will be having drinks and nibbles at Ji Soo Bar across the road. All friends and family invited! No media."

With that, our party relocated to the bar, which had been booked out in advance by Jinseung's parents in anticipation of a favourable verdict.

The evening was warm, and we sat outside on a rooftop courtyard lit by glowing lanterns dangling from potted green trees and fairy lights which snaked around an iron fence border. A perfect ending to a difficult few days.

Jinseung and I stopped by my parents' table first. They had never seemed impressed that I was dating a famous actor until this visit. Seeing the fabulous house Jinseung had bought for me and the beautiful neighbourhood I lived in had opened their eyes to his wealth. Then seeing him in person confirmed how handsome and charming he was, especially in his military attire. Mum hadn't stopped gawping at him since I introduced them. Dad was less obvious, but I could tell he was impressed as well.

We chatted for a while, me playing translator, until Mrs. Woo interrupted us with her husband in tow.

"You still haven't properly introduced us to your parents, Chloe. I'd like to talk to them, but I seem to have forgotten most of my English!"

"Of course, *Eomeonim*. Don't worry, I'll translate."

Seeing my parents with Jinseung's parents was odd, to say the least. The two couples couldn't be any more different. Jinseung's parents were in a class above mine, and the culture gap was clear—the elegant Korean couple and the unsophisticated British pair. Nevertheless, they exchanged polite greetings with my help as interpreter.

"Well, that was awkward," I whispered to Jinseung when his parents finally retreated.

"Come on. It wasn't that bad."

We moved on and chatted with Han Seri and her parents next.

"You have to come to Melbourne!" Seri said. "Adrian and I just bought a house. You're welcome to stay any time."

"Wow. That's amazing," I gushed. "I definitely want to come."

"Am I invited?" Jinseung asked.

"Of course!" Seri said. "Though I don't suppose you can while you're in service."

"True."

"What about you, *Abeonim, Eomeonim*?" I asked. "Do you visit Australia often?"

"We have only visited once," Mrs. Soo said, "but we are thinking about coming to live there once they get married."

Chapter 38

"Married?!" I snapped my eyes to Seri.

She blushed. "*Eomma*! Aren't we getting ahead of ourselves?"

"Don't wait too long. You're already living together," Mrs. Soo said.

"We want grandchildren soon," Mr. Han added.

Seri turned a deeper shade of scarlet.

"What are you saying?" asked a confused Adrian in English.

"Oh...nothing..."

"They're talking marriage and children," I said, grinning.

"Oh!" He chuckled. "Why am I not surprised?"

After visiting every table, Jinseung and I settled down with Bora, Young Jae, and Sangwook, who were huddled close around a basket of fried chicken and fries. Jinseung nicked a chip straight away.

"And they join us at last!" Bora announced, swaying and slurring slightly. She seemed a little tipsy. Okay, *more* than a little tipsy. She leaned close to Sangwook, who touched her arm to steady her.

Young Jae held up a hand to signal a passing waiter. He ordered more drinks for the table.

"Sangwook *Oppa*, give them the update!" Bora said.

"Update?" I asked. "Do you have more news about the Mr. Kim case?"

He nodded.

"Let's hear it, then. If it's okay to tell us, I mean."

"First thing, Kim Sunwoo has been denied bail."

"Sunwoo?"

"Mr. Kim."

I sniggered. "Funny. I never knew his given name until now."

"Good news about the bail," Jinseung said.

"And what of the other suspects?" I asked.

"Jeong Daeshim has been allowed bail since he has been helping with the investigation," Sangwook explained. "We're still gathering the necessary evidence to arrest the others, but progress is being made, and the acting commissioner is fully on board with the investigation."

"And your job is safe?"

"Yes. I've been pardoned for my errors this time around."

"See? I knew you'd pull through," Bora teased, lightly jabbing him in the ribs.

He swatted her hand, though his sheepish smile gave his amusement away.

"What about the video?" I asked. "Did you find it?"

He shook his head. "At this point, I doubt it will ever be recovered. I suspect that, having no further use for it, Mr. Kim destroyed it upon her death."

"In a way, I'm kind of glad," I admitted. "More than anything, Jung Jen didn't want anyone to see that video."

"I agree," Bora said. "It's better left unseen."

"I'm confident we'll be able to obtain enough evidence without it," Sangwook said.

Jina appeared at our table, cheerful and effortlessly glam as usual in gold hoop earrings and a slinky black dress. "Hey, peeps! Mind if I join in?"

"Where were you?" I asked.

"Inside. I know the bartender here."

Young Jae moved over to make a space where she could pull up a chair. "*Noona*, long time no see."

"Thanks. Oooh…" She eyed Bora and Sangwook. "When did *this* happen?"

"This?" Bora asked, blushing.

Chapter 38

"You're dating, right?"

"Well..."

My heart was beating fast on her behalf while I watched with curiosity as to how this would unfold.

"Yeah. Kind of," Sangwook said, making Bora blush harder. "I mean, we've been on dates."

"Those were dates?"

"I thought they were. Didn't you?"

"Yeah, I guess. So...we're dating now?"

"Any objections?" he replied, arms folded across his chest.

"...No."

"That settles it then."

Unable to contain ourselves, Jina and I simultaneously squealed in delight. We got up, grabbed each other's hands, and jumped up and down until we ran out of steam.

"So cuuuute!" Jina gushed.

Young Jae poured everyone refills then raised his glass. "To the new couple."

We all clinked glasses and cheered. I couldn't be more happy for Bora.

As the evening continued, numbers began to dwindle. My parents and Jinseung's parents left in taxis. Soon, only our table of six remained.

"How's everyone getting home?" Sangwook asked, always the responsible one.

"I'm taking Chloe home," Jinseung said.

"Want to share a taxi, Young Jae?" Jina asked. "Your place isn't far from mine."

"Actually, I thought I might go out," he replied. "My friend's DJing at The Sound Cave."

"Ooh. Can I come?"

"Sure. Anyone else...? No takers, huh? It'll just be us."

"Fine with me!"

That left the obvious pairing of Sangwook and Bora. They looked at each other, both slightly pink-cheeked.

"Then, shall we...?" Sangwook asked.

"Do you mind?" Bora replied.

"Not at all."

I couldn't wipe the smile off my face. Those two were adorable.

After thanking the bar staff, we exited and went our separate ways. I slumped into Jinseung's car and pulled the seatbelt on.

"Did you have fun?" Jinseung asked, taking the wheel.

"I'm just glad the trial is over."

"Yeah, me too."

I watched the city lights pass us by—a blur of colourful neon. Where would life take us next? Could I continue working at KAM Entertainment, waiting for Jinseung to be discharged? And what about Jinseung's career? Would his contract still get renewed amidst all the chaos? I let out a small sigh, my breath misting the window.

"Everything okay?" Jinseung asked.

"Just thinking about the future..."

"Thinking about what you're going to do now?"

"Mmhmm. And you. What will you do when you leave the army?"

"Don't worry about me. I'll figure something out."

"Even if your contract doesn't get renewed?"

"I don't know if I can stomach the idea of continuing to work for KAM Entertainment. The whole thing has left a sour taste in my mouth. Even if they do offer to renew my contract, I don't think I'll accept."

I gasped at his sudden declaration. "You won't renew?" I had to ask again, just to be sure.

He nodded, eyes staring straight ahead at the road. "That's right. I won't renew."

"Wow. That's a big deal. When did you decide this?"

"Recently. But I started thinking about it as soon as you told me what Mr. Kim did to you. I felt so betrayed."

I took a minute to consider the implications of his announcement, my fingers twisting the seatbelt. "Does this mean you'll quit acting?"

"No. Maybe I'll sign with a different agency. Or maybe I'll do something completely different. Either way, I feel excited about the opportunities out there."

As he spoke, I noticed the road sign signalling our exit, but we sped past it. "Hey—you missed the turn-off."

"Don't worry. We're going the right way."

"But—"

"We're not going home."

"Then…where are we going?"

The corner of his lips quirked up and he had a glint in his eyes. "Wait and see."

39

I could only think of one reason why we would be driving to Namsan Mountain. The famous tourist attraction, N Seoul Tower, stood at its peak, lit up bright pink, its needle tip piercing the dark expanse of sky. But why would Jinseung take me to one of the busiest tourist locations in Seoul? Unlikely that he suddenly fancied a spot of sightseeing, I would have thought.

Jinseung parked in the carpark by the cable car ticket office. He had taken off his stiff jacket and replaced it with a soft hoodie. He wore the hood over his head, and a black fabric mask to cover the lower half of his face. I wrapped my silk scarf around my neck and burrowed my chin into it. The darkness provided the rest of our cover. A few people milled around the area, but I couldn't see a queue anywhere, and the cable car station was unlit and shut off, the ticket windows closed.

"Looks like the cable cars have stopped running for the night," I said.

"We'll walk up." Jinseung took my hand in his.

We walked side by side along a moonlit path through Namsan Park, lined by trees on both sides, gently sloping uphill towards the tower. Every now and then I caught glimpses of the city below through the branches, like dashes of glitter on a dark backdrop.

The crowds grew thicker until we reached the plaza at the base of the tower. I nervously glanced around.

"Is this okay? There are so many people…"

"We'll blend in," Jinseung said, adjusting his mask. "We're tourists, just like everyone else."

"If you say so."

Most of the shops in the plaza were closed, but the main attraction was the view. I rushed to the fence to lean over and gaze upon the sea of glimmering multi-coloured lights below.

"Wow…"

"It's beautiful, isn't it?" Jinseung said over my shoulder.

"Stunning."

"Have you ever been here before?"

"No, actually. I haven't."

"You never did the tourist stuff, huh?"

"No. So why did you bring me here?"

He smirked. "All will be revealed. First, we must go to the tower."

As he guided the way, we passed fences covered with colourful padlocks—love locks, just like the ones on the bridges across the Seine River in Paris. You could purchase the locks from several nearby vending machines.

"*Aigoo*. So overpriced," I said, peering through the glass at the garish novelty padlocks inside. "We're not going to do this, are we?"

Jinseung pouted. "Why not?"

"It's kind of tacky, isn't it?"

"Well, I guess I'm just a tacky sort of guy. Besides, secretly you want to, am I right?"

I scoffed, but a sheepish smile slipped out.

"There it is. You totally want to."

"Okay. You got me. It *is* kinda romantic."

He produced a bright pink padlock and a black permanent marker from his pocket. "Here's one I prepared earlier."

"*Aigoo*. You really thought of everything."

"Let's write our names." He passed me the marker.

I wrote C.A.G. In my neatest handwriting.

"What does the A stand for?" he asked.

"Alice. It's my middle name."

"I didn't know that!"

"Did I never mention it?"

"No. I would have remembered if you did. *Alice*. Cute."

He took the marker and wrote his own name in Hangul characters, plus a heart in the middle.

"Where shall we put it?" I asked.

"Let's find a good spot."

The fence was already completely covered. Locks were attached to locks that were attached to other locks. Eventually I clipped it onto a lock which seemed to belong to another multicultural couple—Ella and Taehwang. I guess I felt some kind of weird affinity for them.

"There." I stood back to admire it from a distance.

"Perfect."

We both took photos of the lock and a selfie with the two of us standing by the fence. I tried to imprint the exact location of the lock in my mind, hoping that I'd be able to find it if I ever returned.

A group of nearby girls started staring and whispering

between themselves. I wondered if they had recognised Jinseung.

"Come on." Jinseung tugged me away before the girls could approach. He led me towards the tower with purposeful strides. I wondered what would await me when we got there. He clearly had something planned, but what?

My excitement turned to disappointment as we closed in on the tower entrance. The doors were shut, the lights were off, and security guards were turning people away.

I frowned. "It looks closed. I think we're too late."

"It *is* closed. To everyone but us, that is."

"What do you mean?"

"Patience, *jagi*." He approached one of the security guards, pulled down his mask, and passed him a folded-up document he had stored in his pocket. The guard unfolded the piece of paper, looked it over, then nodded. He unlocked the door and led us inside. The place was deserted except for a few staff members finishing up. All of the gift shops and cafes were closed and only a few dim lights remained turned on to guide our way through the building. We stepped into the elevator and the guard pressed the button for the observatory.

"I hope you're not scared of heights," Jinseung said.

"I think I'll be fine."

"Then you're in for a treat."

We got out at the third floor.

"Come back here when you've finished looking around." The guard gestured to us to go on ahead while he stationed himself beside the elevator.

The room was circular with windows along the outer wall providing a 360-degree panoramic view of central Seoul—a sparkling, kaleidoscopic paradise emitting a hazy glow into the sky. I pressed myself close to the cool glass. I felt like I was floating above the world.

"Oh, this is wonderful. Spectacular."

"Pretty special, isn't it?" Jinseung wrapped me in his arms from behind, his chin nestled beside my ear.

I admired the view for a while longer, staring down at the vibrant cityscape below.

"This must be the most romantic thing anyone's ever done for me."

"So, you like it?"

"I do. What made you think to do this?"

"I wanted this night to be as special...as *memorable* as possible."

"All this to celebrate the end of the trial? Wait—is it our anniversary or something?"

He chuckled. "Close your eyes."

I did so, anticipation rising in my chest like an oversized bubble. I heard a slight shuffling sound as he temporarily released me from his arms.

"Hold out your hand," he said.

I lifted my right hand and held it in front of me, palm facing up. My breathing hitched when he placed something there—a small box, smooth and heavy. He closed my fingers around it. "Now. Open your eyes."

I tried to keep my expectations low, but my heart was beating on overdrive. I cracked my eyes open a slit, and then fully, gazing at the box in my grasp—black and glossy with smooth rounded corners.

A jewellery box.

Was this really happening? Was this what I thought it was?

"Go ahead. Open it," Jinseung urged in a low, husky tone.

Hand shaking, I pushed the pin down and the box opened

with a hefty click. There, nestled in a cushion of black velvet, was a ring. A gold ring with a single, multifaceted diamond.

"Is this...?" My voice was hoarse.

"Yes."

"Oh..." My breath came in short spurts as my eyes filled with tears.

Jinseung put his hands on my shoulders and turned me around to face him.

"Chloe." He stared deep into my eyes. "Will you marry me?" His voice wavered slightly, and his cheeks were tinged pink.

I didn't want to leave him hanging, but I couldn't speak because I was sobbing so hard. He had done it. He had proposed. The thing I had never allowed myself to even imagine had really happened. I was in a state of shock.

Eventually I managed to choke it out. "Yes! Yes, I will." I threw my arms around him and pulled him close.

He placed one hand on my cheek, the other on my chin, and tilted my face up so he could kiss me—a long, dreamy sigh of a kiss. His lips were soft, his mouth was comfortable and warm.

"Thank you," he whispered, before kissing me again with more passion, my back to the window.

Fully absorbed in the kiss, I nearly dropped the ring box. I had to break away and steady myself.

"I should put this on," I said, opening the box again.

"Allow me." He plucked the ring from its velvet bed, took my hand, and slid it onto my finger. "This ring belonged to my *halmoni*."

I held my hand in front of me, admiring the way the dim light reflected off the shiny stone. "It's beautiful. It fits perfectly."

Jinseung stroked my hand. "I planned to do this on the day I leave the army, but I couldn't wait."

"I think I'll be emotional enough that day without a surprise proposal. Then again, I'm pretty emotional today as well."

Jinseung chuckled before leaning in to plant kisses on my neck and cheek.

We enjoyed our privacy in the observatory for a while longer before heading back down to the plaza. The crowds had thinned out, likely due to the late hour.

"It's been an amazing night," I said, yawning, "but we better head home. I'm so tired."

Jinseung murmured in agreement. "It's way past bedtime."

As we slowly walked downhill, I found myself gazing at the ring again, entranced by its sparkling angles under the moonlight.

"My parents will be in for a surprise when they see this," I said.

"Your parents already know everything."

"What?"

"I told them yesterday. I asked their permission for your hand."

"Wow. So old-fashioned! How did you manage? Did you write it down in English and say it like a speech?"

"More or less. There were probably mistakes, but they still understood."

"That was very sweet of you. I can't imagine how my parents reacted."

"I think they were confused why I would ask but pleased at the same time."

"Right. What about your parents? Did you tell them as well?"

"Think I could rely on my mother to keep such a secret? No. They don't know. I'll tell them tomorrow—later today, I mean—it's past midnight."

I barely managed to stay awake on the drive home. As soon as we entered our room I dove onto the bed and landed in the soft blankets with a sigh.

"Gonna sleep in those clothes?" Jinseung asked with a smirk.

"No," I mumbled into the pillow.

"Then let me undress you."

I allowed him the task without protest. He removed my clothes with love and care and minimal disturbance to my resting form, then he pulled the covers over me. I felt the bed dip when he climbed in. He cuddled up to me, skin to skin, his hand stroking up and down my arm.

"When are you going back to the army?" I asked. He had told me before, but I blocked it out so I could pretend that he wouldn't be going back.

"Tomorrow afternoon," he replied.

"So soon…"

He began to massage my shoulders. "Chloe, once we marry, you won't have to worry ever again about whether you can stay in Korea. You'll be able to become a resident, if you want to."

"I know. That's a big relief."

"It's not the reason I proposed, of course, just an added bonus. And if you don't want to stay in Korea, that's an option too. We can go anywhere you like. I'm open to the possibilities. You probably don't know right now, but we can think about it. There's plenty of time."

"The only thing I know is that I want my life to be considerably less dramatic from now on. K-dramas are fun to watch on TV, not so much when they play out in real life."

I felt his amused smile against the back of my neck. "I feel the same way."

It had taken a long time, but it finally felt like we were on the same page. Sighing with contentment, I turned over and pulled the covers up closer to my chin.

"Goodnight, Jinseung-ah."

"Goodnight, *jagi*."

My eyes fell closed straight away, and I lost consciousness of everything except the warmth of Jinseung's arms around me and the weight and feel of the smooth band of gold around my ring finger.

Thank you for reading *The Superstar Scandal*.

Find extra content from Sara Martin here:
saramartinauthor.com/links

GLOSSARY

- **-ah/-ya** — A casual title used when addressing a close friend
- **-nim** — An honorific used when addressing someone by their profession
- **-ssi** — A polite title used when addressing someone
- **Abeonim** — Father (formal)
- **Aigoo** — An exclamation expressing surprise or exasperation
- **Aish** — An exclamation of displeasure
- **Appa** — Dad
- **Dongsaeng** — Younger sibling/friend
- **Eomeonim** — Mother (formal)
- **Eomma** — Mum
- **Galbi** — Korean grilled ribs
- **Halmoni** — Grandmother
- **Hyung** — Used by males to address older brothers or older male friends
- **Jagi** — Darling/honey (can also mean myself/himself/herself depending on context)

- **Noona** — Used by males to address older sisters or older female friends
- **Omo** — An expression of shock or surprise
- **Oppa** — Used by females to address their older brother, older male friends, or boyfriend
- **Sasaeng fan** — An obsessive fan
- **Seonbae** — Senior
- **Seonsaeng-nim** — Teacher
- **Unnie** — Used by females to address their older sisters or older female friends
- **Ya** — Hey, oi
- **Yeobo** — Darling/Honey

Printed in Great Britain
by Amazon